The screen door banged, sending pain coursing through Cody's eardrums to every raw nerve ending in his body. With all his strength, he opened one eye a slit to see who entered the room

The princess entered, clad in stonewashed blue jeans, her tailored white blouse tails tied at her waist and exposing a tiny triangle of taught stomach and a dainty belly button, her shirt sleeves rolled up blue-collar-worker style. On her, it looked extremely alluring. Especially when the early morning sun highlighted streaks of molten lava through red hair that billowed down to her slender waist.

She was the angel of his dreams, with hands as soft as a baby's bottom. Hands that had touched him in places that would make a lesser man blush. Just the thought made his blood boil.

But she couldn't be an angel. They usually didn't enter through the front door as this one did. And they were usually quieter.

Suddenly her expression changed and she halted mid-step, her blue-eyed gaze riveting on him. Her eyes narrowed, then widened and he thought he detected a trace of pleasure before it was quickly veiled. She was at his side in two steps, her warm palm on his forehead, then cupping his cheeks.

"Sleeping Beauty finally awakes," she murmured, barely loud enough for him to hear. She walked around so that she could look squarely in his face. Without a trace of shyness, she leaned over him, her breasts brushing his bare arms, making him inhale sharply. Her finger pads prodded his upper left arm, sending shooting pain screaming down his arm to his fingertips and he winced.

"Still sore." It wasn't a question.

"That's...an...under...statement." His words skipped syllables and sounds, his voice sounded crackly due to his cotton-dry throat. It hurt to breathe. It took super-human effort just to twist on his side to get a better look at her. His muscles screamed from the abuse, objecting from even minute exercise. He forced his eyes open wider to study her face. His hand captured her slim wrist and he was surprised when she didn't try to pull away.

"What happened?"

"You cozied up to a rattlesnake that wasn't in the mood for company. I think he was a mite perturbed when you jumped on him with all 220 pounds..."

"One-hundred eighty-five." Cody grimaced at how weak he felt. He wondered how much muscle he had left, if any. Rattlesnake bites were nasty critters.

He inched himself to the side of the couch and let his gaze roam the room, wondering where his not-so-dearly-departed assailant had found its final resting place. But he saw nothing. It was probably behind the couch, or she'd kicked it underneath. It wasn't important, as long as it was gone.

Her hands climbed to her hips and rested there, her elbows jutting out at ninety-degree angles. "Do you think you're strong enough to help me undress you?"

His mouth dropped open and he gaped at her for several moments.

5 stars! ~ Elaine Hopper delivers an intriguing tale of love, suspense and adventure intertwined into one tastefully written romance story. Her ability to move the reader from the edge of the seat and back, again and again, keeps you riveted to the pages until the last word is read. When a novel ends, leaving the reader yearning for more, you know the author has created a masterpiece. Elaine has accomplished this in Lions of Judah.

The story begins with the heroine running from a gruesome past of torture, violence and death. Domestic violence is rampant in our world, and readers will instantly relate to her struggle to mentally defeat her demons. Unfortunately, the mental demons aren't the only ones she has to conquer day after day, scene after scene. She portrays a strong willed character that must let go of her past, and learn to love again.

The hero enters the scene just in time to save her from her first physical demon. Together, they stare death in the face repeatedly. They find themselves in heart pounding situations that are laid in their path time and time again. Will the hero be the ultimate person to save the world?

Don't be the only one among your excited friends who has to say they haven't read it yet. An exceptional plot lays waiting for you among the cleverly written pages in Lions of Judah. Without a doubt, I give this book a 5 star rating.

by Karen Beck
Romancing the Web
http://ritahestand.romance-central.com

Elaine Hopper

Lions of Judah

by

Elaine Hopper

NBI

NovelBooks, Inc.
Douglas, Massachusetts

This is a work of fiction. While reference may be made to actual historical events or existing locations, the characters, incidents, and dialogs are products of the author's imagination. Any resemblance to actual persons, living or dead, is entirely coincidental.

Published by
NovelBooks, Inc.
P.O. Box 661
Douglas, MA 01516

NovelBooks Inc. publishes books online and through print-on-demand.
For more information, check our website:www.novelbooksinc.com or email publisher@novelbooksinc.com

Produced in the United States of America.

Cover illustration by Arianna Overton

ISBN 1-931696-96-9

I'd like to dedicate

LIONS OF JUDAH

to my critique group,

The Rainbow Girls
who are the sisters I never had,

and to

Linnea Sinclair
who introduced me to NovelBooks
and has helped me in countless many ways,
and to my wonderful editors and experts,

Karen, Kathryn, and Gail McAbee.

Chapter One

Without warning, the horse that bounty hunter Cody Richards had been watching reared and bucked, neighing frantically. The young woman on its back grabbed the creature's mane with all her might, but she was slipping fast—right under the deadly flailing hooves.

Lightning fast, Cody vaulted to her side, snatching her out of harm's way. He hadn't been sent to rescue the kidnapped heiress just to witness the horse trample her to death.

She blinked up at him, salty droplets clinging to her orange-fringed lashes. Gritty sand clung to her and now to him, but he didn't care. Despite the sand, she felt warm and soft in all the right places against him and he stared at the lovely vision in his arms, as if an angel had fallen out of Heaven.

When the horse flared its nostrils, snorted and cantered away, kicking sand in their faces, she spluttered, "Just look what you did. You let Devil escape." He looked down at her wriggling in his arms; fire flashed in the most amazing blue eyes he'd ever seen. Her glorious hair cascaded over his arm, haloing her angelic face. "You can put me down now."

Her tone was amazingly regal, even supercilious, for someone with a mouthful of wet sand.

Too bad her manner didn't match her appearance. *So be it.*

"As you wish." Who was he to thwart a woman's commands? Cody dumped her unceremoniously on her derriere and turned a deaf ear on her outraged squeals. Two could play this game. "It was either that or you'd be flat as a pancake, and not nearly so pretty," he drawled, crossing his arms across his chest. "Hoof prints all over your face wouldn't endear you to your husband." He hoped to evoke a response from her. Maybe she'd lead him to Jesse, her boyfriend—the supposed kidnapper Cody'd been hired to find.

Melissa's family, but most especially her fiancé, wanted to put Jesse Elliot behind bars.

Struggling to her feet, she bent, dusting the sand off her faded jeans with jerky, angry dashes. "I bet you're a big hit with the ladies."

"Don't know." His lips quirked into a half smile. "I've

never tried that move before. I haven't had the opportunity to save too many damsels in distress or slay too many dragons." He slid her a sly glance. "Did it work this time?"

Her lips twisted in a grimace, then slowly curved into a wide smile that stole his breath. She eyed him up and down then laughed a sweet, tinkling laugh that he liked immensely. "You don't look like a white knight in that get up. And Sir Lancelot never dropped Guinevere on her ass." She laughed dryly, circling him. "Tell me, is that the new Indiana Jones line of fashion? Drab and dreary?"

So he *hadn't* had a chance to buy a new Brooks Brothers wardrobe while trailing her.

"Could be. You like?" He bowed deeply from his waist in an exaggerated gesture. "Sir Lancelot at your service, Princess; or, to be exact, Cody Richards." Cody straightened to his full height, looming above her just in time to catch her rolling her eyes heavenward before she pivoted on her boot heel. Weren't fairy princesses supposed to wear glass slippers and ball gowns and smell like spring flowers instead of sweaty horseflesh?

Then again, Prince Charmings and white knights weren't supposed to look like Indiana Jones rejects.

Melissa Vanderbilt-Smythe trudged down the beach, her boots leaving imprints in the wet sand. Sticking her fingers in her mouth, she whistled. The horse turned in a smooth U-turn and trotted back to her, stopping a foot in front of her, contrite—if a horse could feel such an emotion. She held her hand out and stood still, waiting for the huge animal to come closer.

"Nice trick." Cody whistled under his breath. "You know your way around a horse." Born and raised in the big city, he hadn't spent much time around the creatures and held a healthy respect for them—especially ones whose nostrils flared and whose black beady eyes glared at him like he was breakfast.

Melissa smiled but didn't say a word. When the horse nudged her shoulder with its wet nose, she clamped her hand on the bridle and stroked him with her other hand.

When she crooned to the gelding, Cody thought he heard angels singing. She owned one of those deep, melodious voices like Garbo, a voice he could get lost in. He shook his head. He'd never had a fantasy about a client or a case before. Now wasn't the time to start. This was a smart young lady and a slippery one at that and he had to keep his wits about him if he wanted to complete his mission and collect his due.

"How about I escort you home? It's not safe for a young

woman to be out here alone at this hour." Not that Cody was sure the Jersey shore and a deserted carnival were ever safe for anyone. But his prime motivation was to get a better look at her house to see if there were signs of her infamous boyfriend. Or maybe they were married by now? Rumor had it that she'd been brainwashed. At least she hadn't become a terrorist. Two years was a long time. He looked for signs of a wedding band but saw none. Her fingers were unadorned and he sighed in mental relief, telling himself his reaction was for her family's sake.

She swung herself up onto the horse and glowered down at him. "Thanks for saving me, but I don't know you from Adam. How do I know if I can trust you?" With that parting remark, she swung her horse around, clucked loudly and dug her heels into his flanks.

Without another word, horse and rider rode into the wind, kicking sand and water on him.

~ * ~

Melissa Vanderbilt-Smythe returned Devil to her friend's stable and brushed him down. With strong, smooth strokes, she whisked the sweat from his black gleaming coat, restoring him to his majestic beauty.

Devil pranced and snorted, sniffing the air full of carnival smells. Odors of hot buttery popcorn and sugary sweet cotton candy lingered in the air, mingling with whiffs of the salty ocean. Seagulls swooped overhead as the surf lapped the shore. All Melissa's new carnival friends were tucked into bed and would be until well past noon. She had the place to herself.

"Thanks for the ride, boy," she crooned in Devil's ear. Delving in her jeans pocket, she extracted a handful of sugar cubes, slightly sticky from being in her pocket so long, and stuck her flat palm under his long nose. His scratchy tongue and the whiskers on his nose tickled the soft flesh of her hand when he scooped them up. Then he nuzzled her shoulder. Love twinkled in his coal black eyes.

When she hugged him, his warmth seeped into her. Except for Devil, Melissa hadn't felt another body warming her since Jesse died…not until the stranger who had saved her just that morning held her in his arms, against his chest.

She only allowed her mind to linger on Jesse, or the puzzling stranger, a moment before she dusted away her memories and pitched fresh hay into Devil's stall.

He ate greedily, as if it were to be his last meal and she

watched in silence, her foot hitched on the railing. She leaned her head on her folded arms atop his stall and watched him, loath to leave. "I'm going to miss you like hell, boy." She drank her fill of him, etching his magnificent form into her memory. "Maybe I'll be back one day."

She couldn't promise. She never could. Who knew what the future held? She couldn't even plan the next hour, much less the next year or the rest of her life. Maybe if not for Nathan, her abusive ex-fiancé, she could go home. At least she could settle down and start a new life. A real life. But as long as she sensed his presence, her life was on hold.

Oppressive loneliness closed in on her. Suddenly claustrophobic, Melissa had to pull fresh air into her lungs before she hyperventilated. The moldy stable air wove around her, squeezing the breath from her body.

"Later. Okay, boy?" She skipped into the deserted carnival grounds, gulping the salty air into her lungs. Morning wind whipped her hair into her face and she stuffed it into the back of her blouse to keep it from getting into her mouth.

She pulled huge, raspy breaths into her lungs and craned her neck so that her nose pointed to the clouds. They drifted together, then apart, like the loved ones in her life. They only stayed a little while before they were wrenched from her. And now, even Devil would be a sweet memory to be tucked away in the book of remembrance she kept deep in her mind. He deserved an entry in her journal. She vowed to make it before she retired for the night.

God, but she was so tired of running, of looking over her shoulder for shadows and glimpses of ghosts. Would Nathan never give up? Would he ever leave her alone?

But that eerie feeling that prying eyes bore into her back came back to plague her. A trap lay nearby with her name engraved on it. If she weren't careful, she'd walk right into a noose.

Nervously, Melissa glanced over her shoulder into monstrous shadows. Although she chose to hide in darkness often, right now she shied away from it; for it could also hide many evils. She couldn't shake the feeling and increased her pace until she fled for home.

Not really home, but a little dilapidated shack that reminded her of a vagabond that hadn't had a manicure or a good washing in at least a decade. But she didn't need much. Just a soft, clean mattress to rest her weary back, a solid roof to keep the rain off her head and a place to keep Jesse's picture and her journal safe.

Melissa spent most of her time outside, combing the beach, riding Devil, doing odd jobs at the carnival. She didn't like to be closed in. It reminded her too much of being shackled and chained by her ex-fiancé.

Checking behind her again, she didn't see the wall of chest in front of her and came up short with a bang. Vice-like arms clamped around her as a sinister chuckle rang in her ears.

"What's the hurry, Sister? Got a hot date?" A raspy voice whispered in her ear and she swallowed a scream, barely reining in mindless fear. Had Nathan found her? Was this man a bounty hunter? Or did he have other more evil, unthinkable, sinister thoughts in mind? "How about with me?" He issued a deep belly laugh then spit a wad of chewing tobacco several feet into the air, that fell and splattered the cement like dried blood.

The rank smell almost doubled Melissa over…or would have, if her captor weren't holding her so tightly she could barely breathe.

Squirming, she struggled to no avail. She opened her mouth to scream and a meaty hand clamped over her mouth. "It'll be a lot less painful if you stop fighting, Miss Vanderbilt-Smythe. We can do this easy or we can do this hard."

His face lowered to within an inch of hers and she fought down the hysteria rising in her chest like bile. God, this Cro-Magnon knew who she was? How she wished her intuition had been wrong. It was hell being right.

"What's it going to be? I can't be taking you back with no bruises or fingerprints on that porcelain complexion of yours. The Reverend won't like that." He lifted a damp handkerchief to her face and she smelled something suspiciously like sodium pentathol.

Her eyes widened as far as they could and she compelled him to an act of humanity with her gaze. She mumbled into his thick palm, "I'll pay you double what he offered if you forget you ever saw me."

With what she didn't know, but it sounded plausible. She had a small nest egg tucked away under her new name, but not that kind of money.

The big man paused, an indescribable emotion clouding his eyes. His thin lips twisted into a grotesque smile as his vile gaze raked over her. "You don't look as if you have a dime to your name. How much you offering?"

Melissa could smell his greed and it sickened her. She'd always hated fortune hunters. They were the lowest scum of the earth. Human snakes. But she lifted her chin a notch and gave him stare for stare, refusing to blink or look away. Summoning her regal bearing and impeccable training, she treated him to her most commanding demeanor. "Unhand me, or you don't get a dime."

He took her measure, his distasteful stare lingering much too long on the slight swell of her breasts barely visible at the open v of her blouse. "How much?" His voice was a growl.

"I told you, I'd double what he offered. I have a Swiss bank account." Bluffing, she adopted an unconcerned, bored look, as her heart raced so fast she thought her chest would explode.

Licking his lips, he relaxed his grip. "Sister, you and I are inseparable until I get my money."

Rubbing her arms where his fingerprints bruised her flesh, Melissa bit back a grimace. The man's filthy touch churned her stomach. She couldn't wait to shower away his stench. Then she'd have to sneak away before her newfound family awoke, and assume a new identity…again. Exhaustion gripped her, threatening her escape.

"Lead the way." He grasped her upper arm, and parted his leather jacket until she spied the glint of steel peeking out, thwarting her plans to run.

He meant business.

She pressed her lips together, her mind working furiously on another plan. She slid a sideways glance at him. He had a thick skull like a Cro-Magnon and he didn't exactly speak like a scholar. He had no cheekbones to speak of, and a blunt, square chin. He was all brawn and no brains. A gold chain glinted around his neck and she thought it incongruous that a large cross dangled from it. He didn't act like a religious man.

She'd save her screams for the bank. That sounded like her best option. All she needed to do was to stay cool, and keep up the pretense until they reached their destination, and pray he didn't have second thoughts.

Watch over me, Jess. I need you more than ever. If he had truly been her guardian angel, he'd provide a solution. He'd save her.

A motorcycle roared from out of nowhere and the big man spun her around.

Richards, the stranger from the beach, raced towards them on his Harley; he kicked the man's arm away from Melissa, and then shoved the barrel chest with a well-aimed foot.

When the man stumbled and released her, a startled expression screwing up his features, Melissa sprinted away.

The man on the cycle circled about, cut her off, and thrust out his hand to her. “Get on!”

Hesitating, Melissa stared at the strong hand before her in invitation, wondering if it represented salvation…or another trap? Out of the corner of her eye, she saw her would-be captor struggle to his feet, his black gaze smoldering on her. His hands out in front of him as if he would choke her when he got them on her again, he started advancing stealthily.

She gazed from the known evil to the unknown quantity and made a split second decision. Taking the cyclist’s hand, she jumped onto the back of the Harley, slipping her arms around his waist.

Jesse, this had better be your sign. I’m trusting you blindly.

She sucked in a deep, hissing breath as the man lunged at them, swearing and cussing all multitudes of curse words she’d never heard, even from the carneys.

The cycle wheelied and spun out a split second before her assailant grabbed for them, falling flat on his face.

Her fingers dug into her rescuer’s hard stomach, holding on for dear life. They put distance between them and the rugged kidnapper.

When she felt safe, Melissa yelled above the wind hitting her square in the face, “Let me off here.” She didn’t trust him; she didn’t dare trust anybody. For all she knew he was in collusion with the first attacker. Like a sting operation, this could be some cleverly laid trap. She’d not eluded her ex-fiancé this long by being dumb or sloppy.

No response. At least none she could hear. She repeated her demand several decibels louder.

When the man ignored her, she pummeled his back. “Let me off!”

Fear swelled in her chest again. Then she felt herself slipping and she grasped his midsection with the force of a steel clamp and girded her legs around the cycle. She clenched her teeth and forced herself to think rationally.

He’d have to stop eventually, and then she’d jump off and escape.

To her amazement, the cycle slowed, and then spurted to a stop in the sand. Her savior twisted in his seat, throwing a lazy smile at her. "I thought I warned you not to haunt deserted places by yourself."

Bristling at his tone, Melissa's ire rose. Swinging her leg off the cycle, she dismounted. Sand shifted beneath her feet, causing her to stumble.

Although he didn't laugh outright, the corner of his mouth tilted up and his eyes twinkled. Nor did he make a move to steady her.

Feeling foolish beneath his mocking gaze and heavy silence, she glared at him as she dusted sand off her jeans. It clung to her hands, the grittiness insinuating itself into the creases of her palms and ingratiating itself under her fingernails.

"Well?" His eyebrows tented and his gaze practically danced.

"Well, what?" she ground out through clenched teeth. She plodded through the sticky sand. It sucked at her feet, making her way difficult. She longed to wipe that smirk off his handsome face.

"Aren't you going to thank me?"

She turned, hands on her hips, taking his measure. She permitted her gaze to roam his length, taking in his strong legs, his muscular chest that felt as solid as Mt. Rushmore, and then his handsome, but mocking face. She met his amused gaze with haughty disdain. "Do you want money for your efforts?"

A mask shuttered his expression so fast Melissa thought she'd insulted him. "White knights don't save damsels in distress for cash."

"What *do* they accept in payment?" She almost kicked herself for playing along with this insanity, for asking such a leading question.

"I can think of a few things." His gaze riveted on her mouth.

She fell back a pace and held out her hand. "You'll have to settle for a handshake."

He laughed outright, but without a hint of mirth. "I guess you want me to strand you on this deserted beach so another creep can attack you?"

She glanced warily over her shoulder. "He's way back there."

"Not if he has transportation." He snorted. "He looked more than a little determined to me. More like desperate."

Her resolve wavered and she peered down the road, her gaze so intense the horizon shimmered. Dust boiled in the distance. Someone was coming. Of course, it could be anyone, but what if it was him? Could she afford to wait around to find out? She might as well play Russian roulette.

Her rescuer held out his hand again and she took it. His fingers closed around hers, strong and warm, and a shiver threaded through her spine. "Let's get out of here."

"What's keeping you?" Her arms crept around him again and he sped off, the cycle's velocity pressing them together.

She laid her cheek against his back to keep the wind off her face and felt his heartbeat, strong and steady. His scent, slightly musky, mingled with the sea and it wrapped around her giving her a false sense of security, probably because it was a clean, male scent, not unlike how Jesse had smelled. It was purely masculine, unlike the ostentatious, almost effeminate, French cologne her ex-fiancé favored.

Finally, when they reached the next small town down the coast, he pulled into a diner parking lot and killed the ignition. Mid-morning bustle kept her from panicking. Too many witnesses mulled about for him to try anything illegal.

She stayed glued to him for several moments, the droning engine still ringing in her ears, loath to separate herself from his warmth, loath to question her motives for feeling so. He reminded her of Jesse, that was all. He was the first man she'd come into contact with since her husband's death. It meant nothing. Really.

He cleared his throat and twisted in his seat, forcing her to lift her head and remove her arms from his waist. "I've saved you twice and don't even know your name."

"You've saved me twice and I don't even know *your* name," she mimicked, allowing her lips to curl into a small smile.

He flashed her a heart-stopping grin, his teeth so white they almost blinded her. "Sir Cody Richards at your service, Mademoiselle." He grasped her hand and kissed it, his lips so warm and firm they should be outlawed.

Although her flesh burned where his lips touched, her heart sank. "You're not really knighted, are you?" Everyone with a royal title in her acquaintance was a dreadful bore. If she never entered society again, or associated with another blueblood, she would die ecstatic.

"What if I were? Does it make a difference?" His eyes narrowed on her, but otherwise, he squared his shoulders and sat up straight and tall in his seat.

Yes! she wanted to scream. It made a huge difference. She'd assume he was teasing her. He reminded her too much of

Jesse, always more concerned about her welfare than his own, to belong to the selfish elite. "You're not," she took a stab at guessing, hoping he'd enlighten her.

"I don't recall answering." He dismounted, then circled her waist with his hands and lifted her off the cycle, swinging her to the ground beside him.

Melissa didn't grace his non-answer with an answer of her own, but instead gazed up at him and realized she had to crane her neck to look him in his eyes. Not a short woman, she rarely had to do that. It wasn't a bad feeling.

He took her elbow, propelling her toward the diner. She dug her heels into the gravel driveway, refusing to budge another millimeter. "Where do you think you're taking me?" She'd stopped being led a long time ago. She wasn't about to start up again easily, and not without full trust in the person she was following.

"I'm starved. Thought you might be hungry, too."

"I lost my appetite." Food was the last thing on her mind after that nasty little scene. Her stomach still felt queasy, as if someone had lit a few bottle rockets inside it.

"The least you could do is share a cup of coffee with me. After all…"

"You saved my life." She chuckled despite herself. "You're never going to let me forget that, are you?" Melissa sent him a sideways glance and couldn't resist asking, "You're not Chinese, are you?"

He stopped short and favored her with an amused look. "Do I look Oriental?"

She studied him intently, dissecting his features. Strong chin, dark blonde, springy hair, deep brown eyes, high cheekbones, and firm lips. "I'd say you look German. Maybe English."

"About three quarters German, with a quarter mutt mixed in. No Chinese that I know of." He scratched his chin. "So why'd you ask?" His black brow lifted enquiringly.

Melissa cleared her throat. "The Chinese believe that if you save a life, you're responsible for it." She cracked a small smile. "I just wanted to make sure you didn't feel beholden to stick around me forever. I don't think I could stand that."

The man's expression sobered and the smile died out of his eyes. He took her elbow in his fingers and this time, she let him guide her into the diner. He chose a booth in the corner and stretched his length the entire seat. When a cute little waitress sashayed up to the table with eyes only for him, he winked at her. Any moment the woman would swoon on their table. Some women had no decorum.

Irritation coursed through Melissa and she moved the condiments lest the young woman collapse before her. Then she scooted further back on her bench to get out of the way.

"What do you want?" Cody flashed her a lazy, sexy smile. It was about the sexiest, sultriest smile she'd ever seen. If she were a weaker woman, like the waitress, she'd probably melt at his considerable charms. But she wouldn't allow herself to crumble.

"Just coffee. Black." She handed the menu to the waitress, who barely tossed her a glance, as if she were invisible. It was a new feeling she didn't much like. Always before, she'd been the center of attention, even at the carnival. With or without her family's money backing her, her presence lit a room. Her fiery red hair attracted male attention wherever she went. Most women seemed to be intimidated by her rare beauty. Not that she minded. She wasn't used to having many women friends. She'd always had more than enough men around to make up for lack of female companionship. Her little sister, Christina, provided all the female friendship she needed.

Thoughts of her sibling tugged at her heart as they did every time she let down her guard. Quickly, she pushed the unwelcome thoughts from her mind. Christina was from another life. Much as Melissa loved her, Christina was part of the past and didn't belong in her future. At least not until Nathan died, and that could be many long years. It was best to forget both Christina and her father. They came part and parcel with Nathan.

Her rescuer ordered half the menu, nothing with less than a few thousand carbohydrates and a cholesterol nightmare. She wondered how he stayed so slim and fit if this represented his typical diet? When his omelet came, he delved into the creamy concoction. Butter dripped from every forkful. Cheese oozed out the edges.

He fixed her with his steady gaze again. "You've still not told me your name."

The truth was, she still hadn't decided on her new alias. She didn't want anything that would attract attention, which meant not too fancy, nor too mundane. No Smith or Jones.

Her mind went blank. Who did she want to be this time? Wholesome, like Molly? Or fancy, like Vanessa?

"You have a name, don't you? I told you mine, it's only

fair if you tell me yours." He stopped chewing as if willing her to speak.

She sipped her coffee, studying him through her lashes. Was he *too* interested? Or was she paranoid? It was a normal question.

"Lisa..." Jesse had called her *Lissa.* She couldn't use such a natural extension of her real name, but *Lisa* sounded enough different that it shouldn't raise suspicion. She glanced out the window, struggling for a last name to go with her new first name. Woods surrounded the little town. "Woods. Lisa Woods." She stirred her coffee, avoiding his probing gaze. "I really need to get back to my house." She tossed a couple of crumpled, faded dollar bills on the table and scooted out of the booth. "Thanks for the white knight routine. I owe you two now."

He stood in a flash, blocking her way, his shadow falling over her. "Don't you want to go to the cops and report that guy?"

Panic palpitated in her chest. The police scared her as much as that bounty hunter had. Maybe more.

"No!"

God, that *sounded desperate. She* was *paranoid.*

"No?" He followed her outside after tossing his own money on the table and leaving half his meal untouched. "Do you care to enlighten me?"

"No." Goaded, irritated, she pivoted on her heel and faced off against him, her hands planted on her hips, her feet at parade rest. "I appreciate your help but I don't owe anyone explanations. I don't know you. Let's keep it that way."

"How do you plan to get home?"

She needed a way to get rid of him for good. "I'll call my husband to pick me up."

Shock flickered across his face. His gaze sought her finger. "You're married?"

"According to my husband and the great state of New Jersey." She crossed her fingers behind her, hoping lightning wouldn't strike her dead on the spot. For good measure, she crossed her toes. She'd offer penance later.

She was Jesse's widow. She used to have a husband so she just hadn't updated the truth. That wasn't exactly a lie, was it?

He picked her up and hauled her to his cycle, depositing her on the seat. "Husband, huh?" His words were practically growled. "I ought to wish him lots of luck."

"What's the big deal?" Melissa seethed, treating him to her most regal glare, but she didn't dismount.

"I'm taking you back to your husband so I know you'll be safe. I couldn't live with myself if I read your obit in the paper tomorrow morning." He climbed on board and pulled on his helmet. He snapped it with jerky movements.

"You sure know how to sweet talk a lady, don't you?" she said, her words so dry she thought her tongue would turn to dust.

"I don't sweet talk married women." Without further talk, he revved the engine and gunned the cycle, his knuckles white he grasped the handles so tightly. It took off so fast, she almost fell off backwards. Fear glued her to him again.

Chapter Two

So, Jesse Elliott lived and breathed. And Miss Vanderbilt-Smythe had married the slob. I'll be damned.

Well, Jesse could have his little vixen and good riddance to the two of them. Right after he delivered Miss Melissa Vanderbilt-Smythe—or Mrs. Jesse Elliot, if she wasn't lying to him—to her beloved hubby, Cody'd call his client and tell him where to find the newlyweds so he could wish them well. And he'd collect his reward and get on with his life.

Cody didn't need bad tempered heiresses messing with his head. Just because she looked like an exquisite angel, with hair filled with sunlight and skin so white it looked porcelain, it didn't mean he had to give her one more thought. Let her husband take her grief. He'd bet his weight in platinum that Miss Vanderbilt-Smythe's attacker was a man on his identical mission. The man merely had less finesse, blundering in like the Terminator and botching the job.

So why didn't he just take the woman to her fiancé here and now? Then she couldn't slip through his fingers again or cause more trouble.

Because, Cody reasoned, he wanted to capture the elusive husband, too. Senator Alexander had promised triple the reward money to get his hands on Jesse Elliott. Triple the money was worth the chance. Then he could pay off his debt and have money to spare.

He'd be done with this whole sordid ordeal. And he'd get glowing references to all his rich friends and his business would explode overnight. He'd move to an uptown office, hire a secretary and buy himself a car. He was getting too old to ride a cycle everywhere.

The return trip took only half the time as he traveled at mach speed, anxious to unload his burden and meet the husband. It would take one heck of a man to stand up to such a strong woman. That, or the guy was terribly henpecked. Cody wondered which he'd find.

He circled the shack she called home, looking for signs of intruders. Even though she was in hiding, he couldn't get over his amazement that she chose to live in such ramshackle quarters after she'd known such luxury. He didn't want to touch the place without rubber gloves.

He killed the engine, his temper escalating by the second. "Come on!" His jaw was so taut he could barely grind the words out. Cody grabbed Melissa's hand and hauled her after him, not really caring that she stumbled and swore behind him.

"I thought you were a white knight?" She tugged at her hand but he refused to release it. He couldn't chance her escaping and being caught by that maniac again. He wouldn't release her except to her husband—or her fiancé. Whichever.

"I *am*." He spit it out with an attitude, and what an attitude.

"You could fool me and the entire free world." She dragged her feet. "What do you think you're doing?"

Cody stopped short and she ran into him, smacking into his chest. She tossed her head back and practically glowing red eyes flashed fire at him. She certainly had spunk. She wasn't the shy, retiring sort. Feral was more like it at this moment.

"I want to meet this husband of yours and congratulate him."

"Why?" Her tone was so suspicious; he took a double take. He thought he saw fear flicker in her eyes. But it disappeared so fast he must have imagined it. "I'm curious what kind of man could put up with a shrew like you."

She gasped and lifted her chin regally. "Unhand me or my husband will deal with you. I *promise* you won't like it."

"Resorting to threats now?" Cody released her so fast that she tumbled onto her derriere. He towered over her, and lowered his hand to her.

Ignoring his offered assistance, she struggled up on her own. She knelt, then squatted and stood awkwardly, rubbing her behind. "You're not a gentleman, Mr. Richards."

"And you're not a lady, Mrs. Woods. We're even. Now, introduce me to your husband and I'll be gone."

She strode to her door and yanked it open. "Honey, I'm home," she said in a singsong voice. She poked her head in the door, looked around, and called again, "Honey? Are you home?" She cocked her head to the side as if listening intently. After a few silent moments passed, she turned, looked up at him, shrugged, and splayed her hands before her. "Sorry. Guess he went to the store. Maybe another time." She started to slam the door in his face, her features a mask of ice.

Cody blocked the door with his foot and shouldered it open. Walking inside the one room shack, he looked around.

He hadn't been exaggerating when he called it a shack. Her poor mother would turn in her grave if she knew her pampered baby lived in a rat hole like this. Paint peeled from the walls—where walls still stood. Plaster literally fell from the one wall in chunks. What was left of the linoleum was scuffed, scraped, and faded so badly he couldn't tell if it had originally been white, yellow, or orange.

The only sign of a man he saw was Jesse Elliott's photograph framed on the bedside table. No men's clothing. No male reading material. No men's shoes.

This didn't add up. Any self-respecting man would patch up the holes in the wall, paint them and put decent flooring down. And where was his stuff?

Cody's detective instincts buzzed. "I need to use your restroom."

With mockery, she half bowed and pointed toward the back door. "Be my guest." She walked to the middle of the room and guarded it like a sentinel.

Inside the small room, he checked the cabinets and under the sink. Still no sign of a man. No shaving cream. No men's deodorant. No medicine bottles with anybody's name on it but hers. And there were three different last names on her bottles. Elliott, Rhodes, and Parker, but not even Woods. *Interesting. Very interesting.*

She was a chameleon, this one. Or an actress. Or an out and out liar. Maybe she was just schizophrenic.

Cody really didn't care. As long as Alexander paid him what he was due. The Senator wouldn't miss it. He could buy several large countries and not miss it.

When he came out, she glared at him. "He must be at work. I'll thank him for you, Mr. Richards." She stalked to the front door and held it open, motioning for him to leave.

He plopped down on her bed, kicking up his feet. He laced his hands behind his head and smiled at her smugly. "I'll wait. You're not safe alone."

She gasped and closed the door. "What'll he think if he finds you on our bed? Get up! Get out! Now!"

"If he's any kind of man, he'll thank me for saving your neck." He picked up Jesse's picture and studied it. It was the same guy he'd seen in all the newspapers when Melissa had first disappeared and sometimes even now on grocery store aisles in papers like *The Enquirer*.

Yep, there was no doubt. He had his heiress.

Melissa yanked the picture from his hands as if he soiled it. "How dare you!" She seethed, practically boiling. He could feel the heat as if she were a furnace turned up full blast.

He grasped her left hand and rubbed her ring finger. "Interesting," he drawled.

"What's interesting?" She yanked her hand away and stepped back two steps.

"The guy's too cheap to give you a wedding ring. I don't care how poor I was, I'd find a way to give my wife a ring."

"I have a ring." She sounded too defiant. Too brave. "My finger's just swollen." She turned her back on him, clutching the picture as if it were a lifeline.

"Uh-huh." He didn't believe her for a split second. Her entire finger was the same shade. There was no white line where the sun hadn't been able to reach.

"It's none of your business. Leave or I'll call the police." She picked up her phone, her finger hovering over the buttons. The air grew thick between them.

He gambled she wouldn't dial. She didn't dare. He didn't move a muscle.

"Aren't you going to leave?" She stared at him; worry pooling around her irises and in the tiny lines around her down-turned lips.

"Nope." He'd call her bluff if necessary. He wasn't leaving without her no matter what.

She slammed the phone down, and then paced the room, glaring at him at intervals.

"You're in some kind of trouble, just as I suspected, or you'd have called the cops."

"You're too perceptive," she muttered. "That doesn't give you the right to bully me."

"I'm not. I'm protecting your ungrateful neck. Consider me a fixture until your old man returns."

"Don't you have anything better to do than harass helpless women?" She slammed dishes around in her sink. Water splashed over the edge, soaking her feet.

"Yep. But I couldn't live with myself if anything happened to you." A strange noise he couldn't quite place alerted him to a possible presence. He sat up and swung his legs over the side of the bed. He cocked his ear to the wind and sat stock-still. His sixth sense told him the wind had shifted and their time was up. "Gather what you need. We're leaving."

She swung around, hands dripping with dishwater planted on her hips. "You can't order me around! My husband..."

"Now or never!" he growled through clenched teeth.

Cody heard it again. Shuffling, like someone creeping around outside the hut, trying hard not to be heard. His hand crept to his belt where he'd hidden his revolver, reassuring himself it was there and ready.

"I don't have to listen to you. The only man I answer to is my husband." Defiance pure and undiluted gleamed in her resplendent eyes. Her jaw jutted forward and she made quite a picture. If things were different...

The door flung wide and the creep who'd attacked her earlier leered at them. Sunlight glinted off a gun barrel that swung from her to him, hovering indecisively at the end of a pudgy hand. "You're coming with me. No more tricks."

Melissa glanced at him, fear filling her eyes, but she held her body rigid, her expression otherwise neutral.

Cody nodded at her. "Do as he says."

"B-but," she spluttered.

"Now! I'm not going to waste my breath on you." The Cro-Magnon crossed the room and yanked her behind him. "You're my ticket out of this dump."

Melissa sent Cody a beseeching look that tore him up. He nodded again. "Do as he says."

Her shoulders hunched in defeat.

When the man turned his back on Cody, smug that he'd gotten his way so easily, Cody reached in his jacket for his pistol. Quick on the draw, he cocked his trigger, his aim square on the man. "Let her go."

The man glanced over his shoulder, his face turning ghostly white.

"Drop the piece."

"I'll shoot her." The man's voice wavered and his hand shook.

"You do, I'll shoot you square between your eyes." Cody adopted his most lethal smile, the one that had served him well through many tight situations.

"Richards," Melissa hissed, her voice quaking and barely audible. She tilted her head at the man's pistol, her eyes speaking volumes.

He had to ignore the plea in her expressive eyes or he'd be lost. He couldn't afford to show indecision, mercy or fear. Any or all would be deadly.

"I'll shoot her. I mean it." Fear laced the big man's words.

Cody's grin widened. Fewer words meant more power. He put his other hand on the gun, squinted his eye and stared along the black barrel.

Sweat broke out on the man's thick forehead. Heavy beads of perspiration trickled into his eyes and he blinked. His hand shook badly now.

Melissa stood regally straight and tall, her shoulders squared, her chest puffed out.

She might be spoiled, but she had spunk. And fire.

Finally, the man tossed the gun to the floor. It discharged, the bullet going through the wall, not that it was much of a wall. A child's toy cap gun could put a hell of a hole through that flimsy excuse for shelter.

Cody ducked, and then dove on the man, knocking him out cold after a short tussle.

"You'd have really let him shoot me?" Fury shook her voice. Melissa crossed the room and holstered the man's gun in her slacks after putting the safety catch on. Her movements were quick and precise.

She'd have been an asset on the force, Cody realized. "He wouldn't have." He reholstered his own gun, keeping an eye on the adversary.

"You're awfully sure of yourself. You a cop?" She peered at him, tons of distrust mirrored in her eyes.

"An ex-cop."

"That figures."

Not a doubt lingered in his mind that it wasn't a compliment. Derision laced her words like arsenic. He fingered his jaw where the man had landed a punch on him during their tussle. Swollen flesh ached at his touch. He winced.

Melissa crossed the room, removing his fingers and examined his face with close scrutiny. "You need a steak on that. But I'm fresh out. Ice'll have to do." She packed a plastic baggie with ice and slapped it in his hand. "Hold that on your jaw."

"Get your stuff and let's go." He glanced at the man on the floor, stirring slightly. "He might have friends." He positioned the bag over his swollen cheek and grimaced when pain slashed at him. It was so cold he felt as if he'd dived into a snow bank face first.

Melissa froze, her gaze pinning him. "There might be

more?"

"Could be. Better safe than sorry. We'll call your husband after we reach safety." He kept an eagle eye on the man in case he stirred.

She slapped together a small backpack with haphazard abandon, sliding Jesse's picture on top reverently.

When a stab of jealousy pierced him, he chastised himself. What business did he have feeling jealousy over another man's wife? Although Elliott didn't deserve her, making her live in this shack and leaving her unprotected.

Melissa's family was right to dislike the guy.

Cody hadn't met him and he couldn't stand the man.

~ * ~

Melissa stared at her rescuer long and hard, trying to size him up.

She'd seen that hard look on a man's face before and it sparked an ember of fear in her heart. Nathan always wore that expression just before threatening her. Oh, they were subtle threats, well masked in civilized niceties. Usually. Twice, he'd backhanded her, dropping his thin veneer of civilization. He'd looked as if he'd rather have strangled her. It had scared her to death. She'd never let another man touch her in that way again.

Cody stuck his hand out to her. "Time's wasting. He won't stay out forever."

She bit her lower lip, her gaze ping-ponging from the cave man on the floor to her white knight. She peered into his deep brown eyes and made a quick assessment.

He didn't look like a murderer and he had saved her not once, but three times. Maybe he deserved the benefit of the doubt. But only because she was running out of choices. Then again, maybe that wasn't the only reason...

Snubbing his hand, she hoisted her pack onto her back then lifted her wildly arrayed hair out of its confines. "No thanks." Something in his gaze disturbed her, although she couldn't define it. But she'd come to trust her instincts. Jesse had taught her that and they'd never steered her wrong yet. "I'll find sanctuary till my husband joins me."

"By then, you'll be dead—or worse." A ravaged sigh escaped his chest and he pushed long fingers through his disheveled hair. Dim light filtered through cracks in the walls, throwing his features into shadow.

Melissa blinked. At this angle, in this light, his silhouette was a dead ringer for Jesse's. She hadn't realized before that this stranger stood about the same height, possessed the same general shape as her husband. He even had the same lack of fashion sense, preferring the early Indiana Jones look as she'd accused earlier. Still, she grudgingly preferred it to Nathan's pretty boy, never a hair out of place, style. She'd seen him in so many tuxedos she'd begun to dream she was engaged to a penguin.

"I'll take my chances." Discussion closed, she pivoted on her heel to leave him in her dust. Instead, grubby fingers bit into the flesh of her ankle and she gasped as she pitched forward, instinctively covering her face with her arms. Her pack slammed into her back, knocking the wind from her lungs, almost rendering her unconscious.

"You're not going anywhere, babe," a raspy voice said from about five feet behind her. She craned her neck and her assailant's furious face swam before her glazed eyes, his features swimming in and out of focus.

She kicked with all her might, putting all her strength into her efforts. "Let go of me!" she commanded in her most impervious tones.

Still, he held tight, ignoring her efforts so easily it was if she weren't struggling.

Suddenly, she pitched forward as if catapulted free of the earth's gravity, and her head slammed into the concrete floor. Black spots whirled before her eyes and she felt herself going in and out of consciousness. Pain like she'd never felt before pounded her head and she could barely see, but she strained to open her eyes so she could see her attacker and elude him.

Fuzzy shapes like furry grizzly bears in various shades of gray filled her vision. As her eyes focused, Melissa realized Cody held the other man in the air about a foot off the ground. His fist rearranged the man's already bulbous nose as blood spurted forth.

With a grimace and a churning of her stomach, she turned her head and inched further away, holding back a groan. When she dared look again through the slit of one narrowly open eye, she saw the giant slump to the floor in a heap.

Cody bent at his waist, his hands on his kneecaps and he inhaled deeply, his head hung low. His chest heaved as he pulled air into his lungs.

Now was her chance to escape both men, while one was unconscious and the other was out of breath. It might be her only chance for freedom.

Stealthily, Melissa scooted to the door, and then crouched

on her feet, ready to dash through the door. If only she could reach her friends at the carnival, they'd protect her. They'd help her find new sanctuary and she'd continue to elude monsters like Nathan and this Cro-Magnon.

Just as she started to stand, Cody's head snapped up and his gaze sought hers. His eyes narrowed to mere slits as if he could read her mind. Not that her strategy would be difficult to ascertain from her proximity to the exit.

"Are you thinking of leaving this party *sans moi*?"

Melissa shook her head slowly from side to side, her mouth set in a grim line, wisps of red hair in her eyes. She pushed them away impatiently, and matched him stare for stare. With her peripheral vision, she gauged how far she remained from freedom and calculated how good a chance she stood of escaping him, wondering if more of the bounty hunter's thugs awaited her outside.

"Who invited you in the first place?" she said after a long silence.

"That's fine gratitude to show a man who saved your neck three times! No wonder chivalry's dead. Women don't appreciate a thing." He dusted off his hands then pulled himself to his full height. His shadow stretched to her feet and she felt strangely caught...and ungrateful.

"Thank you," she murmured grudgingly.

"You're welcome. I think." The right corner of his lips tugged upward and he wore the same devil-may-care grin that had so endeared Jesse to her. Her heart did a little flip-flop that reverberated through her. She felt like the worst kind of traitor, letting a stranger have the same effect, even if minimal, that Jesse'd had on her.

Or maybe, she rationalized, her heart stuttered because he reminded her of Jesse. That was it. That was all it was.

She took several cleansing breaths, forcing herself to calm down, until the giant groaned and rolled over. Fear imploded in her heart and she froze to the spot, her eyes glued on the man's every movement.

"We don't have time to debate this." Before she realized Cody's intentions, he strode to her and flung her over his shoulder, caveman fashion. Her long hair hung in rivulets down to the backs of his knees, fluttering in the cool breeze blowing across the rocks of the Atlantic. Waves crashed ashore below the high cliffs as high tide washed in. Seagulls swooped into the undulating waves, rising back into the skies with squirming fish in their beaks. White capped clouds shifted and swirled into myriads of shapes that all looked backwards from her upside down position. She commiserated with the poor fish, knowing exactly how they felt.

She pummeled his back with her fists, kicking her feet in the air. "Put me down this instant!" she said in her most imperious voice, the one she'd cultivated from a dozen years in boarding schools.

"Gladly, lady! You know you're one giant pain in the ass?" Without preamble, he dumped her on the hard ground before his cycle.

Dust threatened to choke her as she tumbled unceremoniously, limbs sprawled unladylike, twisted and mangled like a Gumby. When her tortured body finally came to a semi-still position, she blew wisps of errant hair out of her eyes, her bottom lip sticking out. "You, Mr. Richards, are no gentleman." She untwisted herself, and stood slowly, unsure if she'd broken any crucial body parts. Once she'd taken inventory and ascertained she was only a little bruised from the incident but not seriously damaged, she faced off against him, the rising sun in her eyes. Why did he always seem to have the advantage of seeing her face clearly while she only saw his in shadow? Did he somehow prearrange this to his advantage?

"And you're no lady!" He swung his leg over the seat of his cycle and revved his engine. He patted his helmet on and strapped it under his chin.

She didn't move a single muscle, just stared at him, keeping her face devoid of expression. Looking over his shoulder for signs of life, all she saw were scampering rats foraging for leftover carnival goodies and sparrows diving for the scraps the rats hadn't dragged off. Not a human soul stirred within sight. Judging from the sun's position still low in the almost cloudless sky, noon wouldn't come for hours. No one would be up. They'd only gone to bed in the wee hours of dawn.

No help would be forthcoming from her carny family.

Ruining her stoic stance, she glanced uncertainly over her shoulder to see if her would-be captor followed.

"Hurry up and choose. Me or him. I know what my choice would be in your position," he drawled, a hint of a New York City accent echoing in his words. No wonder he seemed so cocksure of himself. All New Yorkers thought they ruled everything under the skies.

"Show me some credentials," she finally said, needing

assurance he wasn't a mass murderer.

"You mean that if I carry a gold card or show you my clean driving record, I'm safe?" He chuckled, ridicule lacing his voice. His hand revved the engine and he bounced on his seat. "I'm cutting out of here in precisely one minute, with or without you. Do you really want to tangle with Mr. Bad Attitude in there? I don't think he likes us very well."

She wanted to trust him, knew she needed to trust him, to take a chance, but it went against her basic nature. She'd had trouble trusting anyone until Jesse came along, then he'd been torn from her so cruelly.

"Time's almost up. What's the million dollar answer?" Richards tilted his head toward her shack, a smug smile hovering about his lips. "Me? Or him?"

She looked at the hovel she'd been calling home for the past few months and thought she detected shifting shadows. Fear squeezed her heart, spurting her into action. She sprinted onto the back of his bike before she could think too long or too hard.

"Hang on, Princess." He barely gave her time to encircle his waist with her arms before he pushed the machine into hyper drive, flying into the wind.

Chapter Three

Wind whipped Melissa's hair wildly about her face. She pushed it out of her mouth and her eyes several times before she gave into the sheer pleasure of the ride, letting the wind have its way with her errant locks.

Fragrant woodsy perfume replaced the salt spray in her face, tickling her nose. The sun rose higher in the sky as they rode inland, losing themselves in lush forest that was such a contrast to the sandy, open beach. Traffic grew sparse the deeper they drove inland and she didn't know whether to feel safe that civilization and Nathan's bounty hunters were far behind without a clue to her whereabouts…or scared of her presumed savior.

Her thoughts traveled faster than the cycle. She needed protection and an escape plan in case they were found, in case Cody Richards was a fraud. But she had neither. For all she knew, he was headed to her father's mansion or a rendezvous with Nathan the Nazi.

Was she a fool to be so trusting? But had she really had a choice? The Cro-Magnon was a sure threat. Just the memory of his fierce eyes and hungry expression made her tremble.

Her instincts told her the man to whom she clung would never hurt her. His eyes twinkled with good humor. Laugh lines crinkled at the corners of his eyes. His lips turned up in a ready smile. But most of all, his grip felt sure and warm when he'd rescued her all three times.

Or was she addle-brained from the morning's events?

Oh Jess! What should I do? I can't even trust myself.

Melissa knew she couldn't let her guard down. Not with her would-be savior. Not with anyone. Not even herself. She'd have to sleep with one eye open until she could safely escape.

Cody Richards wound and twisted through woods and country, making her lose her direction. She hadn't a clue where they were. Not that she had anything more effective than bread to trail behind her anyway. She needed to pay closer attention to the road signs instead of daydreaming, she chastised herself. Knowledge was power. Ignorance could be deadly.

When they crossed the state line into Pennsylvania from New Jersey, trepidation wrapped around her. They were headed west. She pummeled his back and yelled into his ear, "Let me off!"

Richards didn't respond. Maybe the wind whipped her words away. Maybe he had a back of steel.

She pummeled harder and she felt the grumble in his chest before she caught pieces of words whisked away by the wind.

"Unless you have a death wish, you'd better stop." The bike swerved dangerously as if to prove his point, forcing her to hold on tighter as if gluing herself to his back. Gravel spun out behind them, then he tilted the bike and popped a wheelie before gunning the monster vehicle deeper into the forest.

Through gritted teeth, she retorted, "I've ridden with Hell's Angels who drove saner than you."

Without warning, he almost jack-knifed the cycle in a near ninety-degree turn down a dirt path hidden from the main road. Low hanging branches swiped at her face, forcing her to bury it in his back. Finally, after she'd declared him completely deranged, he curbed the bike, vaulted off and put his hands out as if to encircle her waist.

Recoiling, she dismounted from the opposite side to put distance between them, quickly backing away, eyeing him and the old, rustic cabin behind him warily. It reminded her of some gangster hideaway.

Humor sparkled in Richard's green-gold eyes. He raked his fingers through his honey colored hair to push it into some semblance of order and sent her a saucy grin. "Scared of me, Princess?"

She backed away another two steps. Why did he call her Princess? Did he know who she was?

She glanced down at her old worn jeans covered in road dust. She didn't look like a princess anymore. Her gowns of spun gold and silver hung abandoned and forgotten in her room-size closet in her father's mansion. Victoria, her mother, would roll over in her grave if she saw her looking as if she'd walked off the pages of *Biker Chick Magazine*. Nathan would order her to change into one of her elegant gowns that cost more than her last year's expenses.

"Me, scared?" She snorted and shook her hair out, pulling a few twigs out of it. Henri, her French hairdresser, would have a heart attack if he saw her crowning glory looking like prime bird nest material, and she smiled at the image of his shocked expression.

When Cody's lips twisted in an I-don't-believe-you smirk, she tossed her head back and informed him haughtily, "But I don't trust you. I don't trust anyone." She backed away another three feet, her glance sliding around the deserted forest. She couldn't even hear a whisper of traffic. Not the drone of an engine or the honk of a horn. They were so deep in the woods, she expected gnomes and leprechauns to come out of hiding.

"That's fine gratitude for saving your pretty neck." He leaned against his bike, folding his arms over his hard chest. "Do I have a dishonest face? Or you're just one of those chicks that don't trust any man?"

"Chick?" She lifted an eyebrow at him. *No one* called her chick. Ire churned in her veins but she quelled it, reminding herself she needed to be in control at all times. She took a deep, cleansing breath and counted to ten mentally, performing abbreviated yoga.

She hitched her backpack higher on her shoulders, strained her ears again for a sign of a vehicle from which she could beg a ride and grimaced when the only sounds that met her ears were animal conversations and rustling leaves. "Thanks for the lift. Sorry I took you out of your way."

"Where do you think you're going?"

"There's got to be a town or a car sooner or later."

"The nearest town's about twenty miles as the crow flies." He looked her up and down with an insolent light in his eyes. "And it's not safe for a pretty girl to hitch a ride. Who knows what types travel a deserted road like this?

"There're bound to be houses…"

"This deep in the woods? Goldilocks, the Seven Dwarfs or Grandma's cottage?" He chuckled sarcastically. "I know these woods. Trust me. There're only a few hunting cabins. And you don't want some shotgun-toting rednecks high on Jack Daniels taking a shine to you."

Surely he was handing her a line? Wasn't he? This was Pennsylvania, not the Outback or the Wild West. Still, what would she do if some grungy backwoodsman got hold of her? So far, Cody Richards hadn't laid a hand on her, except to help. Maybe she was being uncharitable? Maybe she thwarted her guardian angel?

"Who are you? I mean, who are you really?" She narrowed her eyes and gazed into his.

He didn't flinch or hesitate. "Your protector." When she lifted her brow, he added, "An ex-New York cop."

"What are you?"

"Starved, tired and sore. Can't we play twenty questions after we get cleaned up and eat?"

"What are we doing here?"

"Hiding out until things cool off and your husband comes for you."

She cut her glance away from his and felt her cheeks color. In a low, husky voice, she asked, "You own this place? Is it safe?"

He dug in his pocket and pulled out a chain, heavy with keys. "It's locked up tighter than Buckingham Palace, so we won't have to worry about any surprise visitors."

"Why? Are you on the lam, too?" Melissa bit her tongue, furious with herself for her idiotic slip. Jesse had taught her better than that. Where was her mind these days?

"Maybe," he said smoothly. He took a bold step forward. His voice, whisper soft, asked, "What are you running from? Why is that creep chasing you?"

She clamped her mouth shut before she caused more damage.

"From your husband? Does he abuse you?"

She stiffened and lifted her chin. Jesse would never dream of it. But Nathan... She shivered despite the warm summer day; memories of Nathan's temper terrorizing her again as they always did at mention of his name. If he ever caught up with her, Heaven help her.

"Are you running from your husband? Does he hurt you?" Richards asked even more gently, concern in his voice.

"Je...Jeff would never do that." She closed her eyes. How could she be so feeble-minded to almost divulge Jesse's name to this stranger? She couldn't be going senile at twenty-five, could she? Or had the ride deprived her brain of oxygen?

"Who are you running from?"

She rounded on him, feeling hounded. "Are you my priest? Or just incurably nosy?"

"I'm a friend who wants to help." He stretched his hand out as he had earlier and tilted his head at the cabin. "Come inside. We can eat and get some shut-eye. Unless you prefer to stay out here with the grizzly bears?"

Melissa hesitated, staring at his strong, bronzed hand and wondering if it had a hook in it. It looked strong enough to crush her delicate bones and warm enough to make bacon sizzle. But it was those strangely golden eyes that threatened to mesmerize her and made her breath quicken in her chest.

Nor did the sound of grizzly bears exactly give her a warm, fuzzy feeling.

"You have to trust somebody. You can call your husband from the cabin and he can come for you."

When she still hesitated, staring down the road hoping for a good Samaritan to deliver her, he sighed deeply. "Look. If I wanted to hurt you, why would I take you to my cabin so the Feds could pin some crime on me?"

Melissa played out scenarios in her mind and the thought of coming face to face with a grizzly, or a hunting party or another bounty hunter didn't particularly appeal to her. And her mouth was parched from the wind and the sun's merciless rays beating on her face.

She really didn't have much choice. Cody Richards was the only game in town. If he had a phone as he claimed, she'd call one of her friends to come for her. Or she'd wait till he fell asleep and take his bike. She'd leave it in the next town with the local garage and give instructions to have it delivered to him. By the time he got it, she'd be long gone, her memory an echo on the wind.

In clipped tones, she commanded, "If you're lying, Cody Richards, God help you."

She glanced Heavenward. *God's good graces will protect me. Right, Jesse?*

Eyeing the quiet cabin in trepidation, she wondered if this was an elaborate trap. Would Nathan or her father lay in wait inside? Or their agent?

She looked for signs of habitation, as Jesse had taught her. She went through her well-remembered checklist. No smoke coming out of the chimney. No lights. No smells of cooking or gas tickling her nostrils. No movement. No unusual animal or human sounds.

Then, she looked for subtler signs. Trampled grass. Tire ruts. Was the place too tidy for a cabin tucked away from human contact for a couple of years, as Cody had claimed?

She heard a faint buzz and wrinkled her nose. Wasps. She hated nature's winged syringes. She inched closer very carefully and spied the mud daubers' nests painting the front of the cabin, as if a small child had slung mud pies everywhere. Those had to go immediately. She'd tell Cody to clean them up soon as he was rested. A few feet away, a bird nested under the porch overhang with her brood of hungry mouths poking over the edge of the straw.

"Too rustic for you, Princess?" Cody whispered in her ear, his voice deep and raspy. His warm breath tickled her neck, sending long-forgotten, not entirely unwelcome sensations down her spine.

"Stop calling me that," Melissa said through grated teeth. That was her daddy's pet name for her and touched her earliest memory buttons. She turned her gaze on the stranger beside her, wondering again if he were her savior or her captor, but still no closer to the answer. "Does it have somewhere to sleep? Water? Food?"

"I can't promise food. I think I left survival supplies." A wicked gleam lit his eyes and he swooped upon an earthworm and tugged it from its safe haven. He dangled it before her eyes. A grin tugged at his lips. "Take-out protein. Care for a snack?"

"Let's check the pantry first," she said so dryly, her words almost turned like tumbleweeds. Melissa brushed his hand aside and ambled up to the cabin. She peered through dingy, spider web-covered panes as best she could, ascertaining her former opinion that it was deserted. She put her hand on the gun she had *borrowed* from the intruder earlier, just in case a bear rushed out.

Cody unlocked the door and swung it wide. He held his arm out, beckoning her inside. "Ladies first."

"My, my. You're a regular gentleman," she drawled, stepping gingerly over the threshold, still clutching the gun. It was several shades darker inside than out, like a haunted house. "Are there lights?"

He flicked the switch. "Nope. I didn't have time to call the power company."

She sighed in exasperation, turning to spear him with her glare. "Weren't you ever a Boy Scout? Didn't you go through boot camp? Don't you have a generator?"

"Yes. Yes. And no. Real men don't need electricity or generators. Just a little pioneer ingenuity and a strong ax."

"Right." Melissa sized up the dusty cabin, deciding the spiders had staked a homestead claim. Not that she'd be staying long, but it needed a good scrubbing and disinfecting. She turned her gaze on Cody. First things first. "Let's raid the pantry."

"Kitchen's first door to your right. There should be some tinned crackers and Spam ham. Maybe a few cans of tuna."

"Heavenly," she said without a trace of sarcasm. It sounded like ambrosia and her taste buds began watering. She started for the kitchen, but he circumvented her.

"I'd better check it out first, just to make sure we don't have any unfriendly visitors."

Melissa quirked her eyebrow and tilted her neck back to gaze up at him from this abbreviated distance. He was a good half a head taller than she, maybe more. "Who are you expecting?"

"Remember? This is bear country. I wasn't kidding about those critters." Richards took out his gun and cocked the trigger, holding it before him.

He must've been a formidable cop, Melissa thought. She wondered why he quit the force?

"Wonderful." She beckoned him to precede her. "Gentlemen first."

Stealthily, Richards pushed open the swing door as if he suspected an adversary on the other side, while Melissa held her breath.

Wider he opened the door, until they both had a clear view. Late afternoon sunlight streaked through dirty windows. Dust nearly an inch thick layered the counters. Baby spiders hatched in the sink. At their approach, they scuttled down the drain.

Cody laid his pistol on the counter and knelt on one knee. Opening a cabinet, he rummaged around. With a grunt of satisfaction, he finally pulled out a six-ounce can of tuna and one package of crackers. "Pay dirt," he said with satisfaction, a cat's grin curving his lips.

"Is that all?" She leaned over and peered into a black hole of cabinets. "Where's all your survival food?"

"Looks like someone raided it."

"I thought the door was locked?" She heaved a huge sigh, ordering her stomach not to rumble. "I am *not* eating your protein snacks. We have to go to the grocery." She straightened up, brushing her hands down her jeans.

He patted his flannel shirt pocket—then frowned.

She watched with trepidation as he sought inside his pants pockets and swore softly with fervor.

"My wallet must've dropped out of my pants back at your place. I hope your husband isn't the jealous type."

"You have no money?" Melissa closed her eyes and shook her head. "Why are things never easy?"

He pulled his pants pockets inside out and shrugged. "Can you fish?"

"In the dark?" She glanced at the waning light filtering through the cloudy windowpanes.

"Do you have a better idea? You didn't take to the quick protein snacks." He put his hands on his hips and loomed over her, challenge in his eyes.

She pulled the only money she had with her out of her pocket, a ten, and waved it under his nose. "We'll buy groceries."

It was his turn to snort. "What century are you living in? That might buy two days worth if we buy bread and peanut butter."

"I have ways to multiply this. You'll see."

His eyes narrowed speculatively. His gaze roamed over her appreciatively and she felt her whole body blanch. Quickly, before she let him see the effect he had on her, she turned away, found a can opener and a knife. After rinsing them off in surprisingly clear tap water, she spread thin layers of tuna on the crackers and handed him one. She stuffed one into her mouth, and then licked her lips.

"I'm too tired to ride into town tonight. We'll go tomorrow." He wasn't asking her opinion. After cramming a double-layered cracker sandwich into his mouth, he ambled to the living room and threw his long torso on the couch that she had her eye on. *Some gentleman.* His white knight status was in serious jeopardy. Weren't gentlemen supposed to give ladies the couch?

Melissa was debating if she should check out the bedrooms for a soft place to rest her head or if it was safer to curl up in a chair near Cody, when she heard the whisper of a hiss which made her blood freeze in her veins.

"This is heaven," Cody was saying, sighing deeply, oblivious to his unhappy neighbor. Absurdly long eyelashes for a man fluttered over his deeply tanned cheeks. His chest rose and fell slowly as sleep descended upon him.

"I suppose there was a serpent in Paradise." Melissa slipped the revolver from her pants as gently as she could, trying to quell the shaking of her hands. "Don't move a muscle."

"Why not?"

The sinister hiss sizzled and she froze instinctively, her eyes darting about for the snake. "I think you disturbed somebody's nap. And he doesn't want a roommate."

Now she heard a rattle, or at least she thought she did. She held her breath, her chest tight from the strain, her stomach tied in instant knots. Then the snake raised its flattened, triangular head, vertical, elliptical pupils devoid of emotion staring at her as if to hypnotize her. Its rattler tail coiled upward ever so slowly, as if to mock her.

"Damn!" Cody's eyes flew open and he froze to the spot. "Give me my gun."

"Shush. No time."

Melissa pulled together all her courage and peered down the gun's short barrel, getting the slithering snake in her sights. It hovered over Cody, well within striking distance, its rattle escalating. Is that how they sounded when they prepared to strike? She wasn't sure, but she couldn't chance it. She had just started to squeeze the trigger when Cody jerked in front of her sight. If she'd pulled the trigger one second before, she'd have shot him between the eyes.

"Don't move," she hissed, raising her sight a notch until the snake's maniacally grinning face dared her. Melissa ordered her knees to stop shaking. She needed to be in complete control. She could do this. She had to. She owed him.

"Who am I to argue with a woman who's got the drop on me?" His gaze never left the snake. His features lay in sharp contrast, as if etched in stone.

The snake's body writhed as if it relished taunting its prey; sure it had its quarry without a fight. Those cold eyes stared deeply into hers and Melissa felt as if she looked into a bottomless pit.

"What are you waiting for?"

The snake swooped down on Cody just as Melissa squeezed the trigger.

The gunshot rang out, loud and sharp, deafening her. She hadn't realized she'd pulled the trigger, but when the snake swooped down on Cody, she had acted instinctively.

But she wasn't fast enough. Split seconds before she squeezed the trigger, the snake sank its fangs into Cody's shoulder.

Blood spattered his face. Melissa turned away from the most gruesome sight she'd ever seen: the snake's body had fallen between Cody's feet but its head was still attached to his shoulder, and chunks of flesh spattered across the couch and floor; the sight made her sick to her stomach. She dropped the gun to the floor as if it burned her.

A second gunshot rang out and a sizzle of light exploded from the barrel.

Cody jumped and swore as the bullet whizzed within an inch of his head. He glared at her, a dangerous gleam in his eyes. "If you wanted to kill me, why not let the snake do it?"

He swooped down on the gun, emptied it of bullets and

holstered it in his shoulder strap.

"Aren't you going to thank me for saving your life?" She looked at him—anywhere but at the snake—and then decided it wasn't safe to look in his furious eyes either and she dropped her gaze to his dimpled chin.

"For almost killing me, you mean?" he asked in disbelief. "You're one mixed-up lady. I feel sorry for that husband of yours."

Melissa gasped at his crassness, and then winced when he yanked all four feet of the snake's rapidly stiffening body from the couch. Then he turned, glared at her, and sank to the floor, his eyes rolling back in his head.

Chapter Four

As Melissa's shock subsided, as she got her revulsion under control, her gaze focused on the man sinking onto the dusty floor, his pupils dilated, his flesh turning a sickly yellow.

Oh God! In the course of killing the attacking viper, she'd almost blown the man's head off, too. Just a fraction more to the left and she'd have killed him. Jesse's hands must surely have guided hers; his aim directed hers to save the other man.

Jesse, where are you when I need you?

Cody moaned, his baritone voice laced with deep torment. His hand struggled to reach his injured arm to brush away the snake's head that still draped him like a stole.

"Lisa." He said the word with such difficulty that she almost thought he struggled to recite the Gettysburg Address from memory. His hand fell to the floor with a thud as his eyes rolled back alarmingly in his head.

Melissa knelt at his side, putting her ear to his mouth. His respiration was barely audible, fast and weak. She put her lips to his head and was alarmed at his quickly rising temperature. She slipped her arms around his waist and tried to haul him to the couch. "We have to get you to the hospital." But tugging with all her strength barely moved him. She guessed him to stand at six foot three and weigh in over two hundred pounds. Her frame couldn't carry twice its own weight.

She panted, willing herself to perform super human feats, but desire and good intentions weren't enough. She'd already ascertained that the cabin's telephone was dead. The wires had been gnawed through. She and Cody were on their own. She eyed him with trepidation as she gulped in several cleansing breaths of stale, dusty air, trying to regain her strength. She'd be no good to him, weak and shaking.

"Do you have a snake bite kit?"

When he didn't respond, she shook his shoulders gently, her fingers brushing the finally still form of the snake fragment that still sprawled over him. With a grimace, she mustered her courage and shoved the snake to the floor. It fell next to her in a heap and she shuddered in disgust, her skin crawling as if tiny, poisonous spiders crawled up her flesh. She kicked it as far away as she could with her booted foot, and then blocked it from her mind.

Melissa had other, more important things to think about. "Concentrate on my voice. Where's the kit?" She ripped his flannel shirtsleeve off at the shoulder, examining blue-black swollen flesh. Fingers gentle as summer rain prodded his injury and she didn't like the feel of his flesh one bit. This was bad. It could be very, very bad. She would never travel without a cell phone again. If only she had one, she could call for help instead of being this man's only hope for survival.

In a guttural voice, she strained out through tightly clenched teeth, "Don't leave me, Cody Richards. I haven't repaid my debt to you yet. You can't leave the party when it's just getting exciting."

Shadows danced across the rugged planes of his ashen face, muting its features. All she saw was an oddly familiar ruggedness that tugged at her heart. Flashes of Jesse's lifeless face, eerily translucent and lit by flames where she'd last seen him, flitted before her tightly closed eyes and she fought to push them away. Death couldn't visit again; it wouldn't dare show its unwelcome face. Yet she saw the signs of life drain from Cody's body, felt his agonized struggle to breathe. She flung back her head and an anguished cry tore from her raw throat; then she buried her face in the injured man's chest, absurdly taking strength from him.

A trembling hand stroked her hair and a raspy, hoarse voice labored to be heard. "Check…saddlebag."

Her head jerked up; she sniffed and brushed a burning tear off her cheek with the back of her hand. "Where?" Her heart brimming with cautious joy as her gaze sought his. The man visibly fought death. He wasn't giving up. "In the kitchen? On the bike?"

His muscles rippled as if he tried to lift his hand to point the way, but his strength waned. Melissa covered his clammy hand with hers and squeezed it gently, lending him her strength. She saw his lips undulate as if he tried to speak again and she lowered her head, willing him to speak, to guide her.

Please be his guardian angel, Jess. Ill take a rain check for myself.

"Saddlebag. On the bike," Cody Richards mumbled at last.

"Good," Melissa said, applauding him with her tone. "Don't leave. I'll be right back."

She flew out to the bike as if the wind picked her up and carried her. Maybe it did; she couldn't remember. Her fingers fumbled with his backpack, but it was getting tougher and tougher to see. She squinted up at the sky, mentally cursing the twinkling stars. Then her wrist bumped into something long and metallic. Exploring further, her fingers curled around a long, cylindrical object and she smiled. Good. A flashlight.

Melissa felt for the switch and flicked it on, illuminating the contents of the bag. Frustrated, knowing that time was her enemy, she grabbed the pack, hauled it into the cabin, dumped the contents on the wooden floor and shone the light on it. Finally, she discerned the object of her search and grabbed it.

Now, what to do with it? Shining the small circle of light on the back of the box, she read and re-read the instructions, losing valuable time. It was the one commodity she feared Cody had least of. Impatience gnawed at her, brought on by the obstacles in her path; she was on the verge of swearing, but bit back the words her father would have rebuked her for voicing. A well-bred young lady didn't curse and swear, even in dire circumstances. She almost laughed aloud at herself.

Well-bred young ladies didn't share back-woods cabins with spiders and snakes either.

The snakebite kit said, she noted, that she had to drain the venom from the victim's body. And she hadn't long to do it. She had no idea how long it had taken her to find the kit, how many precious moments she'd lost reading directions.

Determinedly, Melissa held the flashlight under her chin, directing the beam of light as steady as she could as she opened the kit and found a venom suction machine. But it wasn't the most serviceable grip; she dropped the flashlight to the floor and heard it roll away from her. The light clicked off and she had nothing to guide her, save a pencil-thin stream of moonlight shining dimly through the gritty windowpanes.

On all fours, she groped in the near dark, scared to feel around, for if there'd been one snake nesting in the cabin, logic dictated there could be more. Many more.

Shivers shimmied down her spine, permeating to her fingertips and toes. Even the top of her head tingled in dread anticipation.

Cody didn't have time for her to be squeamish, though, so she forced herself to his side. Jesse would protect her. He had thus far. So with blind faith, Melissa ran her hands over the unseen floor, wincing when a splinter pierced the soft flesh of her palm. She uttered a sharp cry that was really no more than a small mew, then clamped her lips shut, feeling ashamed for her pain that must be nothing compared to the man's. She blundered forward, breaking through a whisper-soft spider's web.

Despair threatened to overwhelm her, but she made herself immune to fear and focused on the man's need and his complete reliance on her. Finally, her knuckles grazed the hard metal casing of the flashlight and she almost leaped for joy. She'd never been this happy to find her stockings laden with valuable baubles on Christmas morning, and she'd not felt this relieved when she'd found her lost diamond pendant hiding on the back lawn.

Melissa clicked the light on again; it must've switched off when it hit the floor. "Hang on a little longer, Cody."

Again, she shone the light on the miracle box and opened it. She stared at the miniature suction machine that looked as if it couldn't suction a baby's nose and gulped. She was supposed to suck out poisonous venom with this scrap of machinery?

She eyed it suspiciously, but the alternative would be to put her lips to the wound and suck out the venom, chancing self-poisoning. Or tying a tourniquet around the arm and taking a chance on cutting off his circulation; end result—amputation.

And Melissa knew quite well that she didn't have the grit to cut off his arm, no matter what.

She said a fervent prayer to the powers on high, her eyes squeezed tightly shut, her chest so tight with worry she thought it might burst from lungs craving oxygen.

Breathless, thoroughly exhausted, she forced herself to continue, beyond what she deemed necessary, to make sure she got it all. Then she poured hydrogen peroxide over the wound and watched in fascination as it boiled as if in a bubbling cauldron. Her fingers shaky, her head pounding as if someone struck a gong in her head repeatedly, Melissa bandaged the wound as best she could in her flickering light. Then she elevated the injured limb as the instructions demanded, propping it up with a small pillow she'd found on a nearby chair.

Shakier than she'd ever been, her stomach feeling green, she stumbled to the kitchen, scrubbed her mouth, face and hands at the sink as if she'd touched the devil's imp himself. Then she dropped to her knees, her hands still clenched, and offered her prayers and herself to the Lord.

Her mouth moved silently as her heart cried the words clamoring to escape. She didn't need sound. She knew her Maker would hear her, and that Jesse would do everything in his power to help.

Melissa'd done what was in her power; now it was in the

Lord's hands. Well, she'd done the toughest part, but she wasn't finished. She found fever reducer and an old cup, which she rinsed out and filled with water. She carried it to Cody, propped his head on her lap and forced the pill through his lips, then poured water down his throat.

Cody spluttered, almost choking, but she saw his Adam's apple work as the liquid passed down his throat. She repeated the process, raising his perspiration-soaked head higher so that it went down easier this time. She cradled him against her breast and supported him between the crook of her arm and the old couch.

Then she felt him trembling and cursed herself. Even though it was summer, the temperature must've fallen a good ten degrees since the sun set, maybe more. It felt good to her, but to someone running a fever, possibly in shock, it would feel chill. Perhaps downright freezing.

With the gentleness of a new mother, she lowered the man's head to the soft cushions of the couch as she eased herself out from under his considerable bulk. Her eyes now accustomed to the moonlight shining through the windows, she stood over him and looked at him, really allowing herself to look at him for the first time.

Not classically handsome like Nathan, Cody had a rugged attractiveness that she found far more appealing. Like her Jesse. His nose would have been Sicilian-perfect except for a bump and slight turn attesting to one too many fights—with friends like her Cro-Magnon captor, if her intuition was any good. His lips, even in fitful sleep, were strong and wide. It was a mouth that knew what it wanted, a mouth that would never be petulant. A day's growth of beard stubbled his strong jaw-line and blended in with springy hair as brilliant as a new day's sun.

Tremors racked his huge frame, pulling Melissa out of her reverie, and she chided herself for being a poor nurse. The man needed a blanket.

She found a bed blanketed with a dusty cover in the bedroom. Extra cautious, she crisscrossed the bed with her stream of light, and then snatched the coverlet from its mattress with a magician's litheness, her nerve endings screaming in protest lest she touch a spider or another snake. She kept both ears perked and watched the shadows with an eagle eye.

Spooked at the thought of snakes lying in wait, plotting their revenge for their cohort she'd executed, Melissa tugged at the edge of the spread, trying to lay it flat on the floor to ascertain that no suspicious lumps or movement writhed within. Then she shook it as best she could from the corner. Finally satisfied that it was snake-free, she did the same with the blanket underneath and the pillows at the head of the bed and bundled them into her arms before returning to her charge.

Melissa laid the linens on the floor by the head of the couch, and then lifted Cody's head to slide a pillow underneath. Then she folded the blanket over him and tucked him in as if he were a seven-year-old and not a grown, and extremely virile, man.

She brushed her lips to his forehead again and smiled when his flesh felt cooler to her touch. Good, the fever had broken. Her fingers lingered, brushing the stray strands of golden hair off his forehead, then took a last glance at her bandaging job to ensure blood from the wound wasn't seeping through.

Satisfied that it looked clean and secure, she rose to her full height, resting her hands on her hips, surveying the rustic living room as best as she could with the aid of dancing moonbeams.

When her glance lit on the snake's remains, she made a hard and fast decision. She didn't know how long they'd be holed up in this cabin together before she could safely leave the injured man to get groceries. And their earlier search hadn't unearthed as vast an amount of food as Cody had obviously counted on. At most, they had two days supplies. Perhaps three, as she suspected she couldn't eat for a good long while.

They were liable to become mighty hungry way out in the woods like this and she didn't dare leave him alone in this condition. And he wouldn't be able to help her get him to the cycle for at least several days.

Food was food. Jesse had tutored her in the art of survival and he'd drummed it into her head not to be squeamish. The good Lord had put meat on this planet to feed His children and so be it. Granted, if she had a grocery store around the corner, she'd buy steak and chicken soup, but that wasn't an option. She'd take what the Lord provided. And right now that meant rattlesnake meat.

With more forcefulness than she knew she had, Melissa took the pillowcase off the pillow and wrapped the snake in it and carried it outside to the clearing illuminated by silvery moonlight. Then she took the knife from the snake bite kit and began skinning it, telling herself it was no different than skinning a squirrel or a deer. She cut the rattle off for a souvenir to give to Cody when he pulled through this ordeal. She wouldn't allow herself to think *if* he pulled through this ordeal. Even the ghost of the thought made her grit her teeth in determination.

Then she gathered wood from a nearby woodpile, starting a small campfire. She smoked the meat, just as Jesse had taught her. She held it out on a long green stick, watching as the flames sparked and smoked against the velvety backdrop of midnight blue sky.

Chapter Five

Cody drifted in and out of consciousness. Cold sweat saturated his covers.

He couldn't be one hundred percent sure, but he suspected that an angel ministered to him, giving him cool sponge baths, spoon-feeding him mush that tasted like crushed leaves. She seemed to float in and out of his sight, murmuring soothing words to him when the pain ran through him in rivulets.

Then she gave him something that sent him floating on clouds as if he were an angel himself. He could get used to this part.

Little by little, Cody regained awareness. Vague images teased his memory and he could swear the princess was his angel.

Blinding sunlight pierced his eyelids and he opened one heavy lid, then the other. He tried to speak, but his mouth felt dry as stale greenware ready to crack and it had a horrible metallic taste in it. His tongue feeling three times its normal size, he tried to lick his lips. They felt parched and his tongue didn't want to move the way his brain commanded.

He was a horrible mess.

Unaccustomed to being weak or dependent on anyone, he grimaced and tried to swing his legs off the couch and sit up. But that was a mistake and he groaned when pain hit him in the solar plexus, feeling like a cartoon piano dropping on his head. Gently as he could, he lowered his head back to the lumpy, sweat-stained pillow, closing his eyes against the merciless glare.

The screen door banged, sending pain coursing through his eardrums to every raw nerve ending in his body. With all his strength, Cody opened one eye a slit to see who entered the room

The princess entered, clad in stonewashed blue jeans, her tailored white blouse tails tied at her waist and exposing a tiny triangle of taught stomach and a dainty belly button, her shirt sleeves rolled up blue-collar-worker style. On her, it looked extremely alluring. Especially when the early morning sun highlighted streaks of molten lava through red hair that billowed down to her slender waist.

She was the angel of his dreams, with hands as soft as a

baby's bottom. Hands that had touched him in places that would make a lesser man blush. Just the thought made his blood boil.

But she couldn't be an angel. They usually didn't enter through the front door as this one did. And they were usually quieter.

Suddenly her expression changed and she halted mid-step, her blue-eyed gaze riveting on him. Her eyes narrowed, then widened and he thought he detected a trace of pleasure before it was quickly veiled. She was at his side in two steps, her warm palm on his forehead, then cupping his cheeks.

"Sleeping Beauty finally awakes," she murmured, barely loud enough for him to hear. She walked around so that she could look squarely in his face. Without a trace of shyness, she leaned over him, her breasts brushing his bare arms, making him inhale sharply. Her finger pads prodded his upper left arm, sending shooting pain screaming down his arm to his fingertips and he winced.

"Still sore." It wasn't a question.

"That's…an…under…statement." His words skipped syllables and sounds, his voice sounded crackly due to his cotton-dry throat. It hurt to breathe. It took super-human effort just to twist on his side to get a better look at her. His muscles screamed from the abuse, objecting from even minute exercise. He forced his eyes open wider to study her face. His hand captured her slim wrist and he was surprised when she didn't try to pull away.

"What happened?"

"You cozied up to a rattlesnake that wasn't in the mood for company. I think he was a mite perturbed when you jumped on him with all 220 pounds..."

"One-hundred eighty-five." Cody grimaced at how weak he felt. He wondered how much muscle he had left, if any. Rattlesnake bites were nasty critters.

He inched himself to the side of the couch and let his gaze roam the room, wondering where his not-so-dearly-departed assailant had found its final resting place. But he saw nothing. It was probably behind the couch, or she'd kicked it underneath. It wasn't important, as long as it was gone.

Her hands climbed to her hips and rested there, her elbows jutting out at ninety-degree angles. "Do you think you're strong enough to help me undress you?"

His mouth dropped open and he gaped at her for several moments.

"So I can bathe you," she said on a long-suffering sigh.

"Help me to the creek and I'll do the honors."

She eyed him skeptically, her red brow arched. "I doubt you can stand, much less walk. One little riptide would pull you under."

"Creeks don't have riptides." He struggled to swing his legs over the side of the couch again, determined to prove to her how macho he was; that he could do this with a little willpower and mind-over-matter logic. But his legs felt like gelatin and his feet tingled as if a thousand needles pricked them.

Melissa watched with a maddeningly tolerant solicitude that irked him no end. He'd walk to that creek and bathe himself if it killed him. No society princess would mock him or pity him, no matter how angelic she looked. She could play Florence Nightingale on somebody else. Cody Richards wasn't a guinea pig and he didn't need her noble largess.

But his legs had other ideas and wouldn't support his weight. He toppled as he cursed under his breath, and he stumbled against her. Surprisingly strong arms encircled him and helped him to sit back on the couch.

Strumming his fingers through his hair, Cody glared at up her, feeling both grateful for her gentleness and mad-as-hell that she'd witnessed such weakness. Being the man of logic he was, he bit his tongue and decided the less said the better. He wouldn't let her see how much his condition affected him.

"Take off your shirt." Without awaiting his response, she turned on her heel and disappeared through the kitchen door. As he grudgingly removed his shirt, he heard water running. Old pipes groaned in protest when she shut off the water valve.

He was struggling to pull his jeans off his feet when she walked through the door and stopped, her eyes wide in surprise.

"What are you doing?" If she'd meant her words to sound commanding, she missed her mark. They sounded shocked, even a bit husky.

His blood warmed and the corners of his lips tilted up. This just might be fun. Definitely interesting. He liked the blush creeping up her neck, making her porcelain cheeks bloom with life. Nor did he miss her fingers clenching and her body stiffening. Very interesting. Even intriguing.

"I usually bathe undressed. Don't you?" He deliberately let his gaze roam the length of her svelte form, giving it permission to linger on her jutting breasts. Slowly, he lifted his gaze to hers in challenge, allowing appreciation to glow in his eyes.

"How I bathe is none of your concern, Cody Richards." Water sloshed over the rim of the metallic bowl when Melissa stomped across the room, even more when she slammed it to the floor with too much oomph. He'd gotten under her skin and the knowledge made him feel powerful. He wondered just how far he'd managed to get, and decided to find out. He didn't really believe there was a husband and he wasn't going to let a make-believe man deter him.

Clad only in his underwear, Cody stretched out on the couch, propping his feet on the end of the couch

She jumped back as if stung by a wasp, her gaze throwing flame at him. "Don't get any ideas. I'd do this for anybody in your condition."

He leaned forward, breathing on the long slender column of her neck. His husky voice surprised even him. "But you wouldn't jump back like a scared sixteen-year-old virgin for just anybody. Would you?"

Melissa stilled, but he could hear her heart race in her chest as it rose and fell rapidly, just inches from his face. Her musky scent was driving him crazy, almost as if she exuded triple doses of pheromones with his signature on them.

Her fingers closed over the wet washcloth but she didn't wring it out with much fervor; when she slapped the cold, wet cloth on him, it was if she'd thrown a bucket of ice water in his face.

"I don't like strangers getting in my face. *Any* stranger."

"We saved each other's lives. We're hardly strangers." But Cody lay back and enjoyed the feel of her fingers rubbing across his chest, then up and down his thighs. He wondered if she recognized the effect she was having on him, and then realized it was a little hard to hide in his brief attire. She'd have to be blind not to notice and her eyes looked as clear as the dawn sun.

Still, Melissa was doing a darned good job of ignoring him. Maybe too good. If he affected her even a quarter as much as she was affecting him, she must be on fire.

Too soon, the sponge bath ended and Melissa left him, his clothes bundled under her arm in a ball.

Feeling bereft, not to mention chilled without his clothes, Cody was a little perturbed that she'd left him undressed. "Hey, nurse! Why are you kidnapping my duds?"

Melissa stuck her head around the kitchen door, fooling with her hair. Her fingers worked to twist her long tresses into an inverted ponytail that made her look nineteen at most, and he was fascinated that it stayed without aid of a rubber band. She wrinkled her nose. "I'm washing them." She ducked back into the kitchen and he heard water running again. She wouldn't dare…

"Don't I get my clothes back?"

"When they're washed and dry. And they don't smell like a skunk sprayed you." Her voice was muted by the running water. "Cover up with the blanket."

That dashed any romantic notions he'd held. *That's* how she saw him? Or rather, smelled him? Not that he could exactly bathe when he'd been unconscious for God only knew how long. He eyed the blanket with disdain. It was too hot to pull that heavy thing over him in the climbing heat of the day. She'd just have to deal with him as he was. She was a grown woman. Surely she'd seen a man in less than this. His stomach grumbled and his mouth felt parched. "Can I get some water? And maybe a little food?"

"Coming right up!" Melissa said in a singsong voice, suspiciously cheery all of a sudden.

Cody frowned, wondering why she seemed so congenial, when only moments before, she'd been colder than an iceberg. What was he missing? Or was he merely delirious? Maybe she hadn't extracted all the snake's venom from his blood and he wasn't thinking clearly.

She practically bounced to his side with a plate of smoked meat, something that looked like mush with bits of acorn and black berries rolling around the plate. Her other hand held out a long tall glass of water.

He gulped the water down like a man lost for a week in the desert, then eyed the food hungrily. Without ceremony, he snatched the plate from her, popping a berry in his mouth. Nothing had ever tasted better. The gods on Mount Olympus couldn't have enjoyed ambrosia and nectar more than he enjoyed this.

Melissa's hands crept behind her back and distant stars twinkled in her eyes. She watched him closely, her gaze glued to his face.

After Cody devoured the berries, he grabbed a chunk of the meat and bit into it. It tasted tangy if tough and he tried to place the flavor, but couldn't. With his mouth still full of meat, he asked, "What is this?"

Melissa's head moved so slightly as to be imperceptible. "Don't ask."

"Why not?" Suddenly, the meat stuck in his throat and warning alarms whirred in his ears.

"You don't want to know, that's why."

Cody slammed the plate on the floor and grabbed her wrist, dragging her to him, her lips not more than an inch from his. Melissa's breath mingled with his, but excitement was not what he felt. Through gritted teeth, he snarled, "Tell me."

"Rattlesnake." Her eyes met his steadily, unflinching.

Cody coughed and spluttered, turned his head sharply and spit the offensive meat out across the floor. He didn't care that she cried out in pain when his fingers bit into her silky-soft flesh. She deserved to have her backside tanned but good.

"I told you that you didn't want to know." Her features remained devoid of expression but he was sure there was a smirk lingering in the background.

"Are you trying to poison me? Why bother to save me from the thing in the first place?"

"It's completely edible. And we're not exactly rolling in food. You wanted me to try your protein snack, remember? Why is this different?" Melissa tugged at her arm ineffectually. "You're hurting me. Do you mind?"

"Get that stuff out of my sight." Cody flopped back onto his bed, his hunger completely dissipated. He might never hunger again….

"Don't blame me that you brought me to a cabin with no food." She disappeared into the kitchen, her lush curves sashaying in taunting rhythm.

Cody didn't know if he wanted to chastise her or kiss her senseless.

Right now, though, he was too tired to do either.

Chapter Six

Cody hadn't exactly been the ideal patient.

Although he was healing, he was still a shadow of his former self. A shadow covered in a four-day growth of sandy dark blonde beard. He reminded Melissa of a grumpy koala bear. She didn't know whether to slap him or hug him when he grinned lopsidedly at her. She glanced up from her well-worn journal, to which she had always confided her most intimate thoughts.

While Cody slept fitfully, she recorded the way shadows tap-danced over his face, the way the sun made his hair glow like spun gold. How strong, yet vulnerable, he looked in repose. She voiced how her heart ached at the dilemma of missing Jesse, while Cody Richards captured more and more of her attention. *How dare he intrigue her!*

She could've pegged him for a tough New York cop the moment he opened his mouth, or the moment he ripped into action. Yet he was the epitome of the Midwestern, all-American male, all six foot something of him.

This one was an enigma. All tough-guy macho image on the outside, but Melissa sensed he could be smooth as melted milk chocolate with the right woman. She stopped scribbling in her journal to study him, chewing the cap of her pen thoughtfully. With sunlight streaming through the windows that she'd polished to a high shine, his lashes gleamed silvery gold. Stray locks of hair dangled over his forehead. His firm lips curved in a smile as if he were having an extraordinary dream. She wondered if he dreamt of a woman and who she was. A man as incredibly handsome as this one must have a special woman in his life, even if his fingers were devoid of rings.

Melissa's foot, curled beneath her as if she were a sleeping cat, tingled and she shifted her weight in the leather lounger. She put pen to paper again and jotted down a list of what she needed to get done—something she'd meticulously avoided doing since she'd met Jesse. She'd deliberately avoided schedules and routines in favor of greeting each moment like a new friend.

But now she had a responsibility to this man. Cody needed his medicine on time, dressing changes, food and drinks, sponge baths... She felt heat creep into her cheeks at the thought of sponging that hard body all over, feeling his incredible muscles under her fingertips, lathering him with warm, soapy water. She'd not felt a man's muscles in the two years since Jesse died and she'd not realized just how much she'd missed that sensation until now.

She felt incredibly guilty for having such thoughts about another man. Hadn't she sworn to love Jesse forever? Until eternity ended? Until the sun stopped warming the Earth? Until the stars ceased to twinkle in the night sky?

Melissa stopped writing and grimaced at the soppy sentiments she'd spewed forth on paper. Never before had she waxed so melodramatic. With a bang, she closed the book, angry at herself for letting a man get to her. A man she didn't even trust. At least not completely.

Uncoiling herself from the chair, as lithe as a lioness, she padded to the man on stockinged feet, having discovered it wasn't prudent to traverse the splintery floors barefoot. Towering over him, she tried to figure him out, as though if she stood there long enough, and looked at him deeply enough, she could read his mind or his heart.

But of course that was crazy. Even awake, when the windows to his soul were wide open, she couldn't read them. The only man she'd ever been able to read was her Jesse. And learning to do that had taken time and practice.

Melissa glanced at her wristwatch and realized it was time to change Cody's dressing. Gingerly, she lifted the tape from the still spongy flesh, wincing when he flinched, loath to hurt him when he wasn't awake to fight back.

Remembering she'd forgotten to put on her rubber gloves, she backtracked to the kitchen and gathered her medicinal supplies before returning to him. Humming a song her mother used to sing to her when she was little, Melissa soothed herself to a gentleness usually reserved for a mother with her child before touching his injury. She didn't care that she couldn't carry a tune and didn't much care if anyone else knew.

Working at the edges of the bandage little by little, she peeled it loose, lifting it off. She dropped the used dressing on the floor. Leaning over his broad chest, his heat seeping into her, she did her best to ignore the fact that every feminine instinct screamed for closer contact with this man. She berated herself silently, renewing her resolve to keep her distance from him. Nurses didn't allow themselves to think about their patients in that way. It was unprofessional.

Thus, honing her focus on the injured triangle of flesh, she cleansed it gently, taking care to cover it with antiseptic. But the tinge of yellow looked brighter again and twinges of alarm spread through her. She couldn't put off a trip to town. Cody needed to be seen by a doctor.

A warm arm encircled her waist and she gasped, partially in surprise, but mainly from the maelstrom of desire that erupted in her innermost core.

"I thought I was dreaming," he said in a husky, sleep-filled voice. "If I'm dreaming, I don't ever want to wake up." Before she could protest—not that the thought entered her mind—Cody pulled her into his arms.

But desire was short-lived when air-cooled water sluiced them, dousing the flames of desire. Melissa tore herself from him, glad for the wake-up call to sanity. She glanced at the heavens, knowing a jealous Jesse had stopped his rival cold.

"If you didn't want to kiss me, why didn't you just tell me?" Cody struggled to stand, sleep still shadowing his eyes. "I can take a hint."

Melissa backed away, not afraid of Cody but of her reaction to him. She covered her mouth with her hand to hide the smirk she feared lingered around her lips. Cody looked so cute, soaking wet in his T-shirt.

Then he swayed and steadied himself on the back of the couch as he started to crumple.

She dashed to his side, putting her arms around his waist. "You need to see a doctor. Are you strong enough to ride into town?"

"Do you know how to drive my cycle?" His brow lifted with faint challenge as if he thought a woman couldn't handle the power. "I don't trust myself to drive yet."

"I can handle it, if you can hold on." She let her lips firm in a hard line. No man got the better of her. She'd rather die than pass up such a blatant challenge.

"There's barely enough of you to hold onto."

"Don't judge me by my size," Melissa said in a deathly quiet voice. Too many people were sorry for underestimating her. She hoped he wouldn't be one of them. She couldn't respect a man who wasn't her equal. And she wanted desperately to respect this man. But he had to earn her respect.

So far, he was the only man since Jesse who might have a chance.

"I'm game if you are, Princess." He tugged his wet shirt

over his head and tossed it behind the couch. "Can you get me a dry shirt?"

The sight of the man's bare chest made her heart skip a beat, but she forced herself to gaze at his face without looking away. She peered at him long and hard but saw no flash of recognition, no trace of guile. Without a word, she spun on her heel and fetched one of his many shirts and threw it in his face. "Let's go." She pulled his keys out of her jeans pocket and jangled them in her hand. She put her arm around his waist and let him lean on her as he ambled to the bike.

"Are you sure you want to go into town?" Hot breath rasped down the column of her neck and she shivered despite the hot sun glaring on her.

"Why not?" Melissa tugged on the black helmet and pulled down the visor. With shaking fingers, she tightened the chinstrap, and then placed her hands firmly on the handlebars.

"What if one of your friends recognizes you?"

Melissa paused, steeling herself for the feel of his strong arms encircling her waist. Fortifying her reserves against his allure, she said for his benefit, "I still need to call my husband. There's no phone out here."

Cody stiffened behind her. She was almost sorry she'd brought Jesse's ghost between them. When his arms clasped around her middle, they felt strangely antiseptic, detached, leaving her with an oddly bereft feeling in the pit of her stomach.

Words weren't getting them anywhere, so she sped out of the clearing, concentrating on traversing the overgrown trail without killing them on some hidden tree root or low hanging branch.

When they reached the open road, she breathed a sigh of relief, then gritted her teeth. This machine had a lot of power, requiring her full concentration.

Cool wind felt heavenly on her flesh after days of muggy, unrelieved heat with only the creek in which to cool off. When she slowed to pull into the one-road town, she missed the breeze. Her leg muscles were stiff from grasping the machine so hard with her knees. This made riding horses seem like child's play.

Melissa glided to a stop in front of an office that advertised the local doctor who practiced there. Dubiously, she eyed the tiny office. All the doctors she knew worked out of Hollywood-sized mansions. Their receptionists glittered with diamonds.

"We're here," she said in a deceptively bright voice. She

wondered, as she'd wondered through the entire ride, what excuse would hold him when he found out that she couldn't find her husband? She'd painted a lie that was snowballing out of control. When she'd fabricated it, she hadn't intended staying with him this long. She'd planned on being long gone. But she hadn't counted on him almost dying and on her being obligated to stick around. She swung her leg over the side of the cycle and eyed him.

Cody held his arm, his cheeks ashen.

Alarmed, she was at his side in a flash, helping him off the bike, into the doctor's office.

He tried to brush her away. "I can walk by myself." But his bravado was short lived when he stumbled over the curb and started to collapse.

"Sure you can, cowboy." Brushing aside his protests, Melissa helped him inside.

"What do we have here?" a young doctor who barely looked old enough for his senior prom asked as he rounded the door to the waiting room.

"Rattlesnake bite," she said.

The doctor crossed to Cody's side in two long strides and helped him into an examination room. Melissa followed without invitation, as if she had every right to be there. "When did it happen?"

"Four days ago," she said, hovering at Cody's side, loath to leave him.

The doctor's only response was to lift his brows. He filled a syringe with clear liquid. "Let's give him a tetanus booster to be on the safe side." He wiped alcohol on Cody's healthy upper arm and plunged the needle in skillfully. "Why didn't you seek medical attention?"

"We were stranded in the woods without a telephone. I couldn't carry him to the bike and he couldn't walk." Melissa lifted pleading eyes to the physician. "I didn't want to leave him alone. We had a snake bite kit."

"You suctioned out the venom?" The doctor's coat tails flapped behind him when he rounded the metal examining table to Cody's injured side.

She nodded, biting her lower lip.

The doctor crossed the room, stuck one hand in a rubber glove, then the other, tugging it over the tips of his fingers. Crossing back to Cody, he prodded the wound with deft fingers. Without glancing at Melissa, he took the dressing off the wound and peered at it with aid of his penlight.

Cody winced, clenching his teeth so hard she could hear them grind. His knuckles turned white but he didn't utter a sound.

"Does it still hurt?"

"Like the dickens, Doc." Cody slanted a half-smile filled with pain at her. "Do you think you could be a little gentler? Better yet, let *her* do this. I like her fingers better."

The doctor glanced at Melissa finally. His gaze slid over her with a friendly smile. "I don't blame you. If I had a pretty wife like yours, I wouldn't let her out of my sight either."

Cody's teasing glance enveloped her. His eyes danced with mirth.

She turned away to hide the telltale heat rising in her cheeks.

When Melissa could find her voice, she asked, "What's the verdict? Will he live?"

The young man finished rebandaging Cody's wound, then pulled his gloves off and tossed them in the hazardous medical waste bin. "Your husband's a very strong man and a very lucky one. He should've been in a hospital immediately. His guardian angel must've been watching over him."

She leaned against the wall, her arms folded across her chest. "Is he ready to go home, Doc?"

"I'd like to do an EKG to be on the safe side."

Cody listened to the exchange in silence, his gaze shifting from her to the doctor.

"How long will that take?" Melissa asked.

"Not too long. A half hour—an hour maybe. Why don't you get a cup of coffee and a bite to eat at the diner around the corner?" When Melissa hesitated, he added, "I'll have my nurse come get you when he's ready to go."

Cody tilted his head. "You could use some decent food. Go on. I'll be fine."

"Is that a dig at my cooking?"

Her stomach growled. She hadn't let the rattlesnake pass her lips and the canned tuna had run out days ago. She'd subsisted on berries and boiled acorns.

Cody's smile grew wider but he deigned to answer.

"Pleading the fifth?" she asked dryly, pushing off the wall with her foot. To the doctor, she said, "I'll be at the diner."

"He'll be in good hands. Don't worry."

"I won't," she lied. She held her head high and left the office.

~ * ~

But when Melissa faced the greasy spoon, she dug in her pocket, remembering all she had was a ten-dollar bill. One meal would eliminate half that. Then what?

She had a better idea, remembering her promise to multiply their assets. Entering the diner, she made a few quiet inquiries and found out where the hot card game of the night was being held. Looking at her watch, she saw it was dinnertime. Since when did doctors work so late? Not in southern California. Not the doctors of her acquaintance, anyway.

"It's okay," she mumbled under her breath. It fit in with her plans.

Melissa passed a newsstand and spied a national newspaper out of the corner of her eye. Pausing out of curiosity, she flipped the paper open to the society page. She wondered if anyone she knew would be featured on its glossy pages. She dreaded seeing her picture staring at her again—not that she'd seen herself pictured here for a couple of months, when her father or Nathan had gotten it into their head that she might not have died in the plane crash with Jesse after all.

Good. Maybe the bounty hunters will stop seeking me and let me live in peace.

When the waitress led her to the front door and pointed, she spied a group of rakish men in the park across the street.

"They're at the gazebo in the town courtyard. Mosey on over and introduce yourself." The waitress's gaze danced over her. "I imagine they'll make way for you—long as you have money."

"Thanks." Melissa grinned and wiped her itchy palms down her pants leg, excited at the prospect of a game. She'd not played in a very long time.

Several heads lifted and eyed her with anticipation when she sauntered to the gazebo. Whether it was meant for her or for the fact they thought she'd be an easy mark, she didn't care.

Woe be to those who underestimated her. They'd find out their folly soon enough. "Can I join in?"

A tall, balding man with a glint of steel in his eye demanded, "You got any money, honey?" He puffed on a fat, smelly stogie.

Melissa frowned, tried not to gag, and dragged her ten from her breast pocket, achingly aware that all eyes were on her every movement. She waved it in front of their noses. "This is all I have. Will it do?"

The tall man drew the fat cigar from his mouth, blew smoke in her face, and guffawed. "This game is for big stakes. How do you expect to pay us when you lose?" His randy gaze raked over her suggestively.

"You mean *if* I lose, sugar?" She smiled sweetly at him, her eyes stinging from the smoke, then dug around in her pants pocket and pulled out a glittering ruby ring. She tossed it in the center of the round table. It toppled several stacks of red, white and blue poker chips in its wake, before stopping and sparkling invitingly. "Will this do for collateral? My daddy told me it's worth a mint."

Five men stood so fast that they would have toppled their benches backwards if they hadn't been cemented to the floor. They clamored to see the ring. A chubby hand clamped over her mother's ring, dragging it to the edge of the table. An older, balding man snatched it away, eyed it, and then bit the gold band with his teeth. "She ain't lyin'. This is good jewels."

The leader bowed low and swept out his hand theatrically. "Would you honor us with your presence?"

"I'd love to." Melissa smiled coyly and batted her eyelashes at him. Why did men make it so easy for women like her? Didn't they know better? "I'm so glad you let me play with you. I haven't touched a deck of cards in ages."

Greed sparkled in five separate pairs of eyes.

Good, they were hooked. This was her cue to reel them in. "Would you mind refreshing me on the rules of the game? Are deuces wild?"

"Which game?" one brave soul asked. His fingers twitched.

"You mean, there's more than one?" Melissa asked innocently, her eyes wide. She let her gaze roam over each and every man at the table, letting it linger on each man until he blushed.

Only one didn't. He hid behind a cloud of smoke that he puffed from his fat cigar. He blew it in her face and she choked back a cough, refusing to allow him to see that his disdain irked her. Instead, she reached over the table, pulled the offensive cigar from his mouth and ground it out beneath her booted heel. "There's a lady present. Please remember that."

"Let's play. Deal her in." Grudging respect rang in the man's voice.

Melissa reached for her mother's engagement ring, and slid it on her finger for safekeeping.

"Deal already, would ya, Frankie?" The impatient card player chewed a wad of tobacco as he spoke. Filthy brown juice dribbled down his chin. It also coated his teeth—at least what was left of them. "My money's gettin' cold."

Frankie, the former cigar smoker, scowled deeply, his bushy brows drawing together to form a single line. He was definitely a child of the sixties who seemed to be caught in a time warp. He wore what little hair he had left, now almost completely gray, in a long ponytail. A terry-cloth headband with a peace sign wrapped around his forehead, but it didn't quite hide the large, shiny bald spot on the top of his head. One long silvery earring dangled from his left ear. To complete the picture, he wore a tattered denim vest covered in patches and buttons that screamed for an end to war and for world peace to prevail.

"Keep your pants on, JoJo. Can't you see I'm shufflin'? I can't leave the deck stacked the way you had it." To emphasize his point, he winked at Melissa and pushed his thumbs under the cards in a slick maneuver so they splayed in an awesome show.

JoJo's moon-pie shaped face reddened as he lifted his bulk from his bench. Leaning over the table, palms spread flat on it, he gave the evil eye to Frankie. "You suggestin' I'm cheatin'?"

"Hit a nerve, did I, Slick?" Frankie snorted. "Sit down. I'm dealin'." He slid five cards to everyone.

Melissa looked at her cards, spreading them in her hand. "How do we play this game?" She batted her eyelashes at each man in turn and flipped her hair over her shoulder. "What's wild again?" It was essential they thought her to be a novice for her plan to work.

The man next to her, the youngest in the group whom she'd heard called Sally, scooted closer to her and threw an arm around her shoulder. He seemed to fancy himself a lady's man. "Well, darlin', we play five card draw the man's way. There are *no* wild cards." Hot breath fanned her cheek and skimmed down the column of her throat. His touch felt slippery and slimy, and Melissa had to quell a set of shivers lest she offend him.

"Sooooooooooooo…" she peeked at her cards with an exaggerated gesture, "we just play these cards? I have a pair of…"

He shushed her. "No, honey. Don't tell us yet. You get to discard up to four cards and ask for replacements." He sidled closer so that his thigh burned against hers. "You want three cards? Frankie, hit her with three."

She shook her head. She wanted to keep her queen. "I

only want two." She plucked the low cards from her hand and laid them face down on the table. After Frankie hit her with two more, before she picked them up, she asked, "Are we playing partners?" When he said, "No," she smiled sweetly up at him and lifted his hand by his forefinger and dropped it back to his side. Inching a good foot away on the bench, she said, "Thanks for the poker lesson."

Sally's jaw slacked wide as his cohorts laughed and slapped their thighs.

Frankie said, "She told you, Junior."

"Lover boy bites the dust *again*!" a fourth, hereto, silent man announced. A big belly jostled, probably acquired from all the beer he'd been guzzling and all the chips he'd been stuffing into his mouth. Large jowls matched his stomach, and hung down to form a double chin that wobbled when he moved. His hair was thick and wavy, dark brown with only the occasional strand of gray; Melissa judged him to be about forty.

"Stuff it, Louise," Sally growled under his breath, and swiped at him with the flat of his hand.

The heavyset man jerked backward and then shook a chubby finger at him. "I'm *Louis*, got it? I ain't got no girlie name like *Sally*."

Before this game turned into a rumble, Melissa licked her lips and intervened. "Gentlemen," she said, and cleared the sudden frog from her throat. "I didn't mean to start a squabble among you. I'm sure no one would ever mistake any of you for a *woman*. Not me certainly." She forced an appreciative glint to her eyes as her gaze rounded the table. Contrary to her words, she judged them all against Cody and found them sorely lacking in masculine appeal. "How about we play?" She was eager to win so she could eat. She'd not had a decent meal in over a week and her stomach growled at her to skip the foreplay and get down to business.

Fortunately, the men decided her suggestion had merit, as they were eager to fleece her of her ruby ring.

Little did they know that she'd managed to keep it through countless other poker games.

Melissa won the first round with a full house that they put down to beginner's luck or lady luck. Then she folded a couple of rounds and then won again.

After they passed the beer around, she pretended to take a few sips but kept her tongue firmly pressed to the bottle's mouth to prevent the flow of liquid into her mouth. She wanted to keep her faculties intact, as she counted on the fact they would lose theirs. The drunker they became, the bolder she got at bluffing which was her forte.

Frankie and JoJo stared at her cross-eyed and Sally even made a comment about beginner's luck and the mound of cash growing in front of her. She figured it was about time to call it a game and get some groceries.

Relief flooded over Melissa when Cody rode up on his motorcycle and stopped by the gazebo. She'd begun to think there was no way to escape with her winnings.

Cody blinked as if shocked, slumping a little and still looking haggard. He was in need of a shave and a haircut but it was the bruised flesh rimming his eyes that concerned her most. "I've turned this town upside down looking for you. I was beginning to think you'd ditched me."

She couldn't tell if he was on the level but she felt a blush stain her cheeks nonetheless. Truth was, she wasn't sure if she really was going to do just that or not. She'd come so close, so many times. Thrills shot through her when she gazed upon her white knight on wheels. He certainly had a knack for turning up at the right place at the right time.

Well, except for the snake incident.

"You found me." Was that her voice that was so husky? Or was it her imagination that it sounded that way? She did feel a little tipsy. More of that beer must have slid down her throat than she had realized.

As nonchalantly as she could with shaky fingers, Melissa raked in her winnings and then stood. "Thanks for letting me play. I never knew gambling could be so fun." She half twisted and cocked her head at Richards. "I've got to go now. My ride's here."

"Not with all our money, you don't." Frankie snarled and grabbed for her wrist, a menacing glint in his dark eyes. "She fleeced us. She ain't no amateur, first-time card player like she pretended. She's a card shark who just took us to town."

Sally glared at Cody then at Melissa. "You're *his* girl?"

With sudden revelation, Melissa wished she *were* Cody's woman. But she wasn't. She wasn't sure she could be anyone's woman again. Jesse still held a piece of her heart and probably always would. Was it fair to any man to be with him under the circumstances?

"I'm with him," she settled for, letting all of them make their own inferences from her vague statement. The only opinion she really cared about was Cody's, though. What would he make of her statement?

Meeting Frankie's gaze steadily, she said firmly, "I won fair and square. I never even dealt. I have no sleeves on to hide cards, either." It wasn't her fault they assumed she didn't know how to play or was too stupid to live. Well, not *all* her fault. If they had the IQ of a moose, they should blame their parents.

"We've got to go." Cody revved the engine, his expression a granite mask. "We've got a lot of road to eat."

"Leave the pot and go." Frankie rose to an astonishing six foot-five at the very least, blocking out the setting sun behind him. Rays cascaded around his large frame, illuminating the others, but his face lay in shadow. She'd only once seen such a demonic countenance—on Nathan—and she knew she didn't want to mess with him.

But she needed the cash.

Hunger overruled discretion.

"Come on," Cody prodded, a scowl tugging at his mouth.

Grabbing two handfuls of cash, sun glinting off her ruby ring, she shoved the wadded-up greenbacks into her jeans pockets and then vaulted over the gazebo's railing. She stumbled, and then made a dash for the motorcycle. Rough hands grabbed her upper arms in mid flight, just about the same time she heard Cody swear.

"Give me my money, bitch." Frankie grabbed her upper arm and spun her around roughly to face him.

For a split second, Nathan's face superimposed itself over that of the big man's, and then Melissa awoke from her daze and yanked away from him with all her might, almost falling flat on her face. She dragged in several big gulps of air as she backed slowly towards Cody, her hands fisted in self-defense mode. "I've got a black belt so you don't want to mess with me."

Frankie glared at her, emotions flickering across darkening eyes.

She hopped on the cycle behind Cody, wrapping her arms around his middle, whispering out the side of her mouth so that only he could hear. "These guys are about to eat me alive. I hope you can hold up long enough to get us the hell out of here."

He rolled his injured shoulder, grimacing. "I'm almost good as new—for a few hours, hopefully. Doctor Kildare shot me up full of morphine."

"I wish that made you bulletproof, too. Go, go, go!"

"So do I." With a squeal of tires, he shotgunned the

vehicle forward amidst shouts and curses and dire warnings.

Melissa held on with all her might when the motorcycle fishtailed and jumped into the air as it hit rocks and roots. Her fanny ached as if she'd been kicked several times with steel-toed boots and her tailbone felt as if it were about to snap. Overworked legs felt rubbery and longed for a long, leisurely bubble bath.

"Did we lose them?" she yelled into the wind, as close to his ear as she could manage. Loath to disturb their precarious balance, she wasn't about to twist around and look and the rearview mirrors were useless to her. From her angle, she could only see tarmac about two feet behind the rear tire.

"They gave up the chase a few miles back," he yelled. At least that's what she thought he said. "We'll ride another fifty miles before we stop for the night, to be on the safe side, okay?"

Melissa's heart wanted to keep going a thousand miles, maybe even a hundred thousand miles, but her stomach and her backside begged they stop at the next town. She told all her complaining body parts to pipe down and stop being wimps and focused on her arms, which were having a lovely time encircling the ex-cop, and her chest that adored being pressed so intimately to him.

Night had fallen long before they had traveled far enough to suit Cody. Melissa's legs had long since lost all feeling; she wobbled and almost sank to the ground when he set her on her feet.

"Whoa, Nellie! You're not drunk, are you?" He caught her against him and instantly, she felt a swell in his denims.

Alarmed not only at his reaction to her, but more at her own to him, she stepped back and massaged her achy behind where it was coming awake very painfully. Shaking her head, she said, "Not drunk. Saddle sore. I wonder how the cowboys rode day and night?"

"I have it on good authority that I have magic fingers." He closed the distance between them and replaced her hands with his. Slowly, he worked the tension out of her until she felt like putty in his hands.

"That feels marvelous." He put Raul, her masseuse back home, to shame. Who'd have thought a grizzled ex-cop would have such a silky touch? She wanted him to continue, sans clothing.

That dangerous thought brought her up short. She forced her mind back to more logical thoughts and tried to suppress her libido. "Where are we?" She'd lost track of their whereabouts long ago. For all she knew, they'd left Pennsylvania. She focused on neon lights about two hundred feet distant that merely said 'Motel' in large blinking letters and then 'HBO, Cable, Pool' underneath in a vertical line, in a much smaller font. And then 'Vacancy' in large flashing letters beneath that.

"We're at a *motel.*" The way he pronounced *motel* was downright decadent, sending a heat surge into unbearable places.

Trying to cover up her unease, Melissa adopted a sarcastic repose. "Tell me something I don't know. What state are we in? Town?"

When Cody spoke, his breath tickled her ear and caused cascades of desire to pour through her. "We're still in Pennsylvania, in some hick town. I didn't catch its name."

Her stomach complained loudly and rudely, reminding her she wanted food. "I don't see a restaurant." Not even a convenience store.

"I spied a sign advertising one of those mega grocery stores a couple of miles back. After we check in, I'll run there." Belatedly, he asked, "How much money did you win?"

She dug around in her pockets and pulled out wads of cash. "I don't know. Help me count."

They perched on the sidewalk curb and counted. She was pleased when the amount topped three hundred dollars. Maybe she could find another game and multiply her winnings.

For now, Cody decided, they could stay a night or two in this place, which didn't look as if it would be expensive, and then he could tap into his bank account until he figured out where to go and what to do next.

"Let's check in. I could eat a whole cow by myself. If we don't hurry, I think I'll take on an entire herd." Her mouth salivated at the thought of a thick, juicy hamburger, or better yet, a steak."

"Okay, okay. I get the point." Cody put his hand against the small of her back as he escorted her to the motel lobby." I lost my appetite after that last gourmet entrée you prepared." He wiped his mouth with the back of his hand. "My mouth still tastes like I swallowed metal."

Check-in didn't take long and there were several vacancies, she noted from all the keys in the room slots. Big surprise. They weren't exactly on the beaten tourist track. Out in the middle of nowhere would be more populated than this place.

She wasn't thrilled by the knowing look and suggestive remarks the desk clerk made about their disreputable appearance.

His insinuations downright sickened her.

When she whispered to Cody that they should rent separate rooms, he told her unequivocally "No!" Then he'd explained that he wanted to hold onto what small amount of cash they had for as long as possible and promised there were two full-sized beds in the room so she would be safe—if she wanted to be.

His remark set her blood to sizzling all over again. She needed a cold shower.

Cody escorted her to their shabby room and dumped his saddlebags on the corner table. "Wait here," he commanded with authority. She wondered if he'd really been a policeman or a drill sergeant. "I'll be back in a jiff." He leaned forward and she thought he was going to kiss her for a brief, dizzying moment. She puckered her lips and tiptoed up to meet his lips but felt immeasurably sad when he pinched her cheek as if she were a lovesick ten-year-old.

Laughter danced in his eyes as he spun on his heel and left. A low, throaty chuckle hung in the air.

Realization dawned on her. He'd been teasing her, the skunk! So, was he building up sexual tension for later, or punishing her? The mixed signals were killing her.

"Ugh! Men!" She'd forgotten how downright, utterly exasperating they could be. When Jesse got in a mood, he'd tease her unmercifully. He'd goad her until she couldn't take any more.

Like now. Her nerves were so taut, the sexual tension so high, she couldn't stand one more iota of nonsense. Not one more suggestive word, not one more touch, not one more heated gaze. She needed more than a cold shower. She needed a dip in the pool.

Melissa rummaged through Cody's saddlebags and found a large T-shirt. It would have to do. She'd immerse herself, swim laps until she was too worn out to think, and be back in the room and dressed before he returned.

Rushing, she reached the pool in three minutes flat. She ignored the sign that said the pool closed at ten o'clock. Who would be up at two a.m. to care? No one would know she was there.

To her chagrin, the water was luxuriously warm and heavenly, not ice cold as she'd counted on. Nor had she calculated how sultry and romantic the twinkling stars overhead would be. After a few laps, she rolled onto her back and floated, gazing at the heavens. The scent of chlorine wrapped around her, blending with the clean woodsy smells of the forest. Crickets serenaded her and the gentle lapping of water against her lulled her into a timeless reverie.

Paradise. This was absolute perfection. Life couldn't get any better.

Her first clue that Cody was near was when water washed over her face in a wave. Spluttering, surprised, she sank and swallowed about a gallon of chlorinated water.

Strong hands groped for her, lifting her up. "Pool's closed," he whispered in her ear. His hands didn't leave her waist.

"Then I guess you're breaking the rules, too." Their gazes clashed and her lips parted. Her flesh burned where he touched her and her blood boiled in her veins.

"I'm a rule breaker from way back, darlin'."

That shocked her. "But you're a cop. They uphold rules."

"I'm an *ex*-cop. *Big* difference." Cody sighed, long and loud, and released her. Unsteady fingers pushed through his hair, dampening it. "One rule I don't break, however, is to get involved with married women." He turned his back on her and tilted his face skyward. Magnificent, naked shoulders flexed, mesmerizing her.

Her voice deserted her for several moments as she digested the meaning of his words. He wanted her. He was as attracted to her as she was to him. Like her, he was trying to fight it and was winning by a mere thread.

She didn't want to fight it any more, nor did she want *him* to fight it any longer. The only way to resolve his dilemma and free him was to tell him she was widowed. She struck out in a slow breaststroke, stopping behind him. "Cody." Her voice sounded rich and chocolaty. "I have a confession." She curled her arms around his too-tempting shoulders and leaned her cheek against his back, listening to his strong, rhythmic heartbeat.

"Lisa, you're playing with fire. I want to kiss you and if you don't move away this instant, I can't promise I won't."

She could feel his internal struggle to stay aloof. He was losing. Trailing angel kisses from his mid back to his shoulders, she murmured against him, "I want you to kiss me. I want to kiss you."

"What about your husband? Won't he mind?"

Melissa stopped what she was doing and sucked her teeth, gathering her courage. Gently, she pushed his shoulder, turning him to face her. Gazing deeply into his eyes, she said, "My husband wasn't home and he won't be coming to get me." She paused, choosing her next words carefully.

He jumped in. "Where is he now?" He held his hands at his sides. His eyes narrowed to mere slits.

"He died two years ago." Her voice began to wobble, and she admonished herself for her weakness. "I'm widowed." She looked up at the moon and stars that were Jesse's home now. "I wasn't sure I could trust you. A lone woman is more at risk than one who has a husband. Even the pretense of a husband."

"What do you need protection from? Do you know that creep that attacked you at the carnival?" Cody watched her with a cop's skeptical expression. She imagined he was in tune to every nuance of her voice as well.

Telling him about an unnamed husband's death and divulging her true identity were two very different things. "I never saw that man before."

"You mean to tell me that it was just a random attack?" He shook his head and folded his arms across his chest. "You're too skittish, too careful for just one random attack. Is something else going on?"

Melissa stared at Cody, still debating with herself how much, if anything, to tell him. She settled for more half-truths. Closing her eyes, she began to tell her story. "I was engaged to someone else before I married my husband. My ex-fiancé was a horrible, horrid man that wanted to control everything I did. My family adored him. Just about *everyone* adores him. He's a very powerful man." She hesitated long enough to drag in air.

"So you married someone else? Wasn't that the end of it? Is your family angry? Did they disown you?"

She laughed mirthlessly, on the edge of hysteria. "I only wish it were that easy." Melissa shook her head and pushed the sodden ropes of hair from her face. "My ex-fiancé wouldn't give up. Suffice it to say, he kept trying to break us up. So Jesse and I left without the family's blessings, and that snake blackened our names." She turned away now. In a whisper, she continued, "I'm afraid he still wants me back. I can't let him find me."

"So tell the creep to get lost. Report him to the police if he harasses you."

Turning around, Melissa faced off against this incredibly naïve cop. No wonder he'd left the force. He still believed in *good.* They must have eaten him alive, or would have if he'd not escaped. "He owns the police where we come from. He's got my family fooled. But he doesn't fool me."

Cody closed the gap between them and folded her into his arms, rubbing her back and her hair. "You're trembling. You think your ex-fiancé sent that caveman to kidnap you?"

She lifted her chin, looked up at him and nodded. "Yes. That wasn't the first monster he sent to find me. I've always managed to escape them so far. But I don't know how long I can keep running."

Cody swore under his breath. "What the hell did he do to scare you so badly? To keep you away from your family?"

Ashamed that any man could treat her so, that she allowed it for as long as she had, Melissa lowered her face and stared at her muted reflection in the water. Unable to stand looking at herself a second longer, she stuck her finger in the middle of her image and swished it away. "He, uh, struck me. More than once. He scares me more than anything or anyone else. He's *evil*." She couldn't go into detail without breaking down. As it was, shudders coursed through her at the memories swamping her. "I was afraid he was going to kill me in one of his rages. He threw horrible fits whenever he didn't get his way, whenever I didn't obey his word to the letter." She lifted her eyes to those of the man who held her so tenderly. "I *can't* let him get me. I can't go back there ever again. He'll kill me. I know it."

"Oh God..." Cody slumped, dragging her with him to the side of the pool where he rested his back. His legs provided a ledge for her to sit and he held her close to his heart.

Talking half to Cody, and half to herself, she continued, staring off into space. "My husband saved me from him. He gave me the courage to stand up for myself, to leave. I thought that would be the end of it. I thought I could live in peace and go on with my life. But he wouldn't let us. He wouldn't let us." Tears overcame her. Big, sobbing tears that she couldn't hold back.

"What a nightmare. No wonder." Cody shook too as he held her and she wondered why, but was too distraught to give it much thought.

Finally, when she'd shed all the tears within her, when she'd exhausted herself, she gazed up at the man who held her so gently. "So you see, I'm free. But I'm not free. I can't have a normal life, I can't commit to anyone else as long as he's looking for me. He'd want to kill them, too. He's obsessed with me."

"*Too*?" Cody latched onto the word, pronouncing it sharply. "Are you accusing your ex-fiancé of murder?"

In her heart, she knew Nathan was responsible, but not in a way that a jury would ever convict him for. "He didn't pull the trigger, if that's what you mean. Not that he wouldn't have if he'd caught up to us face to face. No, my husband died as we were trying to get away." A cool night breeze skipped over the water's surface and chilled her.

When she shivered against him, Cody set her on her feet. "Let's go inside before you get pneumonia."

Dawn's light was just topping the horizon as she climbed out of the water. They'd been in the water for more than an hour. She'd forgotten all about food or being hungry.

Cody held out his hand and she put hers in it, feeling safer than she had in a very long time. They strolled to their room silently, both in their own world. Cody held out his arms to her after she'd showered and changed, and she curled up next to him on the bed, not wanting to be alone. He didn't take liberties. She was too shaken by reliving her past to start a new relationship tonight.

What was even more odd was that she had the impression he was too shaken as well.

~ * ~

Melissa awoke in spits and spurts. First, the backfire of a truck startled her, sounding like gunfire. But Cody's warm voice, gruff with sleep, assured her they were safe and implored her back to sleep. Large arms gathered her against a chest made for cuddling and curling up to.

Then she'd heard children shouting and splashing in the pool. But the shouts matched the nightmare she was having, not quite yanking her awake. Visions of Nathan tortured her, forbidding her from escaping him in the nether world. Men chased her. Faceless men shrouded in monks' robes, the hoods falling over their faces. The faster she ran from them, the closer they came, levitating, surrounding her, caging her. Screams gurgled in her throat and she thrashed, fighting the men.

"How dare you hide from me! How dare you run!" Nathan's voice, dangerously quiet, resonant, spewed from the monster's lips. "You're mine. I'll have you or no one will!"

With every ounce of her strength, Melissa ran at him, fingernails bared, clawing and kicking. His laughter mocked her as he fended her off with a finger. "Foolish woman. Don't you know I'm untouchable? Don't you know I'm invincible?"

His finger pressed into her forehead, red hot and incredibly forceful, pushing her to her knees. "Bow to me. Worship me."

"Never!" She whispered, seething. "I'd rather die first."

"Death would be pleasure compared to what is in store

for you. First, I will steal all you hold dear. You will have nothing." Nathan smiled broadly, insanely.

Shocked, fearing for her immortal soul, she gasped, awaking with a start. Bolting up in bed, she clutched her throat, panting with fear. Sand and the night's sleepy film clouded her eyes, so she blinked several times to bring the room into focus.

Memories came slower, loath to replace the more recent visions in her nightmare. A new duffel bag sprawled across the floor, unzipped, clothes spilling out. Cereal, shelf-stable milk, the kind that didn't require refrigeration, and several different fruits littered the one round table that dominated the far corner of the room.

A waterfall cascaded nearby, almost muting the television turned low. Then she realized it was the shower pulsating in the next room, not a waterfall, and that Cody was missing. He must have awakened before her—quite a bit before her, seeing that he had been to the store and back while she still slept. Steam fingers wisped from under the bathroom door, substantiating her theory that her companion was showering.

Nathan's voice lingered in the air and she scowled. Either she was still dreaming or delusional.

Then Melissa realized she was neither, that the sound came from the television.

Her eyes opened so fast, so wide as her gaze reeled on the square screen, the air stung them. The sight that met her stole her breath and stopped her heart, far worse than any dream demons.

On one arm Nathan held her sister, who beamed up at him, glowing, her sunny smile spanning her heart-shaped face. Proverbial stars twinkled in Christina's eyes. The superbly manicured hand that rested on the man's lapel sported the largest, gaudiest diamond ring Melissa had ever seen.

She could barely hear the words and thrust herself off the bed in a rush to turn up the volume. The sheet and cheap hotel blanket tangled around her, tripping her, and she pitched to the floor, her knees and hands taking the brunt of the fall. Pain flared through her, but she was obsessed and had to hear what Nathan was saying. Determined, she crawled the last few feet to the box and poked the volume control.

"…the wedding ceremony will take place tomorrow at the Vanderbilt-Smythe mansion…"

"*No!*" Stunned, blindsided, she yelled at Nathan's image, as if he could hear her. "Leave her alone! It's me you want. Me you're after. Don't drag her into our fight."

"What's wrong?" Cody ran out of the bathroom, naked except for a damp towel wrapped haphazardly around his waist. Water dripped from his hair into his eyes, drizzling down his chest. Pure ebony orbs had replaced his eyes as he honed in on her. "Did you fall? Are you hurt?" Kneeling at her side, he tried to scoop her up but she batted away his helping hands.

"He can't do this!" She spluttered, gesticulating wildly with her hands, punching the air as if time and space would part so she could reach her mark. "Leave her out of this, you bastard! I'll kill you if you hurt her. It's me you want." She continued in this vein as the man at her side gazed from her to the TV, his expression stormy, incredulous even.

Cody lifted her and carried her to a chair as if she weighed no more than a cat, and plopped her in it. Then he did the same for himself, his large frame sprawling from the chair. Long legs stretched almost to the edge of the television console. His ankles crossed, and he flexed, then curled his toes.

Meanwhile, the interviewer droned on about the most elite, most high society nuptials of the year—between the Senator, the monster in Melissa's dreams, and her sister.

"Tell us about the ceremony, Christina. This is touted to be the wedding of the century. Some say it's the grandest wedding and reception since Cinderella married Prince Charming," Shireeta Lee, the exquisite reporter crooned as she puckered collagen-filled lips at the camera. The reporter's ebony hair wound into an elegant French twist and her pink satin gown would fit right into the big ball that was sure to be planned for the following night.

"This must be a bittersweet day for you, wedding your dear departed sister's fiancé." Shireeta cast a wholly feminine, appreciative glance at Nathan. "To wed one of the most eligible, powerful senators in the nation is no small feat. You must have quite a guest list. Do you care to share it with us? Rumor has it that the President and his family, Harrison Ford, Tom Hanks, Cher, Madonna, Julia, and at least half the Senate will be in attendance."

Nathan took the microphone, flashing his most charming smile at the lens. "Our guest list is private, Shireeta. Security will be in full force to protect our esteemed guests, but mostly to preserve the sanctity of our special day."

Shireeta favored Nathan with a flirtatious wink. Women found his charms irresistible and the journalist seemed to be no less gullible. "You won't even confirm if the Queen will be in attendance?"

When Nathan shook his perfectly groomed head, his hair gleamed blue-black under the mid-morning California sunlight.

"Well then, will you confirm if you're going to run for President of the United States in the next election?"

Melissa gasped, digging her fingernails so deeply into her palms she drew blood. Fear flooded her.

Nathan didn't want to be President. He wanted to be Emperor. Julius Caesar. Dictator. *Alexander the Great!*

The pun hit her full force and she laughed hysterically, until she felt Cody's stare on her.

Concern pooled around his irises and his lips drew together so tightly they paled, as did his entire complexion. Stress lines tugged at his mouth and eyes, adding ten years to his appearance.

Reflected in Cody's eyes, Melissa saw herself—and froze. Was that crazy woman her? Violently tousled red hair stuck out in all directions. Cody's borrowed T-shirt wrinkled and sat askew on her shoulder. Devoid of make-up, her face was baby clean. Her eyes gleamed red, almost feral. All shreds of sanity had fled. Madness shone bright and clear.

She dragged in several deep cleansing breaths to clear her head. Fury and fear would get her nowhere. Cool, clean logic was needed.

Cody inclined his head at the set, leaning forward, resting his elbows on very hairy knees. "You know those people, I take it?" The inflection in his voice was more rhetorical than questioning. A stray lock of blonde hair fell over his deeply lined forehead and he shoved it away with an angry sweep of his hand.

Nodding, speechless, she gulped. What could she say? Did he recognize them? Didn't everyone? Did he recognize her yet?

Melissa feared that *yet* was the operative word.

Before she found her voice, her picture flashed on the tube. A big, glossy glamour photograph filled the screen, so different from her present appearance and yet, undeniably her. Coiffed, her brilliant hair nearly blinded her. Foundation, creamy and lush, covered the dusting of freckles over her nose and cheeks, to give her a Georgia Southern belle magnolia complexion. Ruby lips pouted as if nothing would ever be good enough for her. Diamonds dripped from her ears, neck, and even sparkled from a tiara crowning her head. Glitter dusted bared shoulders.

A princess.

A fake.

Cody looked from her, to the photograph on screen, and

back, raising an eyebrow. He listened intently as Shireeta recounted the whole sordid, albeit false, story of how Jesse had abducted Melissa and, like Patty Hearst, she'd been brainwashed and had succumbed to her captor's every suggestion, running away with him, indifferent that she broke her family's and fiancé's hearts. It painted Jesse to be an out-and-out criminal, and Melissa to be a spoiled, thoughtless, heartless fool at best.

Clearing her throat, she leaned forward and touched Cody's wrist. "I'm sorry. I didn't tell you everything last night. I-I left out a few important parts." She averted her gaze when he stared straight at her as if dissecting her. "I'm not Lisa Woods. I'm Melissa Vanderbilt-Smythe, as I'm sure you've surmised by now." Squirming under his scrutiny, she was unable to sit still another moment. Jumping to her feet, she paced the floor, her hands linked behind her back. The threadbare carpet underfoot roughed the pads of her feet.

Long, tousled hair, unlike the elegant poufed style in the picture, curtained her cheeks, hiding her face as she studied her toes rather than meet his most assuredly accusatory gaze. A stray fake fingernail lay on the floor in front of her, grossing her out. At least she hoped it was a stick-on nail…and not the real thing.

Cody leaned back in his chair, crossing his arms over his chest. His towel shifted, baring more leg. "So I *surmised.*" Unnamed emotions flickered across his eyes. "Was what you told me true? Did Alexander abuse you? Threaten you?"

Eager to set things straight, she crossed back to him and knelt before him, taking his hands in hers. "Every word. And more." More visions haunted her, making her tremble all over. "He's crazy. He's always on the brink of explosion. Any little thing I did infuriated him. I was afraid to breathe, to move. He was insanely jealous of any man that looked at me. He'd have killed me if I had stayed. And now he's going to kill my sister." She swallowed hard, making a decision. "I can't let him do it." Torn up, quaking inside, Melissa leaned her head on Cody's knees, seeking his warmth and strength.

He stroked her hair away from her face. "How are you going to stop him?" Alarm, barely veiled, rang in his voice.

"I'll have to go back. I have to save my sister."

"Can't you just go to the police and let them do it?"

She lifted her head and sought his gaze. "Who would *you* believe? The upstanding revered Senator of California? Or the crazy runaway heiress?" Melissa laughed without a trace of humor. "They'd lock me in a mental ward and not even listen to a word I said."

"How will crashing the wedding help then?"

"Who said I was crashing the wedding?" She dragged in a huge breath and closed her eyes wondering who was crazier—her or Nathan? "I'll offer him a trade. Me for her. That's what he wants." She could barely expel the stale air in her lungs. "He did this to smoke me out." Her heart plummeted to her knees. "It worked. I can't let her suffer because of me and he knows it. I can't sacrifice any more innocent people. It's time for me to slay my own dragon." Her dream returned to taunt her.

Nathan Alexander wouldn't destroy all she held dear. She wouldn't let him. Finality, promise, rang in her voice. "He took Jesse from me. I won't let him take Christina, too."

Or this rugged ex-cop, who had come to mean so much to her so quickly.

Cody stood, towering over her. "What if I won't let you commit suicide?"

"I'd hate you forever." Fervor rang in her voice and she faced off against him, her jaw set firmly. "Besides, short of tying me up, you can't stop me." She glared at him, daring him.

"Then I'm coming with you. But you aren't handing yourself over to Alexander. I still have a few connections. I can call in some favors."

"Forgive me if I don't hold my breath." Her mind raced, recalling low flying small planes the previous evening as she'd floated on her back. "Didn't I see small planes flying low? There must be an air strip nearby."

"I don't think the two hundred dollars we have left will buy us tickets to California." Cody turned away from her, dropped the towel as if it were a normal occurrence for him to strip in front of a woman, and retrieved his pants.

She tried to turn away modestly, but his posterior fascinated her and her gaze stayed glued to his every movement. The play of well-honed muscles made her salivate. Stretching sinews. Flexing buttocks. Powerful legs. If he didn't get those slacks on in two seconds, she'd swoon right at his feet. She felt as if she'd been without a man for an eternity, not a mere two years.

Dragging her thoughts back to rescuing her sister, Melissa said, "Who mentioned *buying* anything?"

Pulling on his slacks, he hopped around to face her, his leg half in. "You're going to stow away or hitch a ride?"

Stowing away wasn't exactly what she had in mind. Small planes didn't leave much room to hide. "I was thinking more along the lines of *borrowing* a plane."

It was his turn to freeze. Then his jaw dropped open. "You want to *hijack* a plane?"

"Not exactly." Melissa crossed her fingers behind her back, praying that she remembered how to fly a small craft. "I'll fly it. And I'll give it back when we're done and our mission's completed."

If she could land it in one piece.

Otherwise, she'd give back the pieces.

Chapter Seven

Sticking her nail file in the lock, Melissa fumbled with the door handle of the small plane. The locks on this model were a joke and proved no problem to open.

So far, so good.

"You know how to fly that contraption?" Cody eyed the Cessna as if it were a model plane she'd suggested he climb aboard. He stepped back, away from their ticket home.

"Would I say I could if I couldn't?" Her flight instructor had signed off for her but she'd only flown solo a couple of times—unfortunately, not for a long time. Of course, Melissa wasn't about to tell Cody this…or that she was almost frozen solid at the thought of getting near a plane, much less board and fly it.

He shot a wary glance at her, mixed emotions slamming across his face. Good thing he wasn't an actor.

Finally the lock clicked open and she allowed a tiny smile to hover on her lips.

When she screwed up her courage and proceeded to enter the cockpit, he put a restraining hand on her arm. "We can call the authorities and stop this without committing a Federal offense."

That brought a snicker to her lips she couldn't stop. She lifted a winged brow. "Who do you think they'll believe? The next governor of California? Or a dead heiress?"

Cody didn't blink, but gave her a long hard kiss that left her breathless. "Just don't kill us for real."

She scowled deeply at him. "Very funny. Get in."

He closed her door as she strapped herself in. She pulled the belt's cinch tightly about her waist. She felt around under the dash for keys. Finding none, she looked all over, above, below, on the dash. No dice.

"Problem?"

"No keys."

"So now what, Einstein? Can we hotwire her?"

Melissa sent him a scowl. "I don't have clue one which wires to twist," she grumbled at him, her palms itching. Her nerves screamed that they had taken too long already. Each moment they lingered was a moment closer to a jail cell. They might indeed face time behind bars, but after they saved Christina. She'd figure that out later. That was a luxury she didn't have now.

"So what now? Should I spin the propeller?" Cody placed a hand on his door and looked at her expectantly.

She nodded. "We'll have to. Get into position and wait for my cue. It won't work until I can finagle the ignition to the 'both' position. If I can unground the magnetos, we just might get off the ground." Gritting her teeth, she stuck the nail file's tip into the ignition, jimmying it until it turned to the right.

Angry shouts erupted behind them. Melissa twisted in her seat to see from whom and how far away the sound originated. Her blood chilled when she spied burly men running toward them, fists slamming the air.

"That's our cue!" Cody yelled from the front of the plane. "This thing ready to take off yet?" Cody's steady gaze implored her to hurry.

Further jiggling proved fruitless.

"I can't get the ignition into position." Did he think she could work miracles? That she could just say abracadabra and poof, *the plane would lift off by magic? She mumbled under her breath, "One ungrounded magneto will have to do."*

This would only give them one set of spark plugs, not really airworthy but the plane would fly—probably. But without any margin of safety. She turned on the electrical master switch, praying the plane was fueled up, or their efforts were for naught. When the needles on both fuel gauges pointed to full, she exhaled deeply, relief flooding her. "Spin the propeller now and stand clear! It spins so fast, it'll cut off your hand."

She stomped on the brakes so the plane wouldn't roll forward into him and prayed this would work.

The engine merely coughed and spluttered, as if mocking them, the first time he spun the propeller.

Her heart almost seized up as their time ran out. Their pursuers were almost on them, their footsteps hammering the pavement. Cupping her hands around her mouth, Melissa yelled, "Try again!"

Cody propped the propeller with all his strength and jumped back when it caught and became a blur. He sprinted to the door, hopped in, and slammed it behind him. Breathless, he panted, "Get going." He fumbled with his seat belt, his chest rising and falling rapidly.

Between clenched teeth, Melissa muttered, "Trying." She went through her checklist, desperate to remember everything she had learned. Glancing at her directional gyro, she checked it against the wet compass to ascertain it gave her a good reading. Gratification warmed her that everything seemed to be in order. She crossed her fingers that there were no crosswinds. The treetops reached for the heavens, tall and straight, deigning to move, a pretty good indication there was no wind.

She advanced the throttle all the way forward and the plane rolled onto the taxiway. *What would Jesse think of this stunt?* "I hope we have enough asphalt in front of us to take off," she muttered under her breath, lifting a silent admonition for Jesse to guide them safely.

Thunderstorms raged in Cody's eyes. With tightly reined hostility, he cast a glance behind them and commanded, "Gun it."

The plane shimmied as they lifted into the air, their speed well past the manufacturer's recommended takeoff speed. Alarmed, Melissa prayed it wouldn't crack up. *Jesse, help us.* It had been a long time since she'd logged any hours and she struggled to remember how to steady the nose so the plane would climb. When it did, she sent Jesse silent thanks and blew a kiss into the wind, trusting he'd catch it. Thoughts of Jesse no longer tortured her, no longer ripped her heart to shreds. She could think of him with joy, now. Mainly due, Melissa knew, to the ex-New York cop at her side.

"What'd you promise God just now?" Cody's deep voice intruded on her thoughts, startling her. She didn't imagine he'd appreciate her silent plea to her dead husband, so she kept silent, pretending she hadn't heard him.

The plane climbed steadily and she kept a sharp eye out to make sure she didn't go below seventy knots until the plane reached fourteen hundred feet MSL, when she pushed forward on the yoke just a little and eased back on the throttle, setting it to 2450 RPM. She was still paranoid about keeping an eye on the altimeter. Everything looked kosher but she kept glancing at the fuel gauges, praying they gave a correct reading and praying she'd remember everything she'd learned, that she could pull this off. She'd not looked at a plane in two years, not since that fateful night.

As long as they didn't run into bad weather and didn't experience mechanical failure, they'd be fine. Until it came time to land, anyway.

Landings scared her to death.

A sticky-note taped to the control panel with the name of the airport and two frequencies marked ASOS and CTAF caught her attention. Flicking on the radio, she tuned into the ASOS for weather updates and estimated visibility reports. Otherwise, she'd be flying blind in the dark.

"How long till we land?" Cody leaned back in his seat, fingers linked behind his neck, one leg crossed over the other.

Melissa checked their speed again and made a guesstimate. "Take a nap. It'll be a while."

Cody fidgeted in his seat. "I never felt less like sleeping in my entire life. You gotta game plan? Do we just crash the wedding, or you have something sneakier in mind?"

"Don't say that word." It was bad enough to think it, worse yet to say it aloud— tantamount to a curse.

"What word? *Sneaky?* Or *crash*?"

"Crash." The worst word in the English language after death, dead, or die. She leaned over and punched his shoulder and accidentally kicked one of the rudder pedals, causing the plane to jerk to the right. Immediately she rushed to steady it, cursing under her breath.

He grabbed a handhold for dear life and she didn't have to look at his knuckles to know they'd paled. "Whoa, Nellie! I thought you knew how to fly planes?"

"I do." She gritted her teeth. She just wasn't very adept at *landing* planes; not that she would ever admit *that* to an already agitated passenger. She'd get even soon as they landed, when she didn't have to give this flying tin can all her attention. Revenge would be sweet...provided she landed the plane in one piece.

Melissa couldn't think about that now or she'd lose her nerve. She slid a glance to him. "What do you suggest we do? Go in with both barrels blazing? Kidnap my sister?" Nathan would probably be expecting that and have a trap set. "He'll have sentries posted. He's a lot of things. Stupid's not one of them."

"You wanna fly into the wedding, drop a ladder to your sister, and fly back out?"

Her sidelong glance clashed with his mocking one. She clucked her tongue as she shook her head, humor resurfacing now that the plane seemed to be under control. "He wouldn't expect *that*."

"You have a death wish?" Cody turned in his seat, checking out the fuselage. "Any parachutes aboard?"

"Not in a small plane like this. Were you planning to bail on me now? You don't trust me?" They dueled with words, slicing each other. Annoyance crept into her voice, stiffening her frame. She checked the fuel gauge again, praying it would last the duration of their trip. "Got a better plan, law man?"

"Yeah. I think I do." He grabbed the mike and fiddled with the frequency, changing it off her weather updates. His scowl deepened when he still proved unsuccessful after several minutes.

"Here." She snatched the mike away from him and adjusted the radio to 122.8; that was supposedly the CTAF's frequency. When she handed it back to him, their fingers brushed. Even the slight contact warmed her and she longed for more of his touch than she could afford right now.

His fingernail tapped the mike several times and he blew into it before speaking.

Almost immediately, warnings assailed them, each direr than the last.

Melissa sucked in her breath as the threats mounted. "Turn off that chatter before I lose my nerve." She reached over to flick off the switch but his hand caught hers, preventing her from turning off the radio.

He squeezed her hand before letting it go. "Trust me." He put his lips to the mike. "Cody Richards here. Get me in touch with Federal Agent Chet Mulligan, L.A. office."

The person at the other end of the radio implored Cody to confide in him, to land and be taken into custody peacefully. The ex-cop's features shifted to granite, his voice pure steel. "I'll only talk to Special Agent Chet Mulligan Get him." Awesome command reverberated in Cody's voice.

Fright slammed into Melissa. Cody didn't sound like an ex-burnt-out-cop. He was still in top form. She voiced her re-emerging doubts. "You're a Fed and this has all been a lie, hasn't it?" Bitter laughter escaped her lips. The joke was on her after all. He was good. Real good.

"No, darlin'. I ain't no Fed."

Grimacing, she shook her head, watching him out of the corner of her eye. "Who do you think you're kidding?"

"If I was, I would've taken you in the moment I knew who you were."

She pondered that, and then shook her head again. "Not if you were under cover."

"The only person I see aiding and abetting you is me. I'm going to arrest myself?"

Something didn't jive. Faulty logic nagged at Melissa.

Problem was, she couldn't take the time now to figure it all out. It just felt wrong. Her gut told her so.

"If you're on my side, then tell me what you have in mind. *Everything*. Don't leave anything out."

Ahead, lightning bolted from cloud to cloud. Visibility was poor in the overcast sky. Nervously, she glanced at her altimeter again. Her grip tightened till her fingers felt glued to the controls.

"Why this? Why now?" she muttered under her breath.

She climbed higher and suddenly she couldn't see the ground. "Damn!" she muttered under her breath. She descended immediately to an altitude where she could see, even though it meant launching their cross-country flight at an altitude that put them at risk from unlighted radio towers. She prayed they'd all have blinking lights as they should. "Help me watch for radio towers."

Cody's alarmed glance slid to her face, which she presumed must be as ghostly pale as her knuckles. "You sure you can handle this?"

Through clenched teeth, which she commanded not to chatter, Melissa said, "Heaven help us if I can't. Look for towers," she commanded and gritted her teeth. "Not at me."

"Turn back." It wasn't a request. "We can't help your sister if we're dead." Cody's grim expression belied his fear. Shadows darkened his eyes but she would bet hers were onyx with unadulterated terror.

Except she wasn't sure which fear terrified and nauseated her more.

Fear of crashing the plane.

Or fear of confronting Nathan.

Melissa scowled, wondering how far off course this storm would take them, how much time it would cause them to lose.

But Cody was right. They'd be no good to Christina dead.

"We'll have to skirt it. It'd be suicide to fly into that storm."

Melissa wondered for the millionth time why Nathan had fixated on her? What made her so important? She'd never done anything to make her special—just notorious. She'd always been the bad girl. The runaway. The ungrateful daughter and fiancée. She knew she'd have to pay for her sins someday.

But Christina shouldn't have to pay for sins she hadn't committed.

Melissa couldn't allow that.

~ * ~

Cody admired Melissa's loyalty and courage. They were on a suicide mission as surely as if they planned to dive-bomb their target. His lips pursed as he watched the furious sky manufacture more brimstone as Melissa steered the plane away from the storm. He'd never seen lightning from this perspective. While it put the fear of God into every breath he took, it also exhilarated him. It evoked feelings in him similar to the runaway heiress next to him—but with only a fraction of the intensity.

He should have stopped this when he had the chance. Once the wheels had left earth, he'd been at her mercy. To his horror, he realized she was a novice pilot; long on guts but short on experience. Too late he'd read the terror in her eyes, the uncertainty mixed with her determination to plunge forward.

The only things Cody could do now were pray and maintain a façade of calm. It wouldn't do to spook Melissa any more than she already was, than he already had. Even though she was short on pilot experience, it was a whole lot more than he'd had. Zilch. Zippo. He couldn't decipher these gadgets, which might as well be written in Japanese for all he knew, except for the fuel indicator that she kept an eagle eye on—which didn't reassure him very much.

Reasoning with her hadn't worked, perhaps because he agreed her sister needed rescuing, that the Senator had to be stopped. His objections hadn't been as wholehearted as hers, however.

"How much further?"

As the plane had droned on and on through the darkness, she'd ignored any attempts at idle chitchat that had been meant to distract her and lighten the gravity of the situation.

Baby blue eyes didn't waver from the starlit sky. A tiny pulse flickered at the base of her throat. "The storm delayed us, but I'm not sure how much."

Cody cursed this out-of-control feeling. He'd made it a rule never to let that happen. Where he came from, that was a death sentence. Here he was at the mercy of the plane, Melissa and her ex-fiancé. None of the variables were predictable. And even the ones that were, like a plane out of control with an amateur pilot, were not to his liking. If he held cards like this in a poker game, he'd fold.

But as long as Melissa piloted the plane, she held the cards. She lived to gamble. And it seemed she would bluff all the way to the end of this game. No matter that he pointed out the futility.

Cody studied her profile in the dim light from the control panel. Flashes of brilliant light illuminated her. What cherubic features she had—high cheekbones, a tip-tilted nose, and a bowed mouth. Even pale and set in rigidity, it was a beautiful face. Her eyes flashed azure fire the few times she'd glanced away from the sky. What a rare gem.

Up here, a hair's breadth from heaven, it was as if they were alone in the world. No one else existed.

Time stopped.

Against the stunning elemental backdrop, Cody memorized her beauty. Frozen in time, her face would stay in his memory forever. However long their forever might be. He prayed she would never discover his role in taking her home. It wouldn't matter that he had changed his mind. He had lied to her.

Cody knew in his gut, Melissa would not be able to forgive the man who signed up to take money to return her to her abuser and tormentor. Who could?

If only he could keep her away from Nathan and her father. But that was impossible. He pushed the thought aside. Christina Vanderbilt-Smythe needed them. No matter what happened to him, he couldn't let another young woman suffer abuse.

He'd have to accept his due as a man. And pray for a miracle.

The plane dropped a couple hundred feet without warning and hail pelted them from nowhere. When the electrical system flickered, he wondered how many miracles he was due.

"Are we crashing? What happened?" Cody, normally so strong, so sure of himself, felt all heat drain from his cheeks. He was out of his element. Things were out of his control.

~ * ~

Bile rose in Melissa's throat. She knew only too well what it was to crash land and she was going to do everything in her power to land this metal bird in one piece, and get them out of this with their hides intact. Her lips pursed in concentration. Her left hand clenched so hard on the yoke, she feared it would surely fuse to it. Freezing cold wrapped its tentacles around her bones.

"Look for flat ground." The yoke shuddered, jerking in her hands.

"What am I looking for?" In the dim light, Cody squinted

out the window. The knuckles on his hands gleamed stark white. His features turned to pure granite.

"Landing strips. Flat ground."

Miracles.

"How much room do you need to set this baby down?"

Melissa looked out the passenger window, keeping an eye on the horizon. If she ever needed an angel, now was the time.

"At least a thousand feet of clear, flat ground." Not a lot to ask for in a plains state like Nebraska or Missouri or even out in the desert, but here, in the mountains, they might as well ask for a blizzard in the Mojave Desert. Sliding a glance at him, she asked, "See anything?"

His head moved almost imperceptibly. His lips pursed almost till they were blue.

"A flat piece of highway?" Melissa knew she couldn't hold the plane together much longer. It shuddered uncontrollably, as if it would dissolve any moment. She smelled smoke and the engine coughed; they started losing altitude.

"*Damn*!" She slammed the dash with the flat of her hand.

Cody shot her a startled glance. He raked unsteady fingers through his hair. "It's past time to get our parachutes on."

With grim determination she held onto the controls. Shivers scraped down her spine. "Remember? I told you planes like this don't carry parachutes."

"Buckle in!" Jesse had commanded from the pilot's seat. She'd never seen his face so ashen before, more serious despite all the serious scrapes they'd been in together.

Fire blazed out of control on the left wing where lightning had struck. The engine choked, then died. "Put your heads between your knees."

The plane went into a terrifying dive, spinning crazily. Centrifugal force almost ripped her insides apart. She'd known without a doubt they were going to die.

Jesse struggled to pull up on the yoke while their passenger, Beth, had screamed and cried. With his few remaining breaths, he'd yelled above the wheezing, whining plane, "I love you."

"I love you!"

I'll always love you, she'd added silently, a tear sliding down her cheek.

Looking at Cody, Melissa did her best to banish memories of Jesse, to land on the highway, praying the plane wouldn't explode or the fuselage break into bits, as it had the last time she'd been in a plane.

The smoke filled the cabin, almost choking her. Headlight trails lit the silvery gray tarmac worm below, which was both a blessing and a curse.

A blessing, because they acted as runway lights to delineate their makeshift landing strip.

A curse, since innocent travelers could be in their way.

Either she didn't dare land there after all—or if she tried and miscalculated distance, speed, altitude, anything...they could cause one bloody wreck, sensational even by Southern California standards.

Chapter Eight

"Steady, Lisa." Cody squeezed her shoulder, lending her his strength and acting as navigator. "I don't know if we should chance this. Can you hold out for an airport?"

"We don't have a choice." She could barely breathe and her eyes watered. "We have to land *now*. If we fly low over the northbound lanes for a mile or two, the cars should see us and make room."

Still, she was profusely bothered about risking public safety even to save their lives.

"It's a pretty safe bet they know where we are." Hope mixed with trepidation in his voice.

She pursed her lips. His meaning didn't elude her. Police meant help.

They also meant capture, arrest and jail time more likely than not.

At least they'd be alive.

Behind bars, Melissa wouldn't be any help to Christina. This had all been futile. Maybe they should have made the call anyway instead of this flashy, heroic stunt. *Stupid, stupid, stupid!* She always ran, if not *from* somewhere, then *into* trouble.

What is it with me?

"I can't do things the easy way," Melissa mumbled under breath.

That brought a wry smile to Cody's lips and a gleam to his eyes.

A series of small explosions sounding like firecrackers rocked the plane, jerking the yoke out of her hands. The fire that had been small before exploded, dancing against the stark night. The plane took a nosedive. Gauges spun dizzily and she had a massive headache.

A gasp erupted from her chest, a chest that felt as if it was caving in. "Start praying. We're out of time."

Melissa and Cody grabbed their individual control wheels simultaneously, dragging the Cessna's nose up in fits and spurts.

"Land now, with the traffic flow. They can't miss us."

"You know how many blind drivers are out there?" She

ruined her attempt at humor when her words came out weak and crackly.

"I was a New York cop, remember?" His hand moved over to cover hers. "Go for it. It's now or never."

She swallowed convulsively. As much as she wanted out of this flying death trap, landing on a make shift strip frightened her. Face it. It was a scary situation. And with her history…

At least it wasn't her third strike. After this, she'd never board a plane again. She wouldn't even go near an airport.

If they survived.

They had to survive. They had to save Christina from a fate worse than death.

Melissa sucked in her breath and held it until the wheels of the plane touched down on the highway. Cars honked. Headlights flashed at them. Tires skidded as vehicles swerved.

All hell was breaking loose. Sirens whirled. Vehicles honked arhythmically. Metal twisted and screamed as the plane lurched, bounced, and spun out of control. Vertigo nauseated her. But she held on, her gaze glued ahead to peer through the thick smoke that filled the cabin, choking her.

"The plane's going to break up."

"We've got to get out fast. It could explode any second."

It felt like the plane spun for an eternity before it stopped.

"*Get out!*" Cody was on his feet so fast he looked like a blur. He struggled with the door, but it wouldn't do more than protest in a squeaky metal-crunching voice.

Muffled voices from outside, urgent, even desperate, assaulted Melissa's ears. "They're trapped. Anyone got an axe to break down the door?"

"I got a sledge hammer we can bust through the window with."

"Do it!"

"Duck!" Cody yanked her to him, spun her around and shielded her from the shattering glass that imploded the cabin.

"You okay in there?" Faces peered in at them. A policeman crawled halfway in and held out his hand to help Melissa climb out over the nose. Cody hoisted her rear end in the air and shoved her out. The officer handed her over to a line of civilians who carried her far from the plane.

She couldn't stop coughing, couldn't fill her lungs with enough of the fresh air she craved. But she struggled to turn back.

"Cody!" Melissa twisted out of safe arms to turn back and her blood ran cold at the site of flames engulfing the plane, and smoke so thick she could hardly see the policeman sprawled half in the cabin. Only his torso and legs were visible, his lower appendages kicking as if he were in a shark's mouth and a shiver went through her. The plane's shape did look shark-like.

"You can't help him," a kind voice said. "Let the man do his job. It's your friend's best chance." Two men dragged her several hundred feet away from the plane, moving so fast her feet barely touched the asphalt.

Sparks flew and the night grew unbearably hot as if they were on the lip of an active volcano.

Jesse, please save him. I can't bear to lose both of you.

"He's got 'im!" a baritone voice shouted. "Everyone run! She's gonna blow."

Cody and the officer took off at a dead run, their feet pounding the pavement, their chests heaving. Everyone else took cover.

"Get down, Miss. Shrapnel and fireballs will fly everywhere. You aren't safe standing." Her rescuers yanked her down to the ground so hard that gravel bit into her knees. She bit back a yelp when some imbedded in her sensitive flesh.

"Cover your head!"

But she had to see what was happening. Cody was still in grave danger. She watched in dread fascination.

First the plane imploded, and then it exploded, bursting into a trillion tiny pieces and a few very large lethal ones. The explosion rocked the ground and Melissa watched in horror as Cody and the officer were thrown several feet into the grass by the blast. Visions of Jesse tortured her and she cried out in terror, reliving the nightmare that had happened over two years ago.

Just as the man by her side had predicted, metal and fire hailed for a good diameter of two hundred feet or more. Miniature fires littered the ground. A car caught ablaze and exploded when a fiery wing of the plane smashed the engine and cab.

Superhuman strength fueled by angst propelled her up and to Cody's side. "Not again, Lord. Don't you dare do this to me again. You couldn't be so cruel." Why was this happening? Was she a curse? Or cursed? "Don't die on me, Cody Richards. Don't you dare die on me." She stroked his face, gently, the stubble of his beard pricking her fingers and palm.

Oh God! He looked so still, so pale; was he alive? Jesse's face superimposed itself over Cody's for an instant and she stared, open-mouthed.

Melissa groped for the pulse point on his wrist and

couldn't find it no matter where she positioned her finger, no matter how hard she pushed. Unsuccessful, she leaned over him, putting her ear to his chest. Red hair cascaded over her face, getting in her eyes. Annoyed, frightened, she flicked it back, anchoring it behind her ear.

"I love you, Cody Richards. You're staying here. Got it?"

It was very faint but it was there, like distant drums. A sigh of relief whooshed out of her. "Thank God!"

Strong hands wrapped around her, pinning her to his chest. In a very gruff voice, Cody growled in her ear, "I love you."

Melissa jumped out of her skin. Cody's answer almost choked her.

"Wh-what did you say?" She jerked her head to gaze into eyes so dark blue she could have been gazing into the depths of the ocean.

"I love you."

"If you love me, don't die on me. Promise me!" Her lips trembled. "Jesse died when our plane crashed. It was a little over two years ago." Smoldering embers drew her gaze. She well remembered the sites and odors surrounding the event. She couldn't go through this again.

Cody pressed a kiss to her lips, his cold fingers alarming her. "I'm not going to die today. Not here. Not like this. I promise you."

She stared at him, willing his words to be the truth. How had she fallen in love with a tough cop, of all people?

Footsteps crunched on the gravel near Melissa's head and she twisted around. A pair of badly scuffed black polished shoes and uniformed legs spread before her in a military fashion. She looked up, noting hands bolted on lean hips where a gun belt with a revolver rested. A little further up, she spied a tin star and name badge that read "Thacker." Her heart began thudding against her ribs when she stared into a stern chiseled face covered in soot. Slowly the man drew his revolver and pointed it at them.

"You're both under arrest for stealing that plane. Anything you say may be held against you in a court of law. You have the right to hire an attorney..." He Mirandized them as Melissa listened in dread fascination.

"I think he needs an ambulance." She put her weight on her knees then slowly stood, careful not to make sudden threatening moves and to keep her hands in plain view. The last thing she needed now was to spook the cop. They were already in major trouble. She prayed Cody's connections were stellar.

"Do *you* need an ambulance?"

"I think I'll be all right. You saved my life. Thanks." Cody rolled over, rose to all fours then stood, his face scrunched, his nose wrinkling, his lips pulled down. Red stained the front of his shirt and she gasped.

"Your wound's seeping." As soon as they rescued Christina, she would make him rest for a month, maybe even two months, until all traces of the snakebite were gone.

Cody looked down and scowled deeply. "That…or I have a new one."

"I'd better call that ambulance," said the cop.

"*Please*. He needs immediate medical attention." She wanted to cradle Cody in her arms, bandage his wounds but she dare not. And with what?

"I don't feel so well." Cody blinked, swayed and swooned, staggering towards the policeman.

"Stand back. Not another step forward." Officer Thacker tensed.

"Omigod! He's passing out on us." When she went to catch him, a gunshot sang out, whizzing by her so closely she felt the wind part. Gunpowder singed her nose. A scream gurgled in her throat.

Cody dove forward, knocking the gun from their captor's hands and another gunshot split the night. Shouts erupted behind them.

"Call for back up!"

The words barely escaped the man's lips when Cody plunged his other fist into their rescuer's nose, felling him to the ground.

As she assimilated that Cody wasn't as injured as he'd let on, despite the blood, that it was all a clever, calculated ruse, steely fingers grabbed Melissa's arm, almost yanking it out of its socket. "Let's go."

Cries of "Stop them!" and "They're escaping!" and "They killed the cop!" followed them.

"What now? We're trapped. We'll never outrun this vigilante crowd circling us."

"Oh ye of little faith. Get in the car." Cody stooped and grabbed the revolver shoving it into his pants.

"Which car?"

"The black and white."

"You're joking..." Melissa eyed the police cruiser with

trepidation. He honestly expected to steal a cop car and get away with it? The landing must've jarred all his wires loose.

Unceremoniously, Cody shoved her through the open door, clambering in almost on top of her and slammed the door. "Damn! No keys." Stripping ignition wires bare, he tried to start the engine.

Jumping on her seat like a hyperactive four year old, she cheered the car on. "Go! Go! Go! You can do it!" Her nerve endings screamed louder in her ears than her voice.

"Come on. Now or never."

The cop stood and swayed, his hand clasping his bloodied nose. Several civilians held him steady, inspecting his injuries. Several others closed in on them.

"The cop's alive." Her voice held almost a singsong quality. Almost. She was relieved and feeling dreadful all at once.

"But?" Cody fumbled with the wires, marrying them.

"The posse's about to lynch us. Think they'll smash windows or roll the car?"

"Get the gun out of my pants. Wave it at them."

Small sparks under the dashboard gave Melissa a glimmer of hope. They just might escape one more time. Like a cat, they'd expired many lives; she just prayed they might have a couple left.

Melissa grabbed the gun out of his pocket. "What now, Clyde?"

"Shout at them to get the hell out of the way…or get run over!"

Just as she cracked the window and began a yell at the crowd to disperse, the engine rolled over. Tires spit gravel, squealing. People jumped back, flailing fists, shouting terrifying threats. The car lurched forward at light speed.

"What now? Every cop in three states will be looking for this marked car."

"Settle down, Bonnie. We'll ditch it fast." Cody glanced in the rearview mirror and muttered curses.

She twisted around; she had to see what brought on his reaction.

Two cars bore down on them. One man spoke into a cellular phone, his hands speaking faster than his lips. "Better make it warp speed."

"Don't worry, darlin'. I know a few maneuvers that'll turn them on their ears."

"Basic police training 101?" Melissa asked, her words falsely light hearted.

"Basic Brooklyn driving 101. These country boys don't stand a chance."

"Not very sure of yourself, are you? I think that's what I like best about you. Your modesty." *Not.*

"Hold on." His lips, pursed but not as tightly as his fingers strangling the steering wheel.

Before she could open her mouth to question him, Cody jackknifed the cruiser one hundred eighty degrees and plunged toward the other side of the divided four lane highway. The ground dipped alarmingly and they jounced across the divide, the car's leaf springs cracking, the shocks slamming so hard her neck almost whiplashed and her front teeth chipped.

Half Cody's shirt was blood soaked and matted to him, while his face was lily white. He was obviously in agony but he didn't whine or cry about it, the way Nathan would have done. Then of course, Nathan thought he was dying if a bee stung him.

Their pursuers tried to follow. One car skidded into such a spin it fishtailed and crashed into a parked car. The other slowed, turned and tried to cross the median.

"One's still coming." Her fingernails dug into the back of the seat.

Cody punched the accelerator and they swerved in and out of traffic, a wild, mischievous gleam in his eye.

"You like playing cops and robbers. You're in cop heaven." If her words got any drier the Sahara would look lush.

"Just saving our butts."

"Some getaway car. We might as well wear neon signs that say *arrest us, we're criminals*. Or send up flares."

He cut a sideways glance at her. "When did you become so melodramatic?"

"I tend to get that way when cops chase me." Melissa gave an overemphasized shrug. "Sue me. It's one of my silly quirks."

"But riff raff and motorcycle gangs don't faze you. Interesting."

"Stuff it and drive."

Their pursuer's car launched over a hill, flew in the air, flipped and landed on its nose, which folded accordion style as Melissa watched in disbelief. As metal crunched and screamed, she winced.

Chapter Nine

"Well…we lost them. Do you think they're all right?"

"It's not on fire. There are plenty of people to help them." His brow lifted. "Do you think we should chance going back to see?"

Shaking her head, Melissa said, "No." She eyed Cody skeptically. "Do you have a plan?"

"Yep."

She waited for him to magnify his answer but he drove on in silence. When she couldn't stand the silence any longer, she asked, "You *do* have a plan?"

"Soon as I find an exit with a gas station, we'll ditch this bitch and call my old buddy Chet who's now in the FBI. We'll hole up till he can bail us out of this mess."

"What about my sister? She'll be married by then!" Another thought struck her. "Won't there be road blocks?"

"That's why we'll pull off the road before the exit, hide the car in the woods and walk to the station. We'll bypass the road block."

"Oh."

A plan worthy of Jesse. It had merit.

When Cody passed up the exit, Melissa yelled, "You crazy? We can't stay in this car. We might as well give ourselves up."

"Just watch." He slowed until no traffic was in sight, and then yanked the wheel in a hard right toward a thick grove of trees, slipped in between trunks in an impossibly tight fit, swerved in and out—then cut the engine.

"Now we hike."

"Where?"

He got out of the car and stared pointedly at her.

Melissa got out and started to follow Cody into the woodsy abyss, but he stopped dead in front of her and bent over double. She careened into his rear end, noting to her disgust and increasing lust that it was firm and sculpted perfectly. She put out her hands to steady herself but the only place available for them to land was on him. If she had any other choice than tumbling over him, she'd have taken it, but she didn't. Her palms spread over him, spanning his tempting backside.

"Massage a little lower and I'm all yours."

"Cretin." To teach him a lesson, Melissa pinched him. Hard. "Don't you think we should go a little farther before we stop?" They'd barely gone ten feet. Could he be that tired already?

Maybe Cody was injured worse than she'd realized. Maybe he'd suffered concussion and couldn't think straight. She was ashamed of herself and wished she could eat her words. "Are you all right? Are you bleeding again? Are you dizzy?"

"You don't pinch that hard." His laughter was dry as he straightened with an armload of branches and brush. "Grab some limbs and help me camouflage the car. Then they'll never find it."

Without waiting to see if she followed his commands, he plodded to the vehicle that shimmered like a ghost in the night. She stayed put, poised to flee, when a horrible thought struck her.

"Don't police cars have LOJACS? I bet they're tracking us, closing in on us." Suddenly every shadow, every rustle of a leaf took on a new menace. Melissa switched her intruder detector back to red alert and her ears went into super sonic mode.

"Paranoid?" Helter skelter he tossed the foliage on the car. It started to resemble the swamp thing under her watchful gaze.

"Don't you think a big topiary will stand out?"

"Not in the dark, and by morning we'll be long gone."

The moon shone brightly now that the storm had rained itself out and the clouds had dissipated. If *she* could see it clearly, anyone could. Who was he fooling? As an ex-cop, he'd know these things. But he was an ex-*city* cop. Not a good ol' country sheriff. She was sure he knew the ins and outs of the big, tough city as intimately as a lover. But he was pretty green in these woods.

Melissa made a snap decision. Cody wasn't bleeding so she didn't have to play Florence Nightingale. "You can stay here and play around till they catch you. I'm not sticking around for the party. I've a wedding to crash." *With a big sledge hammer preferably.* Pivoting on her heel, she marched ahead, no clue where she was heading. Not a breadcrumb. No light at the end of the tunnel. At least she wouldn't be a sitting duck waiting for the net to be thrown over her.

Not a whole ten seconds passed before a large body crashed through the brush behind her. She was pretty sure Cody was on her tail and closing, but in this case, she wasn't willing to play hunches. Gambling with cards, money and jewels was one thing—gambling with her life was another. Grizzlies, cougars, and coyotes roamed this part of the country. Cops and bounty hunters did, too. Or something more sinister, like the bikers back in Pennsylvania. She had to know what chased her.

Even though she'd been ninety-nine point nine percent sure it was Cody, she still exhaled a long sigh of relief when she recognized his large frame eating up the distance between them. Although she'd been alone since Jesse's death, she didn't relish trekking through these woods by herself. Those crazies in Pennsylvania loomed large in her mind. She was getting paranoid. Of course, most people would be candidates for a straight jacket in a rubber room after the series of disasters they'd been through in the past few weeks. She should be congratulating herself for retaining her sanity. What was a little healthy paranoia under the circumstances? It had been her salvation more than once.

Melissa smiled sweetly and stopped a sudden urge to bat her lashes at him. "Miss me?"

"You can't crash a wedding alone. Bad manners. You need an escort."

"Tell me again what brilliant, fool proof, spectacular plan you've concocted to get us out of here and into Daddy's house? Through the army Nathan'll undoubtedly have posted around the grounds?"

He took her elbow, propelling her forward. "I have connections." A deep scowl marred his face.

"Connections to Daddy? To Nathan?" Suddenly Melissa couldn't breathe. Did he know them? Maybe he wasn't an *ex*-cop after all?

"FBI connections." He squeezed her elbow. "You *are* paranoid."

"You'd be too if you'd been running and hiding for three years. It's not easy to turn it off." Probably no easier than turning off cop instincts. She should ditch him, should've a long time ago. But now her emotions were all tangled up in him; telling her to do something completely opposite to what her head told her.

And the emotions were winning.

Wanting to kick herself for such weakness, Melissa plodded forward, wet leaves and muck sucking at her feet. The occasional branch smacked her in the face.

"Time's up. It's time to face your demons and get on with your life. You can't run and hide forever."

She stopped and stared at him. Did he know how much of

a demon Nathan was? Not the run-of-the-mill, semi-evil specter, but pure, demonic evil?

"You don't know. You can't possibly understand why I'm hiding." Nathan would kill her. He was a lunatic. Her heart raced at the memories of the many abuses and threatened abuses she'd suffered at his hands. It raced so fast it would surely burst. And now, she had to choose between her safety and her sister's. No contest. No way would she submit her baby sister to him. But it didn't mean a small earthquake didn't have her quivering inside. Nathan terrified her. And Jesse had died for nothing to save a woman who couldn't be saved.

Satan and his dark angels must be laughing their asses off. Nathan would be infuriatingly glib, having manipulated her so easily. Why he wanted her when she took no pains to hide her hatred of him, was beyond her.

Since when was the man sane, though? *Since never.*

"You don't have to marry anyone you don't want to. And if he lays a finger on you, you can have him arrested."

"You are soooooo naïve. He owns daddy. He owns the police. He's practically the governor of California and someday he'll be president. I can't fight him fairly and win. He doesn't fight fair."

"Then we have to expose him."

"He owns the media, too." Despair threatened to take over. "Maybe we should kidnap Christina, get plastic surgery, change our identities and move to Argentina."

"Melodramatic, aren't you? You should be an actress." Cody rubbed his stubbled chin between his thumb and fingers. Moonlight haloed his golden hair, leaving his face in shadow. "He can't own *all* the cops or *all* the media."

Melissa wasn't so sure. "If anyone could, it's my *dear* ex-fiancé. The rest he'll charm into thinking I'm out of my mind."

"Don't forget we have an ace in the hole." When she raised her eyebrow and stared at him blankly, he said simply, "Chet."

"Doesn't sound like a secret weapon." What kind of a secret agent name was *Chet*? She'd feel safer with a *James*, or a *Robert*. Or a *Sherlock*, or a *Basil*. But *Chet*? As in *Chester*? She slid a glance at him. "This wouldn't happen if you carried a cell phone. We could've had FBI escort to California instead of almost getting ourselves killed and locked up forever."

"Not everyone's as rich as you."

Disgust wormed through Melissa. Not another man with

a chip on his shoulder? She wouldn't have expected it out of this one. Either they chased her for her wealth or berated her for being spoiled rotten. Looking down at herself, she scowled at her torn, filthy clothes, the thick soot covering her, the mud splashed to her knees. Pulling a twig out of her hair and wading through a mess of others at her feet, she stared at him cross-eyed. Still holding out a strand of hair, feeling like a forest creature, she said, her voice shaking, "Do I look rich?" Lifting her foot high, she said, "Are these designer boots?" Pointing at her ripped jeans, she continued, "Are these designer jeans?" On a roll, she drove her point home, "You saw my house? Was it a mansion? Did I risk my life in that poker game to buy us food?"

~ * ~

Cody claimed to know the way, so she turned and followed him. "You'd better not be leading us into a trap."

"The key word in your sentence is *us*. Don't worry. I don't want to lose my freedom any more than you do."

Had he ever lost his freedom? Did he know what a precious gift free agency was? Had he ever felt like a prisoner in his own home?

How long she stared at him, weighing him, Melissa wasn't sure. What choice did she have? Not only did her heart long for him, but logic dictated she stay in this partnership.

"It'll be daylight soon. It'd be better if we get to that phone while it's still dark."

She knew when she was being told to shut up. Pursing her lips, she followed in silence, quelling the temptation to say, "*Yes, Tarzan.*" Why did this man bring out the sarcastic side in her? Why did they bicker and one-up each other so much?

Up ahead, lights blinked advertising a truck stop, with an all-night restaurant. Neon lights strobed "Eat." *Real original.* At least it was effective. A semi-tractor trailer slowed and turned into the parking lot, its headlights illuminating pre-dawn darkness.

Finally, a phone. He'd better have a calling card or proper change and Wonder Boy Chet had better be there.

"What are you waiting for? *Rapture*?"

When Melissa started to leave the cover of the shrubbery, Cody put a restraining hand on her upper arm. "It could be under surveillance. Wait."

She peered around the parking lot. No black and whites. No one just hanging around. "I don't see anything. We need to move before they arrive."

"No. We're not going to reveal ourselves. I've got a better idea." His gaze darted from one vehicle to another. "There should be a cell phone in one of the cars."

"We won't be conspicuous peering into cars?" She flicked her hair behind her shoulders and favored him with a sugary sweet grin. "It won't be better just to stroll up to the pay phone?"

"Trust me." He turned a full wattage smile on her, making her heart turn somersaults.

"I *never* trust people who say '*trust me*'."

"Stay put. I'll find a safe phone." Before she could glean his intentions, he bent his head and captured her lips in a searing kiss that stole her breath and almost made her knees buckle.

As she started to melt into the kiss, he tore away as abruptly as he'd started the kiss. "For luck." He sent her a mischievous wink, and then slipped into the shadows.

"In case you haven't noticed," Melissa whispered, her fingers touching her bruised lips, "I'm not very lucky." Not that she believed in luck, except for the luck she made for herself.

Cody was barely visible in the darkness, crouched low and moving stealthily. She willed him to hurry, just in case he was right and the joint was staked out.

"Come on, Cody." Seconds dragged like hours. Every noise made her nerves jump. Birds awoke and broke out in morning song. Truckers finished with early breakfast, ambled to their rigs, gassed up, and returned to work. One crushed a cigar underfoot not far from her and the strong tobacco smell reminded her of her grandfather.

What was taking the man so long? They could've walked to the next town by now. Had he been caught? Should she look for him? If he were in trouble, she had to help him.

Wary to leave the sanctity of the forest, Melissa crept along the bushes edging the parking lot, careful to stay low and hidden.

About halfway around the café, she spied Cody being held at gunpoint, his hands in the air. Her heart froze.

Chapter Ten

"What do you think you're doing, Hoss? We don't much go in for stealing in these parts. Throw the phone down and put your hands up, real slow like."

Cody cursed himself for being caught so easily. Melissa must be out of her mind with worry. Skittish as she was, she might've skipped to the next county by now. Perhaps it would be for the best. He didn't want her to be apprehended, too.

Cody dropped the phone at his feet; it thudded heavily on the asphalt and bounced a couple of times, its fancy casing cracked. Bye-bye phone. No more crystal clear airtime for that baby. If left alone, he'd have *borrowed* five minutes airtime and replaced it unharmed.

"All I wanted to do was make a phone call."

The tall trucker laughed and nodded his head at the phone stands. "Pay phone's right there. You don't expect me to buy that."

Nearby, the leaves rustled and twigs cracked.

Cody sensed rather than saw her, but his gaze darted past the big man. What was she trying to do? Get caught herself?

"Real slow, walk to those phones. We'll just call the sheriff."

Sunlight broke over the treetops and he saw Melissa. She held a large, wicked-looking branch that she raised above her head like a club. His breath caught in his throat. She aimed to attack his captor but she was no match for a man holding a gun.

She had more guts than brains—not that he didn't appreciate her sterling intentions. But it wouldn't do either of them any good if this over zealous trucker went off half-cocked.

Cody could only think of one thing to do. "She's going to hit you in the head."

Melissa glared at him, her mouth agape.

Startled, the man looked and Cody took the opportunity to whirl on the ball of his foot and kick the man's gun out of his hand. It flipped end over end into the air, sunlight glinting off the barrel. He prayed it wouldn't discharge and lodge a bullet in one of their hearts. It was risky, but he hadn't had much choice.

"Duck!" he yelled to Melissa. But she couldn't stop the

momentum of her swing that nearly hit him in his injured shoulder, seconds before his fist found the man's face.

They wrestled on the ground, which Cody was sure would grab attention from inside the diner.

"Get out of here," he told her. The trucker threw a hefty punch himself that caught Cody square in the chin and made him see stars.

"I'm not leaving you." Melissa drew Cody's pistol, stood over them with the drop on them. "Get up," she said to the trucker, deadly quiet. Her feet spread at parade rest, her arms stretched out, the pistol cocked. Sunlight made her red hair glow. Her features lay in shadow. "Put your hands over your head."

To Cody she said, "Make your phone call."

~ * ~

As the call was going through, the man on the ground tried to scoot away unnoticed.

Melissa clucked her tongue. "Tsk, tsk, tsk. Leaving the party already?" She cocked the pistol aimed at his heart. The metallic sound rang ominous in her ears. "I don't think so."

The trucker froze, his gaze glued to hers, his features immobile, his eyes distrustful. Each second that passed, the sun rose higher in the Pacific sky and she grew increasingly nervous they'd be noticed or someone would miss their new *friend* and send a search party.

Melissa chanced a glance at Cody, annoyed that he seemed to be in the middle of catching up with his old buddy. "Swapping war stories?" she asked dryly. Annoyed as she was, she couldn't help but notice how the sunlight burnished his hair or how lean and virile his physique was in silhouette. Before she knew it, he pirouetted and was tackling their would-be captor, who was once again poised for escape.

"You going to kill me?" The man's eyes were deep, dark pools of fear. His lower lip trembled.

Shocked, Melissa's jaw dropped wide open and shame flooded her. "No. We won't hurt you. We only want to get away."

The man's eyes widened. "You must be those criminals the cops are chasin'. The ones who landed that plane on the highway and then stole the cop car."

Cody scowled at her. With his finger, he sliced the air in front of his throat.

She cut off what she was going to say, her gaze ping-ponging between the two men.

Cody jerked his head to the side, at a semi-tractor trailer that stood with its rear doors opened and seemed to be unmanned. Its manifest was packed loosely and Melissa wondered if she read his intentions correctly. *Hitch a ride?* If that wasn't what he meant, she'd be sure to suggest it. A grim smile clamped her lips firm and it was her turn to nod, but nearly imperceptibly. First, they had to figure out what to do with their uninvited guest while they slipped out of town.

In a hoarse whisper, she asked, "What about him?"

Cody looked at the sweating man long and hard. Then he whipped off his belt and advanced on him. Sun glinted off the belt buckle as the ex-cop coiled the length of leather around his hand.

"What're you going to do with that?" Melissa and the man asked in unison.

A half-smile played on Cody's lips. "Tie him up so we can leave in peace."

"Bears roam these woods!" The man's complexion paled even more than it had at the click of the pistol. "Mother fuckin' grizzlies! And cougars. They'll rip me apart!"

A wicked gleam stole into Cody's eyes. He rubbed his jaw thoughtfully. Although there were only a few silvery hairs in his newly grown stubble, they fascinated Melissa and she could hardly rip her gaze away from them. They gave him a distinguished air despite his Indiana Jones wardrobe. "Naaaa. Only if they're hungry." Cody pretended to study the man. "You look too scrawny to be tasty."

Melissa's lips twitched. *Fine time he chose to be a stand up comic.* "You can't do that," she told her companion succinctly, with more than a hint of regal bearing. She lifted her chin high and favored him with her most supercilious glare.

Cody kicked at the dirt with the toe of his boot. So much for getting under his thick skin. He'd probably ignore the Queen. "He'll wriggle free long before the coyotes start sniffing around him."

"Or the rattlesnakes?" Honey dripped from her voice as she taunted him. He could sure dish it out but she'd see if he could take it. She watched him closely for his reaction.

He turned a few tints lighter and she offered him her sweetest smile. So he wasn't as impervious as he pretended. Real life emotions, including human fear, hid under that ultra tough exterior. She was glad to know that. Very glad.

"Coyotes? Snakes?" The man's voice broke. His eyes

rolled back in his head then closed as he slumped. His head smacked the pavement, making her grimace. He'd have a doozy of a headache upon awakening.

Cody nudged the still form with his toe. When it lolled, lump-like, Cody grunted. "Wimp. He fainted dead away. Guess he won't be needing my belt."

Wryly, she said, "Good. You need to keep your pants *on*."

Cody grabbed her hand and tugged sharply, propelling her toward the trailer. Just the touch of his calloused flesh on her tender palm sent shivers coursing through her and made her pulse skip several beats. "Your carriage, Princess. Better get in before the chauffeur returns. Sorry it's not first class." He winked and his cheek dimpled. "We're fresh out of rose petals."

Melissa rolled her eyes at his sarcasm. "Cut the bull. You get a lot of dates this way?"

Warm hands spanned her waist. Long fingers dug into her flesh. As he lifted her into the trailer bed, his breath tickled her ear. "You want a *date* with *me*?"

Hot flashes strafed her spine and Melissa was suddenly moist in a most intimate area, causing her to remember the last time they'd been alone together in the motel. The truck bed didn't look nearly as soft as the other bed had. Still, her body flamed to life.

Before she could suitably reply, Cody hauled himself up next to her, the muscles in his arms bulging from the strain. "Crouch low behind those boxes in the rear corner."

As she did his bidding, she wondered if they were caging themselves in a nice, neat package for the authorities? It went against Jesse's teachings for her to put herself in a corner with no way out. She felt like a mouse that'd just sprung the cheese, waiting for the bar to drop.

"I don't think this is such a great idea. There's no back door." She eyed the steel walls that loomed high and ominous, mocking her.

Footsteps and whistling came out of nowhere and Cody yanked her down beside him, putting his forefinger to his lips. His arm encircled her waist, drawing her so close to him, his heartbeat drumming against her chest.

The door banged shut and a deadbolt clicked loud enough to be gunfire. Not a fissure of light remained. This was darker than any nightmare she'd ever had.

A horrifying thought struck her. "Will the air run out?" Her lungs retracted in response and Melissa felt as if she were on the very edge of hyperventilation. "Will the trailer fill up with carbon monoxide?"

"The air shouldn't run out and the trailer shouldn't fill up with monoxide. We're safe now. The cops will lose our trail."

She swallowed the big lump threatening to block her throat. "What about your friend *whatshisname*? Chad? Chase?"

"Chet?" His breath tickled her throat and cheeks and a delicious chill coursed through her.

She nodded, her hair brushing her cheeks, and then remembered he couldn't see her. "Chet. Is he bringing the cavalry to our rescue?" Uncomfortable in her cramped crouched position, Melissa contorted herself into a sitting position, immediately missing Cody's warmth.

"They'll meet us at your father's house. They're staking it out by now."

The truck rumbled to life and started to roll. But in which direction? Toward which town? Every little bump was magnified a few hundred times so that she sympathized with the Princess with the pea under her mattresses. Except she didn't imagine the princess could get a concussion from her pea; she and Cody *were* in danger of banging their heads on the trailer's bed hard enough to knock them out.

"Chances are about a hundred to one he's headed toward L.A."

"Chances are higher than that. L.A. gets the lion's share of the commerce. If I were a betting man, I'd bet we're headed towards the City of Angels."

"I'd take that bet any day." Gambling fever boiled in her veins at the mere mention of a possible bet.

Cody's hand grabbed her ankle and she nearly yelped in fright. Her heartbeat raced at least ninety miles per hour. Then his other hand followed and he *climbed* her vine-like. When a hand accidentally, at least she presumed it was accidental, came in contact with a very private area, she screamed and jerked.

Immediately his hand lifted. "Sorry, Princess. I misjudged my distance." He settled and stretched beside her, his long, muscular leg pressing against hers. "I'd never be so crass." In a husky voice he added, "I'm much more charming than that."

Still processing his words, she was blindsided when sharp teeth and firm lips nibbled her earlobe. She almost melted when the tip of his tongue lathered it so sensually that she was about to swoon. She fought to hang onto her senses and her logic, but she was fighting a losing battle. "Well?" Her voice was husky.

"Deep subject." His chest pressed her to the floor of the truck, crushing her against him, as one hand entangled in the hair at the nape of her neck and the other rubbed her far arm. Her nipples hardened immediately. She could barely pull air into her lungs, but whether it was because of his weight on her, or the way he incapacitated her, she didn't know.

It was more and more difficult to think, to speak coherently. Her lips yearned for a much more dangerously provocative assignment, but Melissa forced the words past her lips anyway. "We'll miss the wedding if we're in here too long. If we're headed the wrong way." *They'd miss the honeymoon, too.*

Cody's lips continued their mindless assault, nuzzling her throat. Against her pulse point, he murmured, "Soon as we stop, we'll find a phone and call Chet to send a helicopter. We'll be there in no time." Long fingers whispered down her throat to the swell of her chest, caressing it but moving no closer to her breasts that strained against the material of her imprisoning blouse.

Her nipples tightened unbearably, straining to be free, to feel his caresses, begging for mercy. Full-blown thoughts scattered as she turned into his embrace, her lips seeking his.

"You're so beautiful." His lips moved against her flesh.

Meteors of desire showered through her and she arched her back toward him, aching to feel more of him. Yet, she couldn't resist calling him on his faux pas. "*Liar*. You can't see a thing in here." Mirth laced her voice.

His tongue flicked over her burning flesh. "You smell beautiful. You feel beautiful. You taste beautiful." His fingers unbuttoned her blouse and pushed her bra away from her breasts, freeing them to his seeking mouth. His lips closed over her nipple and suckled it. Lower, the hard ridge of his swollen evidence of his desire pressed against her thigh.

Melissa moaned deep in her chest and latched her fingers in his hair, pulling his head closer.

Then the truck hit a pothole, jouncing them unmercifully. Her head banged the floor so hard she bit her tongue and tasted her blood. His teeth nipped her in a sensitive area and she jerked away.

Her senses restored, she pushed Cody away. Huskily she said, as she redressed herself, "This isn't such a great idea. He could stop any minute."

His warm frame still pressed against her. His arm encircled her waist. In her ear, he said, "It doesn't feel like he's slowing down."

"We have things to discuss." Melissa turned her head and spit out a mixture of blood and saliva.

"Such as?" His fingers still played devil's advocate, trailing up and down her arm, making it difficult to think.

This was going to take a good dose of courage and moxie. Melissa willed herself not to back down. "Remember when the plane crashed and you were lying so still?"

"Uh hmm." His breath fanned her cheek.

"And I thought you were dead, like Je..." It wasn't politically correct to confess love for one man while bringing up a former love, so she clamped down on Jesse's name.

"Um hmm." He wasn't exactly helping her out. If only she could see his face, she could read him. Perhaps if Cody were to give more complete answers, she could gage his reaction by his voice. As it was, she was flying blind.

She inhaled deeply, fortifying her courage. "And I told you I loved you?"

"I couldn't hear you. Could you say that louder?"

"I love you."

"Louder."

Totally frustrated, she screamed into the darkness, "I love you!"

"I love you, too," he said against her hair, pulling her back against him. "How can the wind not love the rain? The world not love the rainbow? You breezed into my life and I was forever enchanted."

Melissa twisted her head toward the sound of his voice. "I didn't know you were a poet."

"Neither did I." Cody laughed with a twinge of self-consciousness. His arms tightened around her, practically squeezing the breath from her. "Seriously. I'll understand if you really didn't mean it, if fear made you say that... Like when people make promises to God they don't really mean."

"I meant it...with all my heart." She lifted her mouth and placed a gentle, promising kiss on his lips. The stubble on his chin and cheeks scratched her but she didn't care. When he started to deepen the kiss, she withdrew.

"But?"

"But nothing. Except we hardly know each other. One day you burst into my life, saved my butt, not just once but several times. We've barely talked...I know nothing about you, you know nothing about me."

"What do you want to know?"

"A million-trillion things." She searched her heart for the most important questions. "Why'd you stop being a policeman?"

A deep sigh erupted from him and he rolled onto his back, pulling her with him. "My younger sister disappeared. Her name was Theresa. The sheriff's department in our town didn't take the investigation very seriously. They dragged their feet for months while our family went out of its mind, crazed."

"Did they ever find her?" Her breath was trapped in her chest that swelled with sympathy.

"Just *pieces* of her." Bitterness and fury warred in his voice. His breathing shallowed and his heartbeat galloped beneath her ear.

"I'm so sorry." She stroked his cheek and Cody pressed a kiss into her palm that almost melted her bones.

"That's not the end of it." He paused for a long time and she wondered if he was too choked up to continue.

"You don't have to go on." Some things were too painful, too personal, to verbalize.

As if he hadn't heard her, as if he were in a different world or on a different plane of existence, he continued his story, pathos entwined in his voice. "They finally found the perp…"

"The what?"

"Perp. Perpetrator. Murderer." Moroseness filled into his voice. "But the creep got off on a lousy technicality."

"And that's when you stopped being a policeman?"

"Blame me? What good is the system when the bad guy gets loose to rape and murder other young girls?"

Melissa gasped. "Is that what happened?"

"Yes."

When he was silent for a long, long time, she wondered if he'd fallen asleep.

Then he began again:

"Terry was only nineteen, a college freshman. She was very bright—going to be a doctor. She had a full scholarship and hoards of boyfriends. Everyone loved her. She was the pride of our family."

"I'm sure they were proud of you, too," she said quickly.

"Terry was going to save the world. Until that bastard got hold of her."

It was her turn to comfort him, so she wrapped her arms around him and cradled him.

"Life is funny," she mused, under her breath.

"How so?" Gruffness attacked his words and she suspected he fought off tears.

"Look at me. I had the means to become someone important, to do something worthwhile, and I ran away from it. I chucked it all and disappeared, living only for myself."

"You loved your husband so much?"

"With all my heart." A sigh tremored through Melissa and she snuggled closer into his warmth. "But that wasn't all of it. Not by a long shot."

"Care to tell me about it? I'm a good listener."

Memories fought for recognition, flitting through her mind before being eclipsed by other more poignant memories. They were like a disjointed movie, some clips fragmented, some very clear. Some were brighter, clearer, scarier than others.

That's where she began.

"As I told you, I was engaged to marry Senator Nathan Alexander, a very powerful, influential man. He was obsessed with me." Her voice dropped to almost a whisper. "He thought he owned me. He monitored my every move. He tried to mold me into the perfect politician's wife. He tried to censor my thoughts and my every word. And when I didn't obey him, he was furious! So livid he—he…"

Melissa buried her face against Cody's strong chest, trying to dam the flood of horrific visions assaulting her.

Cody's hands grabbed her shoulders, much as Nathan's had and she lost control, flailing her arms before her, striking him. "Stop it! Stop it!"

"My God! What did that animal do to you?"

Cody's voice brought her back to the present. "He-he threatened to kill me, more than once."

"Unbelievable." Cody pulled her even closer to him. "So you ran."

She shook her head. Tears escaped from her eyes and trickled down her cheeks. "Not at first. Daddy didn't believe me—or maybe he just didn't want me to mess up his perfect plans."

"Surely you're wrong."

Melissa tried to pull away from him, and the dagger he'd just twisted in her heart. Her wry laugh was filled with disillusion. "See. *You* don't believe me either." His lack of faith, of understanding, floored her. He couldn't be the man she'd believed him to be if he could side with her father and Nathan on this. As such, she wanted nothing more to do with him.

"I didn't say that." Cody dropped feather light kisses on the top of her head. "I just can't imagine a parent turning a blind eye to abuse and torture like that."

"Believe it." Conviction made her voice steely. It turned her stomach over.

"So how'd you get away?"

"I was on a vacation with Daddy, Christina, and Nathan when I met my husband."

"And it was love at first sight?"

Jesse's face flashed before her eyes and she chuckled. "Hardly. I thought he was quite the pest. And way beneath me. I still thought I was quite the princess." Her lips twisted into a grimace. *Some princess she'd turned out to be.* Now it was an insult, not a compliment.

"What happened?"

"Well…one night, after Nathan had been particularly nasty…"

"When he beat you?" Cody's voice was deadly quiet.

"Uh…yes. I-I was contemplating my…*life*."

Ending my life, actually. My only way out.

"Jesse followed me again, being his usual pesky self. He made me laugh despite my rotten mood. He showed me that money didn't guarantee happiness. That I didn't have to live in fear and unhappiness."

"Then you fell in love?"

"Not right away, but I suppose that was the start. Daddy and Nathan hated Jesse. They did everything they could to buy him off—then to scare him away. But he refused to leave me at their mercy."

"This Jesse was quite the hero. Not the criminal the papers painted him to be."

"Yes, he was a hero. He saved my life…more than once. I owe him my life. And now—I can never repay him." Melissa stared up into the darkness, hoping Jesse knew how deeply grateful she was to him.

"He doesn't sound like he wanted to be repaid. I imagine he'd be happy just knowing that you're happy. That you've stopped hiding and resumed your life."

"I think I'm ready." A tremulous smile played around her lips. "Except Nathan's still after me. He wants me back and he's using Christina to flush me out."

"You're doing the right thing. It's time to take a stand. For you. For Christina. For the world." He rubbed his chin against her cheek. "We can't let the Senator get away with this. He's got to be stopped."

"If this truck ever stops. I'd swear we're heading to New York nonstop."

"Then we have time to, uh, *snuggle* some more." His lips captured hers, his tongue forcing her lips apart and delving deeply inside.

Stunned, Melissa lay still beneath him for several seconds before her blood boiled, her womanly core ignited with flame, and her flesh sizzled wherever he touched her.

"We have to be ready to get out of this truck alive, without being captured. How do you propose to do that?"

"The trucker can't unload everything at once. He'll take a few things, put them away and come back. We'll have time while he's putting things away."

"What if he has a whole crew waiting for him? What if he saw us and the police greet us?"

"Well, darlin'. If the police greet us, we go peaceably, then we use our one call, to phone Chet. He'll straighten out the mess. If there're truckers, maybe we can bluff our way out."

"How?"

"Maybe by admitting we climbed in here to get a little amour and got locked in before we could get the driver's attention. I think once they see how pretty you are, they'll believe that."

She felt nowhere as sure as he sounded. "How's the snake bite?"

"Well, it's still there. It's healing up pretty good, considering what we've been through."

"Considering what we've been through," Melissa said dryly, "It's pretty darn good we're still walking and breathing."

The truck slowed and turned, and she lost track of what she was going to say. "This may be it. Get ready." She heard the unmistakable cock of Cody's pistol and chills skated down her spine.

"Be ready to run. But not until I tell you. Stay down and don't make a sound." Underneath them, the truck lumbered slower and slower, the engine straining to pull its weight at a lower gear.

She shifted around to a sitting position, using her hands to feel around the boxes that would hide her from view, wishing she had even a little light to see her surroundings.

The truck whined to a stop and Melissa felt as if she'd

lost her sea legs when the road motion stopped beneath her. Her ears strained to hear any evidence of the rear door opening to free them. How she both wished for it and dreaded it, not knowing the outcome.

"Follow my lead," Cody whispered in her ear, his breath tickling her sensitive lobe. "Don't show fear."

No fear. No fear. She repeated this mantra, trying to instill it into her soul. Fear could be paralyzing. It could also keep one from doing something very stupid. In this case they'd already done several very stupid things. Boxing themselves into this truck topped the list. She didn't have a good feeling about it.

Time dragged, each second stretching into an eternity. When the back door finally opened, the sunlight streaming in blinded her. She had no idea if the truck had been stopped five minutes or several hours. Her cramped legs voted for the several hours guess.

"Ready?" Cody squeezed her hand, offering assurance. "Remember, follow my lead."

Melissa nodded, squinting, trying to peek over the top of the nearest box.

"Keep your head down. That orange hair of yours will give us away." His bulk looked incredibly cramped and contorted in the squatting position he'd adopted. His gaze focused intensely on the door as it opened wider, and a tall silhouette reached inside to grab a box.

He pushed her head down so that was all she saw. "Stay down!"

"How many people are there?"

"Only one so far."

She prayed their luck held, that they only had to contend with one lone trucker, that they could just sneak away unnoticed. Time ran short. She hoped they hadn't missed the wedding already.

"Now where are we?" she mumbled under her breath in an aside to Cody. The way things were going, the African jungle wouldn't surprise her. Still, when had things gone easy in a long, long time? Maybe she was just one of those people who was destined to have a hard life. Maybe she attracted trouble.

"You're in Oakland California, and in the custody of Captain Miguel Lopez of the Oakland P.D."

The raspy voice grated on Melissa' spine, making the hair on her arms stand up.

Chapter Eleven

Looking at Cody who stood tall and proud, eye-to-eye with this new nemesis, Melissa hissed, "I told you we were going north."

All he said was, "Chet," with a knowing smile.

Some mantra. She was tired of hearing about this super fantastic, miraculous Chet, agent of agents. She needed to see him with her own eyes, hear him speak, but mostly see his Midas touch in action. Raising her chin regally, staring into Cody's marvelous eyes, trying to ignore those magnificent lips that could leave her breathless, she said, "Don't tell me, tell *them*."

Cold steel handcuffs snapped, the key sounding like a thunderbolt, demeaning her as it cramped her muscles.

"Save it for the station." The police officer pulled a plastic-coated card from his shirt pocket, squinting at it. "I hereby advise that you have the right to remain silent, that anything you say can be used against you…"

"Skip it. I know the drill."

Lopez turned his squinty, wizened gaze on Cody. "You a cop, son?"

"A lifetime ago. NYPD."

Lopez clucked his tongue and shook his head. His eyes rolled heavenward. "Mother Mary, why do you keep sending them to me?" Lowering his gaze to the ex-cop, he peered at Cody closely. "You're not on the force now?"

"No, Sir."

"If you don't mind, I'll just finish reading this to the young lady. Can't stop the wheels of justice." His voice buzzed like a drone bee in her ear.

Now that Melissa wasn't hiding from Nathan or her father, that she was ready to take them on, with her teeth if she had to, a little namedropping couldn't hurt. So what was a little fib? "When my *fiancé* Senator Nathan Alexander hears about this, he'll have your badge."

"Senator Alexander, the California gubernatorial candidate?"

Never had she witnessed a paler countenance. All blood must've drained from the man's face. All trace of his cocky attitude melted away.

"I'm working with the FBI on this case. Let me call Special Agent Chester Mulligan. He'll straighten out this mess."

The cop looked at Cody with renewed interest, but not a wholly trusting expression. His squinty black eyes were mere pinpoints of light, his nose scrunched. However, Melissa was sure the Captain's expression was a whole lot more trusting than her own. Her glance ricocheted to Cody's face so quickly it must surely cut him to the bone. He was working with the FBI on this case? *Her* case? Had he been clever enough to deflect her anti-cop, anti-agent detector? She'd had her doubts but he'd managed to trample each and every one, first by saving her, not once, but several times, then by making her fall in love with him. Had she been so stupid and naïve? So desperate for companionship or love?

"If you were with the FBI, why didn't you say so before now?" The man poised, his handcuffs in mid air, seemingly uncertain whether he should cuff a possible special agent. Lights flickered across his eyes, his mini CPU projecting all possible scenarios. Would he or wouldn't he lose his badge over this? How did he proceed from here? Lopez was an open book to her.

Too bad Richards hadn't been also.

Taking a deep breath, Melissa faced off against the man she'd dreamed of spending the rest of her life with. She cleared her throat to get the officer's attention. Instilling a note of regal haughtiness in her voice, lifting her chin several notches higher, she plied him with her most disdaining voice, honed from the crib. "My fiancé, Senator Nathan Alexander, won't be at all happy to know how you've treated me." Able to drop the masquerade she'd played for so long, she turned up her volume, purring, "I'm Melissa Vanderbilt-Smythe, of the Los Angeles Vanderbilt-Smythes, and I demand you release me."

"Fiancé?" Cody's voice was deadly quiet, deathly cold; his shoulders stiffened but the air crackled between them as his gaze turned stormy, pitch black. If he knew wizardry, they'd surely hurl lightning bolts her way.

Drenching him in her sweetest, most innocent voice, she countered. "FBI Special Agent? Case?" She failed. It came out so sugary sweet she thought she'd go into a diabetic coma. Bitter bile rose in her throat. Growling, her stomach clenched in knots.

"Senator Alexander?" The man practically bowed, rusty, inexperienced, but Melissa recognized the gesture for she'd had a belly full of tin soldiers like him in her past life. She knew the gesture wasn't meant for her but for the snake, Nathan. He had this man cowed and bamboozled like he did the rest. Why did his charismatic charm work on everybody but her? Why did they not see through that slimy façade to the dangerous morass of hatred and power-hungry greed that lurked barely beneath the surface of his civilized veneer?

Then lights blinked on in Lopez's eyes as he obviously processed the rest of what she'd just said. "Melissa Vanderbilt-Smythe. The missing heiress?" He circled her, as she stood tall and regal for inspection.

"Is there any other?"

"But she's dead. You're dead." The man's eyes took her measure.

"Do I look like a ghost?" *Duh* hung in the air. Technically, Melissa supposed her Jesse was a ghost, although she thought of him as her guardian angel. Maybe the man did speak to ghosts. Who was she to say? However, she knew she was alive.

"N-no. No ghost looked like you. But I have bad news for you." Shuffling his feet, the policeman fidgeted. His gaze flitted everywhere except to connect with hers. "Your fiancé's about to marry your sister."

"Then don't you think you'd better get me home?"

Hopefully, Cody's FBI friend would get here fast. Hauling in a huge breath, Melissa reminded herself for the gazillionth time that her mission now was to save Christina. Her own redemption would come later. She'd gamble that she could find another way out once she got Christina clear of the bombs. She could only handle one thing at a time.

"If I may ask, where have you been all this time?"

Her CPU crashed, the screen in her mind going blank. She'd not thought this far ahead.

"She's been suffering from amnesia, thinking she was someone else. I found her in New Jersey."

Tiny wrinkles in Lopez's face smoothed when he smiled for the first time. "I'm sure your fiancé will be delighted to know you're alive and well."

"Alive, yes." *Well?* She might never be well again if she lost the bet. Even if she didn't lose this bet, she might never forgive Cody his deception. "Aren't there bears in these woods?"

"And snakes." Cody's lips smirked in a self-deprecating manner.

A smile hovered on her lips despite herself. He'd hate

snakes all his days now because of her. He'd also make sure to fix all his own meals and feed himself. She let her glance slide over him. "One huge snake for sure."

"I suppose you're anxious to reunite with your family. Won't they be happy to have you back?"

The officer practically ran to his car and grabbed his radio. After jabbering into it, he couldn't move fast enough to unlock the handcuffs, tripping over his feet as well as his tongue, after he'd heard her daddy's name.

Melissa favored the man with her brightest, socialite smile, which she'd practiced from the cradle and which didn't hold a trace of real warmth. She tried to instill some friendliness in it, but between thoughts of Nathan, she wasn't in a very warm and fuzzy mood.

"We're tired and dirty and I'd really like to get to my sister, if you don't mind." Tilting her head at the police cruiser, she asked, "Do you mind if I sit?"

"Of course not. Right this way." The man fell all over himself escorting her to the car, opening the door and being the perfect gentleman.

Mentally, Melissa rolled her eyes. This type of behavior annoyed her. In truth, it always had. What made her different from the rest of the world? A few greenbacks in her daddy's vault? A famous name? Nothing of real importance. She'd discovered she liked being independent and standing on her own two feet, being valued on her own merit, not her rich family's.

Cody followed her, sliding in the other door, his gaze never leaving her. His thigh touched hers, scorching her as if no clothes separated them.

The policeman popped his head into the cruiser. "Good news. Your FBI friend is going to rendezvous with us in a few minutes."

"Soooo, you're working with the FBI?" She should've known not to trust him or anyone. Just because he had a pretty face and lips to die for didn't make him trustworthy.

"No," Cody said, disgust ringing in his voice. He crossed his heart. "I swear to you I'm not working with the FBI—at least not until now. But we're out of options. Do you want to reach your sister in time or not?"

He had her there. She was revealing herself in a couple of hours anyway, and then Heaven help her. It was either that, or rot in some small town jail.

Dragging in a deep breath, Melissa let him off the hook—

sort of. "Okay. Do I have a choice? But if I find out you've lied to me, I never want to see your face again." Did she imagine that his complexion turned ashen? It was hard to tell in this shadowy forest.

Finally, a helicopter hovered over them, blowing her hair wildly about her as she climbed out of the police cruiser, making her squint. She put her hand over her eyes to watch the descent as Cody struggled out to stand beside her.

A tall debonair man with flecks of gray in otherwise dark hair alighted from the helicopter. His twill slacks and white dress shirt were totally incongruous with the forest or with their own dust and grime.

Melissa slid a glance to her companion. "Is that the infamous Chet?" As the man was closing in on them fast with his long stride, she kept her voice low.

"You're the infamous one, sweetheart." An enigmatic smile tugged at Cody's lips as he stuck out his hand to pump Chet's. "Man, are you a sight for sore eyes. I thought you'd never get here."

The men tussled for a moment, obviously glad to see one another. But when Chet touched Cody's wound, Cody stumbled and moaned, clutching at it.

Concern clouded Chet's hazel eyes. "You okay?"

Melissa stepped between the men, taking charge. "Sit!" She nudged the big lug to the forest floor and pried open his shirt.

Chet whistled long and low behind her, his shadow falling over both of them. "What happened to you?"

"What hasn't happened?" Melissa muttered under her breath as she unbuttoned Cody's shirt and slid it off his shoulder.

"Snake bite." Cody glowered down at his chest, his fingers getting in her way as she tried to examine his shoulder. "It's a long story." Cody's chuckle held little mirth. He fidgeted as Melissa pried a bandage loose to peek underneath and ensure he hadn't started bleeding again. It would be a wonder after the day they'd had.

She sucked her teeth when she saw that pus oozed from his wound. Half twisting, looking up and over her shoulder at the tall man towering above her, she asked, "Do you have a first aid kit? He needs a fresh dressing. Then he needs to get to a hospital."

Cody's hand clamped down on her wrist, stilling her ministrations. "No time. Your sister." His labored breathing alarmed her. Looking up at his friend, he half-smiled, half-grimaced. "How long will it take to get to the Vanderbilt-Smythe estate in that contraption?"

Chet glanced at the helicopter and circled his finger at the pilot, who at once restarted the engine. The propeller spun slowly at first then gained momentum, drowning out sound.

Melissa saw the men's lips move but only heard gurgled voices, picking up bits and pieces of words. But it was unmistakable when Cody grabbed her elbow and pointed at the chopper that it was time to go. One part of her wanted to shout *hallelujah* that this ordeal was almost at an end. Another part was worried sick about the ex-cop. He was deathly pale and trembling all over. A hand to his forehead had told her he was burning up with fever.

The sun inched higher in the sky, ticking away precious time. The wedding drew ever nearer and with it, her sister's fate loomed darker.

"Duck!" Chet yelled when they approached the vehicle. Dust, leaves, and dirt hurled through the air, smacking Melissa in the face. Too late she shielded her head with her arm to prevent dust from flying in her eyes. Blinking rapidly, tears cleansed them but couldn't prevent them from stinging.

Finally, Chet and the pilot grabbed her under her armpits and hoisted her inside the cab as she struggled to climb aboard. The noise was deafening until they slammed the door behind Cody, who was last in.

He squeezed his bulk beside her and leaned his head against the cushions, catching his breath. His legs were so long he couldn't stretch them out in the cramped quarters, but had to scrunch into the tiny space.

Bile rose in her throat and her nerves screamed as the bird lifted off the ground. Hadn't God warned her twice that she shouldn't fly? That she should keep her feet firmly planted on the ground? Melissa didn't realize she trembled until Cody whispered in her ear, his breath hot and ticklish, "It's all right. Glenn knows how to fly this chopper. We're almost finished."

His arm crept around her shoulders and drew her to him.

She snuggled against his warmth, letting her arm encircle his waist. They seemed to skim the treetops and for the most part held a steady course. But when the craft dipped and swerved, her heart stopped and she burrowed closer against the man…if that were possible.

Chet turned in his seat. "So you're Melissa Vanderbilt-Smythe? I didn't buy your death. The pieces didn't add up."

"I'm Mrs. Elliott now." She shook his hand.

Chet's eyebrow rose a couple of notches as his gaze fell on Cody's arm around her. He cleared his throat gruffly and looked uneasy. "That was that bloke that kidnapped you, wasn't he?"

"Jesse didn't kidnap anyone, least of all me." Anger snapped in Melissa and the hair on the back of her neck prickled. "He saved me. We ran away and married because we loved each other and because my father would never have accepted my marriage to him." She leaned forward, ready to do battle for a cause long dead.

Cody tried to pull her back by her shoulders but she was just getting started. "Daddy and Nathan, my *fiancé*." She spat the word *fiancé* with venom. "Told everyone who would listen that Jesse kidnapped me or brainwashed me…"

Chet's eyes narrowed. "California Senator, Nathan Alexander, right?"

"God help the people of California! He's a crook and a reptile. Worse, he bullies defenseless women." Her chest heaved and her heart hammered against her ribs so hard it was a wonder they didn't crack. She dreaded seeing Nathan even as she chafed at the time it took them to get to the wedding.

"He'd better pray I don't get my hands around his neck." Cody tensed beside her, his thighs straining, the muscles in his arms cording. His hands clenched and unclenched, his knuckles whitening.

Alarmed, Melissa laid her hands over his. "No, Cody. He's not worth it."

Cody's gaze sizzled on her. "I won't let him touch you again. If he tries, I swear I'll kill him." Menace underlined his every word.

Chet exchanged glances with his pilot, his expression masked. The helicopter circled over a small clearing that boasted a couple of buildings, but no city, no mansion.

This wasn't L.A. This wasn't her home. Her blood turned cold as the chopper descended. Her hands tightened on Cody's and she whispered in his ear. "What's going on? This isn't Daddy's estate."

Cody scowled, his eyes darkening. He whispered back, "I don't like this. Follow my lead."

Chet looked at them. "We're having to lay over. It'll just take a few moments." Although his lips curved into a smile, his eyes remained veiled. His frame held a rigidity that belied his easy words.

Melissa felt a trap and there wasn't a blessed thing she could do to escape it. Not as long as they were airborne, anyway. Was the agent trying to cash in on the reward on her head? Or seeking promotion?

When she spied the familiar man on the ground, she sucked in her breath. Her stomached churned. *Oh no!* The Cro-Magnon who had tried to kidnap her back in New Jersey. How'd he get here? She didn't realize that her nails dug into Cody's hands until he unlatched her from him and she saw the angry red welts she'd left. As if the man didn't have enough scars caused by her. But she hadn't time to worry over minor abrasions. Their very lives were at stake.

Chet's grin widened, showing his teeth. She wasn't surprised when he leveled a pistol on them, aimed straight at their heads.

Chapter Twelve

"What's going on, Chet?" Cody's voice had never sounded deadlier.

Chills scraped down her spine as acid burned her throat.

"You're working for Nathan, aren't you?" Melissa glared at the FBI agent, wondering if he were really an agent. The pieces were falling together. "How'd he buy you?" A snarl decorated her words. "With money? Or promises of power?"

Cody nudged her in the ribs with his elbow, a silent ixnay on the ordsway.

But she intended to have her say; even if they were the last words she ever spoke. "You know he's broke, don't you? His family fortune's gone. Why else do you think he wants to marry into my family so badly?"

The gun moved so that it faced her squarely and she could stare straight down the scarred gray barrel where ridges were emblazoned. Obviously, it had been used before.

The helicopter bounced a couple of times when it landed, jarring her teeth and she bit her tongue. Salty blood trickled down her throat, coated her teeth, and turned her stomach. But it didn't make her nearly so nauseated as did the site of a glib Nathan Alexander, surrounded by his henchmen. They looked so mismatched, Nathan in his white shirt and tie, and his men in black monks-type robes. They weren't his normal entourage that usually accompanied him. *She'd seen them in her dream.* She didn't believe in the mystical or ESP, but this was too odd to be discounted. The coincidence creeped her out.

"Stay by me," Cody said between clenched teeth. His thigh twitched against hers.

Chet clucked his tongue. "You'd do best to remember, old friend, to mind your own business and forget any ideas you might have about this pretty lady."

"What's in this for you?" Cody lifted his chin and glared down his nose at the turncoat. His nostrils flared.

"I'm just doing my patriotic duty, bringing in two criminals. You should never have kidnapped her or forced her to steal that aircraft and cross state lines. You're looking at Federal offenses."

Melissa gasped, enraged. “Cody didn’t kidnap me and you know it!” And it had been her idea to *borrow* the plane. “Agent Mulligan did.”

“It’s your word against mine. Who do you think they’ll believe? The FBI agent with the flawless record? Or the infamous runaway heiress who shacks up with her abductors?” He cocked the gun, his glare unflinching.

His logic was flawed but she didn’t have time to reason it out. Not when the Cro-Magnon man opened the door and Chet ushered them out at gunpoint. “Follow me, Brother Larry.”

Brother’s Larry’s smirk disgusted her; his teeth were brown and filthy from chewing tobacco. The memory of his assault made her ill. The only thing that kept her from vomiting all over his feet at the vile memories was the cold steel poking her in the back.

“Well, well,” the voice from hell grated on her ears even though it was cultured and polished, a true politician’s voice. “At last I catch up with you; and I have the privilege of introducing the Lions of Judah to you.”

“Lions of Judah?” Melissa and Cody mouthed simultaneously.

“My apostles,” Nathan said glibly, looking for all the world like another David Koresh. “Brother Larry, Brother Chet, and Brother Glenn you already know.”

Brother Larry’s vile gaze raked Melissa up and down, sickening her to her core.

Nathan sauntered up, taking her chin between his manicured fingers. He clucked his tongue, shaking his head. Dark humor gleamed in his eyes as he turned her face one way and then the other. “I see living with the dregs of humanity has taken a toll on you. You’ve lost that porcelain veneer I found so engaging. Your dear departed mother would have heart failure were she to see you in such a state.” He clucked his tongue and shook his head again. “I suppose it’s nothing a day at the beauty salon can’t remedy.”

Scorched by his reptilian touch, Melissa tried to yank away but he held fast, hurting her. If it meant he’d never touch her, she’d never have her hair fixed again, never wear make-up again. The price would be well worth her gain.

She spat in his face with as much force as she could, and then grinned, squaring her shoulders. “And I see your taste in company hasn’t improved.” She cast a supercilious look around the group of scum. “Aren’t they beneath even *your* reptilian standards, Nathan?"

Brother Larry advanced on her, his hand up and ready to smack her in the face.

Melissa glared at her would-be attacker, breathing hard, trying not to show fright. Monsters like him thrived on fear. They could smell it.

Cody lunged for the man, and then froze when a shot rang out behind him.

"Not another inch, Richards, or you're a dead man." Chet's voice was devoid of all warmth. He sounded like a killing machine. "Get back and don't be so stupid again. That was your final warning."

Nathan caught Brother Larry's wrist and twisted it. Daggers flared in his eyes. "No one touches her but me. You try that again, *you're* a dead man."

"My hero," Melissa drawled, doing her best not to let them see her wince or tremble. The sarcasm in her voice was impossible to mask. "Are you saving the pleasure of roughing me up for yourself? Have you missed our little *sessions*?"

The tick in Nathan's right eye went spastic, but other than that, he remained remarkably controlled, as if he kept himself on a tight leash. Apparently politics had taught him some measure of self-control.

He wiped her spit off his face and leaned forward. His hot breath on her face sickened her. "I've missed you in my bed. I wanted to rip that Jesse Elliott into little pieces for stealing you from me, for touching you."

Melissa shuddered at the thought of intimacy with the man in front of her. She'd rather die a thousand horrid deaths than let him make love to her. "He was a million times more man than you could ever be."

"I doubt you'll think that after we're married."

"She'll never marry you." Cody tensed beside her, ready to lunge for the man's throat. When Chet pushed the gun in his back and Brother Larry cocked a rifle on him from the front, he relaxed.

Nathan strolled over to Cody. "You trying to pick up where that Elliott left off? Maybe I should take you apart limb by limb."

Cody's eyes narrowed. "I'd like to see you try. By yourself. Without your henchmen. Just you and me in hand to hand combat."

Melissa froze, her gaze glued on the men. Would Nathan accept the challenge? Even if Cody won, he'd be a dead man.

And she had no doubt he could beat Nathan in a fair fight with his hands tied behind his back.

But Nathan didn't fight fair. Nathan's men would see that Cody died.

"No Cody! He'll kill you."

Brother Larry's lips curled back from his teeth. "The Reverend can't lose. Not with God in his pocket."

"Amen." Chet said with fervor, shaking his head.

"Hallelujah, Brother!" another man said, sounding about ready to break into an old fashioned revival.

Cody scowled at Melissa.

Nathan smiled, his left cheek dimpling. He was a pretty boy and it was no wonder he could fool his constituents. It was too bad they couldn't see under his civilized veneer like she could, to his dark soul. She'd tell them if only they'd believe her.

"See how much faith she has in you, lover boy? She knows I'm more man than you'll ever be, no matter what she says."

Melissa remembered Christina. The sun climbed high in the sky and the hour had to be drawing near. "Aren't you going to be late for your wedding?"

Nathan grinned ear to ear. "Don't you mean *we'll* be late for *our* wedding?"

"Never, Alexander!" Cody spat on the ground near Nathan's feet.

"What makes you think I'll marry you, now or ever?" Melissa injected all the haughtiness, all the disbelief she could drag up from the depths of her soul into her words.

Nathan nodded to Brothers Larry and Chet. "Tie him up. If either make a threatening move, kill him."

Aghast, she sucked her teeth and stared at the devil in the three-piece suit.

Nathan put a finger under her chin and tilted her face so that she stared him in the eye. "Either you marry me this afternoon, or your boyfriend dies. And don't think for a minute it'll be a quick, merciful death." He pointed to Larry. "You see Brother Larry, here? I see from the fear in your beautiful eyes that you remember him well."

Brother Larry grinned, sending dread throughout her. The man was the devil incarnate. Pure evil gleamed in his eyes, infecting everything and everyone around him.

Nathan continued, trailing his finger down the column of her throat to the swell of her breast, where he let it linger to her disgust. "Larry loves to make human sacrifices. He lives for it."

"Don't marry him for me, Lisa." Cody strained against the ropes and handcuffs restraining him. "You can't marry that monster."

A tear clung to her eyelash at the sight of the man she loved chained up like a wild animal. More tears clogged her throat. She couldn't let them torture him. She couldn't let him die.

Melissa glared at Nathan. "How will you tell my father, my sister, and your constituents that you're marrying me and not Christina? Won't they be more than a little curious? Won't it look suspicious?"

"No, Lisa." Cody's voice sounded defeated. "Don't do it."

"The press release is already written and just waiting to go to the journalists. Everyone knows I never gave up hope of finding you alive, that I never stopped loving you."

"You mean you're obsessed with her! Threatening her isn't love."

Nathan motioned at the FBI agent with his gun. "Brother Chet, shut him up!" He frowned, prowling, the gun moving back and forth in his hand. "I'm tired of hearing his mouth run."

Curious, she asked as Chet gagged Cody with a strip of cloth, "What if I refuse to marry you still? If I let you kill him?" Melissa prayed her bluff would work. "Would you kill me, too? Torture me?" She knew she took an awful chance and she quivered inside but she stood tall and firm.

Nathan gestured to Brother Larry. "No." His voice sounded deceptively meek, which worried her more than his earlier display of bravado. "I have no doubt you'd choose death, my brave little fool."

"Why would you want to marry someone who feels that way about you? You could've had my family fortune by marrying my sister in some small, quiet ceremony. I'd have never claimed my inheritance. You know that." She peered into his face, examining it. "You're a raving lunatic, aren't you?"

Rage boiled in Nathan's eyes and he struck her face hard, sending her reeling in the dirt at the base of the helicopter. He loomed over her in three angry strides. "Don't ever call me a *lunatic* again!" He yelled over his shoulder, "Bring out our ace in the hole."

Horror flooded her when Larry's men dragged out a bound, gagged, and sobbing Christina from the rustic cabin one hundred yards away. "What're you going to do with her?"

"Same thing your friend will get if you don't cooperate. Only we'll have some fun with her first.

"No!" The word was ripped from her throat. Squeezing her eyes tightly shut, Melissa whispered in a hoarse voice, "You win, *Reverend*. I'll marry you."

Nathan crouched down in front of her, his pants legs hitching up at his knees to show an expanse of black sock. "And you'll have sex with me and pretend to like it. You'll give me heirs. You'll be the perfect hostess for my political soirées, and you'll support my bid for president of the United States."

"*President*!" Shock flushed through her. "My God! You *are* demented."

Fury flickered in his eyes again. "And you won't ever call me crazy or demented or lunatic again."

When he held out his hand to help her up, Melissa shunned it and struggled to her feet unassisted. She dusted leaves and dirt off her jeans. "Can I see my sister now?" Her voice had a hard edge.

"Make it quick or we'll be late for our nuptials. The press and the president are waiting. It'll be the affair of the century." He followed her and nodded to his men to ungag Christina. "No funny stuff."

Melissa hugged Christina as if she'd never let her go. Tears flowed freely from both women, "I'm so sorry I put you through this. I had no idea. I love you so much."

"You're really alive," Christina said simultaneously through broken sobs, her voice incredulous. Puffy red eyes scoured Melissa. Her nose ran and her lips were chapped and swollen. Twigs and leaves were woven into the silky tresses of her blonde hair. "I missed you so much. I thought I'd never see you again."

"I'm here. I'll never leave you again." Melissa crossed her heart with her finger and sent up a silent prayer. "I swear."

Through hiccoughs, Christina said, "You can't marry him. He's crazy."

"Shush! He'll hear you. I know he is but I've no choice. Don't worry about me."

"But I do." A fresh flood of tears ran down Christina's ashen cheeks. "He'll make you miserable. He'll hurt you." Embarrassment flooded her eyes. "I know why you ran away now. You weren't hiding from Daddy and me, were you?"

Melissa shook her head as she wiped away her sister's tears, choking back a healthy dose of her own. "I'll be more miserable if I know he hurt you or Cody. I couldn't live with myself." She sneaked a glance at her intended. "Besides, someone has to stop him from becoming president."

"*President*?" Christina about choked. "No! You can't let that happen."

"Not if I can help it. Don't say a word, promise?"

Christina tried to smile but failed dismally. She shook her head, dislodging a couple of twigs. "Promise."

"Break it up." Brother Larry yanked Melissa away rudely, hurting her upper arm with his meaty fingers. "You've had time to get reacquainted. The Reverend says it's time to go."

Melissa looked at Cody, such a pathetic sight: bound, gagged, and helpless. Raising her voice, she asked, "Can I say goodbye to Cody?"

Emotions warred on Nathan's face. Finally, he said in a gruff voice, his face contorted with thunder, as he jerked a thumb at the bound man, "Make it quick."

She knelt next to Cody and gazed deeply into his eyes. Her heart broke and she struggled not to cry anew. "I love you, Cody Richards. I'll always love you till the day I die." Melissa leaned forward and kissed his cheek, allowing her lips to linger on his stubbled cheek, to inhale his scent for the last time. "Don't do anything stupid on my account. Don't be a hero."

Cody's eyes spoke volumes. To her dismay, they grew moist and misty. She couldn't take it if he cried. Her own composure was too frail.

A shadow fell across them and she glanced up into her fiancé's face. Storm clouds brewed in his eyes. "How touching. The star-crossed lovers saying their final farewells. Should I boo-hoo?"

Melissa rose to her feet, fury infusing her. Her fingernails dug into the palms of her hands as her fists clenched. "Stuff if, Nathan!"

"Is that anyway to talk to your beloved fiancé? To God's mouthpiece? I think not."

Nathan grabbed her elbow and thrust her into the helicopter with Brother Chet and Brother Glenn and squeezed in next to her, where Cody had been on the way here.

The scent, the feel of him sickened her and she turned her face away from him, unable to look at him another second in the creepy robes he'd donned while on the ground. Melissa pressed her nose and hands to the window, staring down at Cody and her sister whom they'd left behind. She watched until she couldn't see them anymore.

Forcing herself to turn back to Nathan despite the nausea the sight of him gave her, she looked him straight in the eye. "I need proof they'll be safe before I marry you."

Brother Chet lifted a silvery brow. "I don't think you appreciate your position."

"*Au contraire, Monsieur.*" Melissa glared at the Benedict Arnold. "I think I do. I don't care to live if you hurt either of them." She turned a scathing glance on the man beside her. "Especially not shackled to *you*." Turning her wrists upward, she held them up to him. "You might as well kill me now, while everyone thinks I'm still dead, or I'll scream what vile scum you are to anyone and everyone who'll listen."

Nathan just chuckled. "You still have spirit, my dear. I can't wait to get you in my bed."

Melissa sneered. "I want them both at the wedding, unharmed and freed. That's my deal."

Brother Chet's hand tightened on the back of his seat. "I don't like it, Reverend. They'll sing to the press."

"Not if they know what's at stake. Radio Brother Larry and tell him to meet us at the wedding with little sister and the cop."

"I still don't like it. Richards is a wild card…" Brother Chet raked his fingers through his hair.

"And this one likes to gamble, don't you?" Nathan snatched her wrist without warning and hauled Melissa against him so that his torrid breath scorched her neck. "Just remember, that this time, you're gambling with your lover's—and your sister's—lives. Don't underestimate me."

"I won't." She considered clawing his eyes out, then grabbing for the controls and crashing the chopper. She'd sacrifice her life, but at least those she loved and the people of California would be safe from Nathan's dementia.

But Nathan must've intercepted her glance at the pilot and gleaned her thoughts. An evil grin dawned over his face. "If you're thinking of making us crash, be advised that Brother Larry has orders to send lover boy and little sister to their Maker in the event of our untimely demise."

Melissa wanted to scream! Nathan's evil knew no bounds. She'd have to figure out a different plan but for now, her mind was a blank.

~ * ~

Cody chafed in his bondage. He'd never been so helpless, so enraged, or so scared.

This Brother Larry character was insane. Cody wasn't sure how tight a rein Alexander kept on his apostles, or for that matter, if the man had a shred of sanity left himself. Mainly, he was scared for Melissa and Christina. He'd seen what monsters like these could do to women and the thoughts sickened him. Unbidden images of his sister's lifeless and mutilated body came to mind. He shuddered, remembering the horror of it, and it took everything in him to lock the images away in his mind again.

He couldn't even talk to Christina as he was still gagged. His lips, teeth, and tongue had never ached so badly in his life. His arms had never been so sore. Blood seeped from his shoulder wound and he was afraid he'd pass out any moment. His vision was getting blurry and he was feverish.

"You're hurt," Christina whispered. She looked so much like her older sister, except she was a paler version with her white-blonde hair, gray-blue eyes, blonde eyelashes, and pale flesh. She looked washed out.

Of course, even after what she'd been through, she looked terrific.

Another helicopter started up.

Without warning, Cody was yanked up from behind and he stumbled, falling on his face, as he couldn't catch himself with his hands. The dirt and moldy leaves tasted bitter on his tongue and he spit them out.

"The Reverend requests your presence at his wedding. Too bad you forgot a gift."

Cody's fists itched to deck the idiot. But he schooled his temper into some semblance of quiet, knowing he'd do neither Melissa nor Christina any good dead.

"Get up!" Brother Larry jabbed him in the back several times.

The man was overconfident. Perhaps he planned to kill them, so feared no reprisals. In fact, Cody wondered why he was still alive. Neither Alexander nor his ex-buddy, ex-agent *Brother* Chet could afford to let him live. That meant this was a temporary reprieve only, so he'd better think of a way to escape and fast. But handcuffed and gagged, he was helpless. If he were truly being taken to the wedding, they'd have to free him for at least a few minutes.

"You Feds think you're so smart. You think you have it all figured out, don't you?" Brother Larry's voice was raspy and gruff.

If Cody could talk, he'd point out he was no longer a *Fed*, but it seemed to be a blessing he couldn't answer and stop the flow of Brother Larry's confessions. He listened intently, all the while highly aware of the frightened woman at his side, whom he willed not to faint or panic.

"You and your little red-headed friend interrupted our sacred rituals. I couldn't believe my eyes when I saw the gods delivered the princess straight into our hands."

"*Princess*?" Christina almost choked on the word, echoing Cody's thoughts. "Are you talking about my sister?"

"*Sacred ritual?*" Cody's gut almost erupted. Could these be the same monsters that ravaged and murdered his sister? Or any of the other children he'd found over the years? Fury unlike he'd never known nearly ripped him apart.

"Reverend Alexander promised us a high priestess with flaming, flowing red hair and blue eyes. We've been searching for her for more than two years. The Reverend near tore apart the whole country."

God save them! Melissa! She was in more danger than he'd ever imagined. His skin prickled with disgust. These religious fanatics that practiced human sacrifice were the worst, the scum of humanity.

"The Reverend was all set to meet us in Pennsylvania, then you had to help her escape and make us follow you back here."

"But the wedding was scheduled to take place on Daddy's estate in L.A." Christina's brows drew together and her nose wrinkled.

"Plan B to smoke her out. And it worked. This was too easy to be fun." Brother Larry punched the seat, making Christina flinch. "Little Miss High-and-Mighty insists you be at her wedding or she won't play nice. I'll teach her to mess with my plans."

Not if he had his way! Cody glared at the psychotic monster. It was his fault Melissa was in danger, his fault Nathan had caught up with her. It was up to him to save her and put these madmen away where they'd never hurt anyone again. He couldn't forgive himself for not seeing the reptile Alexander was before.

His stomach grumbled, reminding him he'd gone without food for almost twenty-four hours. Nor had he had any water since early morning and his mouth was parched.

Impatience gnawed at Cody's gut as he watched forest turn into desert and desert merge into city. Finally they'd reached the City of Angels—although it felt anything but angelic.

Seconds ticked into minutes as he willed the chopper to reach its destination. It seemed as if forever had passed before they hovered over a sprawling estate and mansion.

"We're here," Christina said, relief oozing from her.

Brother Larry drew a gun on them and cocked it. The sound reverberated in Cody's ears. "We're going to take the handcuffs and the gag off, but don't think you're free. My men will be watching your every move and we'll shoot to kill if you try anything funny. One less Judas in the garden won't be missed. *Comprendez-vous*?"

Cody nodded, biting on his gag to keep from growling.

Nathan, Melissa, and Chet met them when they landed. He nodded to Brother Larry. "He give you any trouble?"

"Got him under my thumb." Brother Larry kept his revolver aimed on them.

"Untie them and clean them up for the wedding." Nathan pointed to Cody. "You'll be the best man, so you can see what I'm taking from you first hand." Leaning his head back, he laughed maniacally, all trace of sanity absent from his voice.

Brother Chet pulled the gag off him and uncuffed Cody. His voice came out rusty his throat was so dry. "Reverend, Senator, or whoever you are, you're *nuts*!"

Melissa's eyes widened with trepidation and she stiffened, watching intently. God but she was beautiful, even scraped up and dusty, with her glorious hair mussed and billowed about her pixie face. The thought of this monster touching her, marrying her, enraged Cody.

Thunder flashed in Nathan's dark eyes as he walked up to Cody and struck him hard. "No one calls me crazy!"

Cody's jaw stung where the man's hand connected. He bit his tongue and swallowed bitter blood. Wiping a trickle of blood from the corner of his mouth, he squared his shoulders, wincing when pain radiated from his wound. "What's in this for you, *Brother Chet*? You into his demonic religious rituals and human sacrifice, too?"

Nathan's gaze turned murderously on Brother Larry. "You've been running off at the mouth? You've been talking to cops?"

"*Ex*-cop." Cody enjoyed watching Brother Larry squirm. It was almost worth being dragged here against his will.

"*Witnesses*!" Nathan's eyes narrowed at Chet. "Hose him off and stick him in a tux." To Brother Larry he said, "Keep your gun on him. He tries anything, shoot out his knee caps." Grabbing Melissa's elbow, Nathan propelled her before him. "You come with us, Little Sis," he said to Christina.

Chapter Thirteen

"Who's going to guard us while we dress?"

Melissa wrenched her arm out of Nathan's clutches and marched regally to the house she'd sworn never to enter again. Little things she'd forgotten about threatened to choke her up. Her mother's flower garden. The height marks on the wall depicting her and Christina's growth since they were toddlers. Her grandmother's oil portrait. All things she'd pushed out of her mind since she'd left.

The house and grounds were decorated for the wedding of the century. An artist carved an ice statue of a leaping dolphin. Rose petals littered the ground. White gardenias adorned rows of seats in the garden by the gazebo, where a pulpit had been erected.

Melissa wondered where her father and the servants were and what time the guests and press would arrive?

Nathan guided them upstairs to her old room where her mother's wedding gown laid majestically on her bed. White satin slippers and a long gauzy veil lay next to the dress. Otherwise, her room was just as she'd left it.

"Brother Larry has instructions to meet us at the ceremony in half an hour. Our esteemed guests are arriving now."

"Where's my father?" Melissa stood fast, her arms crossed over her chest, refusing to budge another inch. "What have you done with him? Brainwashed him, too? Or did you make him disappear?"

Nathan leaned over so that he was nose to nose with her, his beady eyes glaring into hers. "What's this brainwash talk? We're just bringing people closer to God and saving their souls."

"Corrupting their souls is more like it." Melissa refused to back down, even when his nostrils flared and he practically breathed fire.

"I'll forgive you this time for you know not what you say. But you'll be instructed in our ways just as soon as you're Mrs. Alexander."

"Where's Daddy? Why are you sidestepping my question?"

"Why, he's getting ready to give the beautiful bride away as we speak."

Before Melissa realized his intent, he pressed his lips to hers hungrily, groping at her. She jerked back away from him, wiping his slime from her mouth with her arm, coming up against the wall. Squirming, she finally broke loose.

Nathan's eyes were inscrutable as he stared at her. "You'll be begging for my kisses sooner than you know. You won't even remember lover boy's name."

"You may claim my body, but never my heart. Is that what you want? To be shackled to a woman who detests you?" Melissa lifted her chin regally, her hands balled on her hips. "I could never love you. The more I get to know you, the more I loathe you. You're a pathetic excuse for a human being. God would never chose you as His prophet."

Lunging at her, he grabbed a handful of hair at the base of her neck, twined his fingers in it, and yanked with all his might, nearly breaking her neck.

"From this moment forward, you are to honor and respect me, to think of no other man, no other husband, no other leader, but me. When I kiss you, you will kiss me back." Nathan twisted and pulled harder. "Understand?"

Bent nearly double, every muscle, every sinew in her neck and back screaming for mercy, Melissa grated through her teeth, "Understood." At this rate, her teeth would be turned to mortar within the week. She eyed her mother's gown and then the monster; she was sick to death she was being forced to desecrate it in a ceremony by his side. Her mother's memory deserved better. "Aren't you going to let us get dressed? Unless you want to marry me in my ratty blue jeans?"

Nathan shook his head. "What do you take me for? You'd climb out that window the moment I turned my back. We'll be married in less than an hour; a little preview won't make much difference. Besides, it's not like I never saw it before."

"That's before I knew what a fiend you are." Melissa glanced at her gritty, grimy self. "Can't we at least shower and clean up? Or do you want to look like a fool to all your society and political friends? If I'm to be a trophy wife, shouldn't I look like a million bucks? You are marrying me for my money, after all, aren't you?"

An enigmatic smile curved his lips, but he didn't reply. "Leave the bathroom door open while you shower. Hurry it up. I have to get into my tuxedo as well."

Melissa didn't wait for a second invitation, but scurried into the bathroom and slipped behind the shower curtain to undress.

He could see her silhouette through the translucent curtain, so she did her best to keep her backside to him. It was still better than stripping in front of him without any barrier. She showered in record time, washing the dust and leaves from her hair as well. She had to suffer parading in front of him in her underwear to reach the gown, but she told herself it covered more than her bikini. Still his burning gaze devoured her, giving her the heebie jeebies, and she did her best not to let him see her tremble.

When Melissa and her sister were dressed, he nodded. "Very lovely, ladies. You'll do us proud. My turn."

They met Brother Chet and a few of Brother Larry's men in the hall and he escorted them downstairs. She had no doubt that at least one of them carried a loaded gun. They had the strangest brand of religion she'd ever come across.

When they reached the bottom of the stairs, she spied her father, decked out in his tux, his hair several shades grayer than she'd last seen it. His shoulders were hunched, too, and his face was lined with wrinkles that she didn't recall. Sudden, unexpected tears blocked her throat and her heart flipped over.

"Daddy!" Melissa broke loose of Brother Chet's hold on her and flew to her father's waiting arms, hugging him fiercely. When she finally broke loose enough to gaze into his eyes, a flicker of alarm jolted her. His eyes were hazy, as if he were drugged. A hoarse moan ripped from her throat. "What have they done to you?"

Chapter Fourteen

Cody kept his mouth shut and his eyes and ears wide open. He watched for any opening he could get to escape, but thus far, one hadn't presented itself.

Hushed male voices drifted to Cody from the corridor, just outside the room where one of Alexander's men guarded him as he dressed. He inched closer to the door, trying not to make it obvious that he was eavesdropping nor to make it look like he was trying to escape. He valued his knees. Thus far, he only caught snatches of words and thought he heard Chet's voice.

The word *president* sent dread spiraling through him and he knew he had to hear the rest. There was no telling what Alexander and his Lions were capable of. No limit to their evil.

Chet's voice became clear. "We've recruited one of the President's Secret Service agents who's planted a bomb in his car. We'll wait till he's safely off the estate, too far away to pin the blame on any of us, and detonate it by remote control."

"What about your friend in there? We can't have a loose thread hanging around." Brother Larry must mean him. Who else would he mean?

"I have the perfect plan. We'll let him go with the President—let him think we're letting him go. He'll be so glad to spill his guts to the old man that he'll get cocky and we can blow them up together." Hands clapped together.

"I like the way your mind thinks, Brother Chet." Brother Larry sounded happy to be maiming and torturing again.

"That's why I'm in the Bureau."

My God! They planned to kill the President! But Nathan wasn't next in line to succeed. The Vice President and Speaker of the House would have to die, too. Then there'd have to be an election. There must be more to their plan. Cody shuddered to think what it might be. He'd underestimated them already. It seemed their evil—and their delusions—knew no bounds.

"Hey you! Get back here!" The man's greasy blonde hair fell across his eyes when he jumped to his feet. His pistol automatically jerked up, too.

Cody lifted his hands over his head. "I'm not trying to escape, man. I was just startled by a noise out there. Sounds like someone fell. Maybe you should check."

"Brother Larry, is everyone okay out there?"

Brother Larry and Chet blocked the doorway. "All's fine, Brother Daniel."

"No one fell? Nothing dropped?" Brother Daniel favored Cody with a suspicious glare as he rubbed his chin thoughtfully.

Cody spread his hands, palms up. "Guess I'm hearing things."

Chet walked over to him and straightened the corsage in his buttonhole, releasing the sickening sweet scent Cody found almost overpowering.

"You know, when I recommended you for the job to the Reverend, I never figured you'd be stupid enough to fall in love with the girl. You knew she belonged to the Reverend, did you not?" Chet shook his head, clucking his tongue. "Since when did you get stupid? You were the best."

Cody reeled. He couldn't have heard what he'd just thought he'd heard. "*You* recommended me?" He had to laugh but it was humorless. "Excuse me if I don't thank you."

"Shacking up with the girl wasn't part of your assignment." Chet checked his watch. "It's time. Serves you right for meddling where you don't belong."

Cody didn't think a reply would earn him any brownie points so he followed in silence, flanked by Brother Larry and Brother Daniel.

"Since when did you grow a conscience, Richards?" Chet whispered in his ear.

He must be referring to that incident back in New York when Cody'd overlooked a certain offense by the mayor. But that had been a minor infraction and nothing like this. Still, it had led to him getting kicked off the force when the scandal broke wide open, the real reason he'd left, not the reason he'd told Melissa. Chet had been part of the NYPD but moved up to the FBI shortly thereafter. Still, they'd remained friends. At the time, Cody had been grateful that Chet kept up the friendship after what had happened.

Now he knew why. Either larceny didn't bother Chet or he was just stringing Cody along until he needed his services. The funny thing was, that was the only time in his life Cody had veered from the right side of the law and he'd been caught. Chet, it seemed, had gone way overboard, and he was still one of the exalted G-men.

This would be hilarious…if it weren't for the fact that the president's life, and perhaps the entire country was in danger.

"When did you start following Charles Manson? Is this another retaliatory statement against Waco?"

Chet didn't answer, just tossed his head and moved away. So did that mean yes? God, he was sick of these religious fanatics who thought an eye for an eye meant it was okay to murder innocent people just because the government screwed up. It wasn't okay that innocent people had died at Waco and it wasn't okay that innocent people died later in retaliation for Waco or any other tragedy, government made or not.

The irony of the situation struck Cody full force. He, the exiled cop, was the only one in a position to save the President of the United States, and the FBI agent was trying to bring down the country. Well, at least he had the knowledge. He wasn't quite in position yet and was still clueless how he'd get into such a position.

His mind on the President, Cody wasn't looking for Melissa, but when he caught a glimpse of her from the corner of his eye, the vision of her took his breath away. He stopped dead; so enchanted was he that Brother Daniel ran into his back, almost knocking him over.

Chet turned and whistled under his breath. "A real beauty, she is." He clapped Cody on the back. "Eat your heart out. Maybe next time you won't mess with the boss man's woman."

Cody drank his fill of the glorious vision, ignoring his ex-buddy. Melissa's hair was loosely twisted into a French knot at the nape of her neck and was softened by wisps of hair allowed to hang down at her ears and around the elegant column of her long throat. The gentle ocean breeze caught the wisps, lifting them so that they framed her angelic, heart-shaped face. The dress she wore had probably been stark white at one time but was faded with age. The style suggested the dress was made in the 1960s. Opalescent seed pearls glinting in the afternoon sunlight adorned the complete bodice in intricate designs. The long skirt hung in folds, swirling around Melissa's ankles, and then trailed her gracefully. Puffed sleeves showcased her slim shoulders, then slimmed to hug her arms with more of the intricate beadwork. She wore make-up for the first time in their acquaintance and she looked like a porcelain doll, with foundation hiding the natural highlights of her face. Her eyes were rimmed with dark blue eyeliner, making her eyes look too large in her face. Or maybe her face was pinched because deep down she wasn't the happy bride outward appearances would shout.

Cody preferred her without the make-up, he decided, and he wanted her to wear that dress for him, not for the Reverend.

He had to force his attention away from Melissa so that he could watch the President. He studied each aide and guard, wondering which one or ones would betray their leader and their country. Could it be the too tall, too slim man who looked to be fiftyish, with sparse hair and large ears? Could it be the All-American college boy with blonde hair and blue eyes that looked as if he'd played college ball? Could it be the boy next door with dark red hair and a smattering of freckles across his cheeks? Or could it be the one that looked like the hard-bitten cop, who was paunchy and balding and didn't wear his suit very well?

Cody knew looks could be deceiving. It could be any or all of them. Money and power talked and many could be bought. The idea nauseated him, but he was realistic enough to live in the real world. Or maybe they'd not been lured by money or power at all, but sucked in by Alexander's charismatic religion. How many people would kill the President if they thought God had told them to do it? A far sight more than would for money or power. So the real question was, how many people thought Alexander worked for God? That he was a spokesperson? A prophet?

Cody had nothing against God or real prophets. He had been known to attend church on Sundays and get down on his knees to pray and to pay an honest tithe. He'd done a whole lot of repenting for his transgression of turning a blind eye to the mayor's illegal activities. But he didn't believe that Senator Nathan Alexander or any of his *brethren* were true disciples, or that they followed God's word and precepts. They were monsters in religious robes, spewing false doctrine, hypnotizing the unsuspecting with visions and promises of glory and exultation, when what they really delivered was eternal damnation. Just breathing the same air they breathed sickened him to his core.

Nathan strutted up to them, resplendent in a tailor-made tux. His black hair was slicked back into a ducktail and he'd put on a spot of make-up so that his complexion looked pasty. Attaching a diamond cufflink to his wrist, he looked like a gangster. A gangster would probably be less deadly than the religious fanatic he was.

Or maybe there was no difference in how far they'd go to achieve their goals or how much regret they'd feel over their actions.

Cody followed his gaze and realized the grounds were full and that nearly everyone had taken seats in front of the gazebo. There must be a thousand people, a good two hundred of them press, no doubt from society and political papers nationwide. Cameras flashed about every two seconds.

"It's time." Nathan adjusted his bow tie, his Adam's apple throbbing. His pulse jerked in his neck, but other than those indicators, he was calm and collected, as far as the world could see. He darted a piercing gaze at Cody. "No funny stuff at the altar. One word out of you and the girl and the President get shot. A lot of innocent bystanders may get hurt, too. You don't want that on your conscience, do you?"

"You got a lot of nerve calling yourself a man of God and a man of the people." Cody faced off against the bridegroom, wanting to rip him apart with his bare hands. They were roughly the same height and even roughly the same build, but Cody was a lot more solid and well honed than the other man. He'd win a fair fight with little effort.

"Tell me something, Alexander. You got it all. You're a senator. You hobnob with the President. You've got movie stars here." Cody's glance slid to Leonardo DiCaprio and Liz Taylor strolling arm in arm, their heads bent close together. Earlier he thought he saw Julia Roberts and Richard Gere. "You've got it all. Why give it up for this sorry bunch of losers?"

Brother Larry bristled behind him but the huge man's voice was remarkably controlled. "You're talking about worldly concerns, and sins of the flesh. Fame is only important to help us gain our ends…"

Cody intercepted a narrowed warning glance from Nathan to his apostle.

"Why do you want to marry a woman who so obviously hates your guts? Are you that hard up?" He lowered his voice. "Or do you honestly believe she's your sacred priestess just because she has red hair and blue eyes?"

Nuclear explosions flared in Nathan's irises when his gaze pinpointed Brother Larry.

The man cringed, stepping behind Cody.

What was he now? A human shield?

Cody pushed. "What will you do with your *priestess* once you have her? Sacrifice her to your gods in some bizarre ritual?"

"Shut up, Richards," Shadows fell across Chet's face as they fell into line beside Nathan at the altar. His lips and teeth barely moved so that he reminded Cody of a ventriloquist. He kept his voice low, too, so that the preacher couldn't hear him and Cody had to strain to catch his words.

"Why? You can't afford to let me live anyway."

The preacher frowned and said, "Shush." The man folded his hands before him, which all but disappeared in the folds of his long white robes. A gold and purple sash draped around his neck, falling to his wrists. Thick wiry eyebrows drew together in a single line. His nose had a large bump on the bridge and flattened on one side as if he'd been in a fight or an accident.

Chet tossed him an evil half smile. "Be warned that if you try anything, the girl will be shot."

"Your boss won't like that." Cody was confident that his ex-friend lied. The Reverend was obsessed with Melissa. He hadn't searched two years for the missing heiress to shoot her, had he?

Chet's features turned to granite when he whispered in Cody's ear, "Then they'll be together in the Celestial Kingdom."

Cody's blood chilled in his veins. Was he to presume Chet was a loose cannon? It sure sounded that way. He must have delusions of power, too. Why hadn't he picked up on that till now?

The organ belted out the first strains of the wedding march and Nathan loosened his tie, dragging air into his lungs. He looked even pastier than before and his pupils dilated.

All eyes turned on Melissa, exquisite in her wedding gown; they probably missed the groom and even if they noticed his pallor they would probably put it down to normal wedding jitters.

Cody had never seen a lovelier vision. She was an angel fallen to earth and he couldn't take his eyes off her, couldn't breathe.

~ * ~

Melissa felt as if she marched to her doom. This wasn't her wedding. It was her funeral procession. Life with Nathan would be death. No. It'd be worse than death. Pure torture. Agony. *Hell.*

His handsome face masked a soul of pure evil. His smile was that of a crocodile, ready to ensnare the unwary. His mind operated on a different wavelength and his heart was pure steel.

Her feet couldn't be more leaden and they didn't want to cooperate. They didn't want to take her to her doom.

The sea of faces swirled before her. None of her real friends were in attendance…if anyone from her past life could be deemed a real friend. They were all Nathan's friends, or rather, his cultivated elite. People who could propel his career: movie stars, millionaires, and politicians. Several state senators, the mayor. And even the President. An impressive group and yet, no one who really mattered to her except her father, her sister, and Cody. She could care less about prestige and fortune. The *beautiful* people had lost their charm. They lacked substance. Yet she wondered how even they could be so blind to Nathan's evil? How they could be taken in by his charisma? She wondered how many followed his teachings? How many believed he was a prophet? Surely not the President?

Her gaze was drawn to the man she'd dreamed would be her bridegroom; Cody. His intense gaze bore into her, inflaming her.

Staring at Cody, not watching where she was going, Melissa stumbled over her skirts.

A murmur went up in the crowd as flashbulbs blinded her. Polka dots danced before her eyes, making her blink rapidly to regain her vision. She forced a strained smile to her lips, cursing Nathan yet again.

The cogs spun in her mind. What would happen if she denounced Nathan and his group of evildoers in front of everyone? Would he really shoot Cody and Christina in front of all these witnesses? In front of the press and the President?

Melissa gnawed her lower lip till she tasted blood. Could she chance it?

Beside her, her father floated along as if in a trance, zombie-like. His speech was sluggish and slurred. His steps lacked purpose. His hand on her arm was clammy. How long had Nathan been drugging him? Is that why he'd been on Nathan's side before? Or seemed to be? Had she missed seeing the indications?

Guilt stabbed her. Had Nathan drugged and manipulated her father all along? Had she blamed her father for deserting her when she'd really deserted him?

Oh God! She was sick to her stomach. This couldn't be her life. She'd been born to privilege and glamour and she was supposed to have a fairy princess life. At least that's what her father and society had told her.

Now that she was an adult, Melissa didn't lust after money, fame, or glory, but she'd dreamed of being happy. Of marrying the man she loved and raising their babies together. She could be blissful in a shack on the poor side of town, but not caged in Nathan's gilded mansion, taken out in public only to decorate his arm, while in private she would be maltreated and unloved.

Please help me, God. Jesse, watch over us. She'd not spoken to God in a very long time other than to blame him for Jesse's death, but Melissa lifted a fervent, silent prayer now. She wasn't sure He'd listen but it was worth a try. *Don't let Nathan get away with his evil plans. Don't let him hurt anybody else.* Dreamy eyes devoured her, but it was Cody's gaze, mixed with passion and pain, that tore her apart. He should be her groom. He was her match.

She divorced herself from her body. It was the only way she could get through this ordeal without breaking down and screaming. Detached, she seemed to watch her father kiss her cheek and say goodbye to her. Fascinated horror replaced acute sadness when Nathan took her hand in his and her father stepped back from the altar to take his seat of honor in the front pew.

The music faded out, leaving an expectant silence. Only the birds and ocean waves dared interrupt. Melissa was only vaguely aware of the preacher clearing his throat and loosening his collar with pudgy fingers. A slight breeze ruffled the parchment page in his Bible, whipping it over and lifting the golden ribbon that held his place.

Bells rang in her ears so that she missed every other word the preacher said, and the words she caught were blurry. The wind ruffled loose wisps of hair into her eyes and mouth but she didn't try to brush them away. It'd be futile anyway. The wind was being mischievous today, taunting her, but also cooling off her heated flesh.

The preacher's lips moved as the muscles in his jaws flexed. Each word he uttered wrapped a little tighter around her as if he bound her in unbreakable chains. Well, wasn't he doing exactly that?

"Do you, Nathan Adam Alexander, take this woman to be your wedded wife? For better, for worse, in sickness, in health, from this day forward, till death do you part?" The clergyman's voice buzzed in her ear, an annoying sound that should've been the most beautiful words on earth.

"I do." Nathan smiled at Melissa, baring his teeth, his lips stretched wide. He still reminded her of a crocodile, deadly and vile. The pad of his thumb rubbed over her knuckles, grating on her nerves.

The preacher smiled up at her, the sun reflecting off his wire rimmed glasses. *"Do you, Melissa Victoria Vanderbilt-*

Smythe, take this man to be your lawfully wedded husband? For better, for worse, in sickness, in health, from this day forward, till death do you part?"

Cody bristled beside Nathan while Christina sobbed quietly at her side. Melissa paused, her gaze dueling with Cody's unfathomable one, darker than she'd ever seen it. The words stuck in her throat. She couldn't utter them, not even to save her life.

Nathan scowled. "Answer him!"

When Melissa remained silent, Nathan growled, snarling, his lips barely moving. "Say *I do* or your sister, lover boy, and your father get shot. What do you choose?"

"Well?" The preacher lifted his brows and widened his eyes. "Do you take this man to be your lawfully wedded husband?"

Brother Chet patted his chest and then opened his jacket fractionally. Afternoon sun glinted off his pistol barrel.

Trapped, she sighed, squeezing back stinging tears. To Cody she mouthed, "I love you forever."

Cody mouthed back, "I love you."

Hanging her head, she whispered in a hoarse voice, "I do." A hot tear plopped on the back of her hand and rolled off into the grass at her feet.

The preacher expelled a huge sigh of relief and his face relaxed into a smile. Turning to Nathan, he said joyfully, "If there are no objections," he paused, looking at the guests, his gaze lingering on Cody who fumed silently, and then continued when no one spoke up. "You may now kiss the bride."

Nathan's arms wrapped around Melissa, drawing her against his chest. His breath rasped sickly sweet on her arched neck as he bent her backwards over his arm. Light bulbs flashed in her eyes as reporters and photographers knelt on the ground in front of them, their cameras poised.

Bile rose in her throat, threatening to bubble over. When she struggled against him, splaying her hands over his chest to push him away, he hissed, "The President's watching and the press are taking pictures. *Kiss me*."

Melissa hawked up the phlegm in her throat, considering spewing it at him. But she caught the glint of sunlight on Brother Chet's revolver pointed at her father and thought better of that action. Swallowing her spit, she almost choked. "I may be married to *you*, but I'll always love *him*."

Nathan ground his lips against hers while his tongue sought admission to the cavern of her mouth, but she kept her lips firmly shut, refusing to allow him access. He thrust her from him in disgust, his lips twisted grotesquely. He chuckled maniacally.

She stumbled and would've fallen if not for her sister catching her. Clenching her fists so hard that her nails dug into the tender flesh of her palms, and squaring her shoulders, Melissa glared at her new husband. "I hate you. I'll always hate you."

"I'm not the only one you should hate, Miss High and Mighty." Nathan glanced over his shoulder at Cody, venom coating his eyes. "Try turning that hate on the man who tracked you down and brought you to me—for cold hard cash."

Melissa froze, her blood congealing in her veins. She couldn't breathe. Confusion and pain twisted her thoughts.

"Cody?"

That one word held a lifetime of hurt and disbelief.

"None other." Glee swam in Nathan's words as harsh afternoon sunlight hit him full in the face. "Richards is my hired man. I paid him very well to find you and deliver you to me."

"This can't be," she mumbled under her breath, going over every word to make sure she didn't misunderstand or hear incorrectly. Her heart imploded as the sincerity of the words penetrated her brain. "My first instincts were right. I shouldn't have trusted you." Lifting her eyes, her gaze clashed with Cody's. Raising her voice, she directed her words to him. "I should've let you rot from that snake bite." Marching to him, she slapped him hard. "I never want to see you as long as I live. Don't ever come near me again!" Hitching up her long satin skirts, she pivoted on her heel in preparation to run down the aisle. Nathan's ring shackled her finger so that she could hardly breathe. Bits of her heart scattered on the ground around her, blending in with the cloying rose petals.

How could she have been so stupid? How blind? He'd had cop written all over him. If she never saw him again, it'd be too soon.

~ * ~

Cody closed his eyes, vertigo assailing him. He should've known Alexander would tell her, but he hadn't seen it coming. If only he'd told her first that he'd been working for her fiancé and explained that he was trying to save her, trying to reunite her with a loving, caring family.

"Move away from Mrs. Alexander." Chet brandished his pistol at Cody, his lips curled back in a snarl. Cocking the pistol's hammer, he thrust it in Cody's face.

"What's going on here?" the President's voice boomed above the sea of excited chatter behind them.

"Mr. President, we have to evacuate you now." The Secret Service men rose, encircling their chief, reaching for their own firearms.

Chaos broke out. Wedding guests rushed to escape, some trampling others, some screaming. Folding chairs collapsed when brushed against. People stumbled, falling to their knees, ruining expensive gowns.

Cody seized the opportunity and thrust Melissa at her groom, and then kicked his leg in a high arc, knocking the weapon from Chet's hand.

A bullet exploded in a flash of light as the weapon hurled to the ground, end over end. Cody ducked and rolled, grabbing for the shiny black instrument where it landed in the grass.

Chet dove for the gun, too, landing on Cody, knocking the breath from him. Fighting his way up, Cody's left hook caught his ex-friend in the jaw. Bone crunched as Chet's eyes rolled back in his head.

But the man recovered quickly and put his hands around Cody's throat, squeezing.

Strangling, Cody tried to pry the deadly fingers from his throat. He couldn't speak, only grunt. He tried to jab his knee into his adversary's groin but was pinned down. Thwarted, he shoved the heel of his hand as hard as he could against the underside of Chet's nose. The other man howled his rage as he grabbed his face.

Choking, spluttering, Cody stretched for the gun. This time his fingers found the polished metal. Rolling to his knees, he clasped the weapon in both hands, seeking out the Reverend. What he saw turned his blood cold. The Secret Service men were hurrying the President to his car. Worse, Alexander was forcing Melissa in the same direction.

"Stop!" Cody shouted. "Release her or I'll shoot!"

Jumping to his feet, he swung swiftly to catch Brother Daniel and Brother Larry sneaking up on his rear. "Uh, uh, uh. You'd best rethink that. Drop to your knees. *Now!*" He didn't care if he sounded like a son of a bitch so long as he castrated their attempt to overtake him. Jerking his head at Christina, he said, "Take their weapons. You know how to use a gun?"

Christina gulped but nodded her head. Her eyes were huge in her ghostly white face. "Daddy and I shoot skeet a few times a week."

"Good. Shoot to kill if they threaten you." To Brother Larry he said, "Try anything funny and I'll aim for your knees." He drew out the *n* sound, deliberately casting red herrings.

Precious time slipped away. He couldn't let either Melissa or the President get in that death trap of a limousine.

Nathan beelined for the opposite side of the vehicle, dragging Melissa by her arm. The wedding gown was torn, the beadwork ruined, the sleeves tattered. Beads scattered to the ground. Melissa's elegant hairstyle was a memory as red locks tumbled out of confining pins. Her white satin slippers were strewn on the lawn and her toes peeked out through rips in her stockings.

Growling, primal, protective urges swelled in Cody. "Let her go." He motioned with the gun as he advanced on them.

The coward did just the opposite, pulling her in front of him as a human shield. "Back off, Richards." Nathan wound his fingers in the hair at the base of Melissa's neck and yanked. "I'll snap her neck."

"Your constituents are watching, Senator. Or need I remind you, *Reverend*, that God's watching, too?"

"Let us go, Cody." Melissa's voice warbled and her lips trembled. Terror flashed across her fear-darkened eyes. "I'm not worth getting hurt over. Get the President out of danger."

The man in question was being ushered into the car and Cody's heart stopped. The agents were pulling firearms on him now that they believed their leader to be secured.

"Drop your weapon and put your arms in the air!"

No choice; Cody complied. But he shouted, "There's a bomb in the car! Get the President out of there now!"

The agents didn't waste a motion helping their chief to safety. "Did you plant it? Are you threatening him?"

The idiots! They thought *he* was the threat. Or maybe that was the mole trying to shift blame on him? He made note of the tall skinny balding man with the too-thin nose.

Three revolvers leveled on him. "Put your hands up." The thin man crouched, aiming straight at him. Sunlight glinted off the barrel. "Now!" He spoke into the microphone by his mouth as he squinted against the sun.

As he tossed his gun aside, Cody said, "The Senator's behind the assassination attempt. Mr. President—at least one of your guards planted the bomb on Senator Alexander's orders."

"Preposterous!" The thin agent tensed both hands on the

gun. "You expect us to believe the Senator's trying to kill the President? Who are you that we should believe you?" A haughty glint gleamed in the man's eyes.

"He was kicked off the NYPD for taking bribes." Nathan gloated, smirking.

Didn't anyone else think it odd how he treated his bride, Cody wondered? Dragging her across the lawn caveman-style wasn't exactly a promenade.

Melissa turned accusing eyes on Cody. "You told me you left because you couldn't get justice."

"That, too." Cody scowled, wishing he had the opportunity to explain everything to Melissa in private; that she would listen. But he didn't have that luxury right now, not when their lives lay at risk. "I overheard their plans. He aspires to be President. He plans to kill you and I don't know how he planned to get rid of the VP."

"He's delusional." The agent scoffed. "The Senator's beyond reproach."

"The Senator's crazy!" Melissa glared at her husband. "He's the most pathetic, vile excuse for a man I've ever met. He thinks he's a prophet and apostle."

Nathan narrowed his eyes. Daggers shot from them.

"Shut up!" he hissed. "Don't say one more damned word."

"How touching; the *loving husband*." Sarcasm dripped from Cody's lips. "What happened to *love, honor, and obey?*"

His arms ached from stretching them over his head so Cody wiggled his fingers to keep the circulation flowing. Still, his shoulders protested the strain, the muscles kinking up. "The Senator's paid off at least one of your men to betray you. One of them put a bomb in your limo. You leave in that, and you won't ever see the Capitol again."

"Drop and spread 'em," an unfamiliar voice rang out. "Let Melissa go." Melissa's father held a smoking shotgun pointed at Nathan's chest.

Nathan yanked Melissa in front of him, using her as a human shield, his lips curled into a snarl.

Cody swore under his breath, ready to strangle the Senator with his bare hands. "Release her, Alexander."

"If you let me go, I'll make sure they set you free. Just don't hurt anyone." Melissa's eyes were widened and darkened with fear.

Nathan pushed her into her father and sprinted, running with all his might. He climbed the chain link fence and jumped to freedom on the other side.

A shot exploded and Cody jerked to the right. Gunpowder tinged his earlobe. The bullet had just missed him as he turned to follow the escaping villain. If not for his excellent reflexes it would have hit him square between the eyes. He somersaulted then jumped to his feet and sprinted for cover as more shots rang out. One set sounded like a cannon.

A trembly Christina stood over Chet, who lay still at her feet. Blood puddled around his chest where a dark red stain splotched his white tuxedo shirt and cummerbund.

"Is he dead?" Christina's voice rattled in her chest. Shaky hands waved the gun loosely at the brethren who rushed to their fallen brother's side.

They froze grotesquely in place, as if they played the children's game Red Light Green Light. Rage and pain contorted their faces.

"Let us see to him, try to save him," one begged.

Cody joined Christina and Melissa and took the gun. Kneeling beside the prone figure, he searched for a pulse. Finding none in the wrist, he pressed his fingers to Chet's carotid artery. Still nothing. He lifted his eyes to the women and shook his head.

"Let us pray over him." Brother Larry knelt at the dead man's side, moaning. "The Creator can raise him from the dead." He chanted an alien mantra, his eyes rolled back in his head.

An ashen pallor fell over Melissa's face as she stared at the fence Nathan had climbed just moments before. She put her hand to her throat and swayed. "We let Nathan get away."

Instantly alarmed, Cody jumped to his feet and took her into his arms. She was ice cold. "It's okay. It's over." He stroked her hair, crooning in her ear. Sunbeams danced on it as if it were spun gold. He looked around and spied the Reverend dashing away. He called to the Secret Service men and pointed after the Senator. "The ringleader's getting away."

"Oh God. He'll be back. He won't let me go that easily."

"You can get an annulment and we can be together now." He tried to stroke her hair, shaking. That was too close.

Melissa pulled away and stared at him, pain pooling around her pupils. Shaking her head, her glorious hair haloing her face, she dragged in a shuddering breath. "No, Cody. You *lied* to me. You were helping *him*." She notched her chin higher, regally.

His heart flipped over in his chest. Reaching out, he touched her arm and it tore him up when she yanked back and folded her arms across her chest.

"Let me explain. I thought I was helping a loving fiancé and a distraught father save their loved one. I didn't know all the facts."

Confusion spread over her face and she bit her lower lip. Indecision lit her eyes. Emotions warred on her beautiful features. She breathed deeply, her chest heaving. After an eternity she finally said, "You could have told me this before when you found out what a beast he was, when I told you what really happened." On a sigh she added, "But you didn't. You still lied."

Beside himself, his gut twisting, Cody searched his heart for the words to say, for the gestures to make, to convince her how much he loved and cherished her and why she should forgive him. What would sway him if he were in her position? Could mere words soften his heart and overcome his doubts. He voiced the emotion uppermost in his heart. "I love you."

Tears clouded her eyes, making them sparkle. They shimmered on her eyelashes and hung precariously. "And I love you. But I can't trust you, thus, I can't contemplate a future with you."

~ * ~

Her father took Melissa in his arms, tucking her head against his shoulder. "I've missed you so much. I thought you were *dead*." His voice cracked on the last word.

Her heart shattered and with it, her composure fled. The tears she'd tried so hard to dam broke loose on a sob and flowed. Curling her arms around her father, she drank in his warmth and sniffed his scent—a heady mixture of deep woods and mint that was his own special combination. He felt so thin, so frail, she could feel his ribs; although only two years had passed and he was only about fifty, he seemed to have aged twenty years.

Unbearable grief consumed Melissa. How much had he suffered because of her? Not that she regretted a moment spent with Jesse, but she shouldn't have cut off her family. She should've seen how Nathan manipulated them. She should've tried harder to get her family to accept Jesse.

Something she'd do again in the future should the situation ever arise again.

Cody her heart cried. But he'd lied to her! He'd helped the demon that'd wanted her for unspeakable things. Just glancing at the shell of the FBI agent's body sent shivers through her. Evil still emanated from it. She wished it were Nathan lying there, that the evil would be buried. But the evil remained. The Lions had to be stopped at any cost.

Separating herself from her father, Melissa squared her shoulders and sucked in a deep breath for fortification. Grabbing her father's hand she pulled him behind her, unwilling to lose physical contact with him. When she brushed against Cody, her nerve endings screamed and her flesh tingled. Her traitorous body still yearned for his touch. Her unruly heart longed for him, too. But she remained stalwart, letting logic rule her.

"Lisa?"

A heart full of heartache throbbed in that one word, almost but not quite circumventing her firm resolve to give this man up. It hugged her and made her long for impossible things, such as babies with his marvelous soulful eyes and long, dark eyelashes. Mischievous little boys that would play cops and robbers, cowboys and Indians, as she was sure he had as a tyke. Exquisite little girls that would adore him and be adored in return.

But she guillotined those thoughts, stamping them *dangerous*, and filed them in cold storage. Perhaps they'd never be retrieved. Maybe she wasn't meant to find her soul mate while still on Earth. Or most probably, Jesse had been it and now Melissa had to forge her path alone, forgetting love, marriage, and babies.

But Jesse's image was fading from her mind and he was securely tucked away in a tiny corner of her heart. Cody's face flashed before her, clear, solid, and vibrant. His voice rang in her ears. His scent wrapped around her.

Yet she'd be the worst kind of fool to ignore the facts and chance another betrayal like Nathan.

"No, Cody. Whatever we might have had is over." Forcing her feet forward, she left him behind with all her hopes and dreams. As soon as this nasty little scene was over, she'd face the blank slate that was her future.

"Mr. President!" Purpose rang out in her voice and infused her step as she embraced her mission.

The handsome and debonair man with silvery hair lifted his wise, commiserating eyes to her. "Yes, my dear?" He opened his arms to her and she accepted his consoling hug in disbelief she was touching the President, much less embracing him. "I don't know yet what just happened, but I hope you'll fill me in."

Diplomacy made her check her tongue and delve for appropriate words. "Thank you. Much as I revere life and shouldn't speak badly of the dead." She pointed at the dead agent. "But he was a traitor to you and to our country, Mr. President.

Worse, he reported to Nathan Alexander, who is a vile, evil, and dangerous man." Her flesh crawled just saying his name and a chill skipped through her. Suddenly, she was very, very cold and had to rub her arms to instill some warmth in them. "He planned to murder you and I think he planned to offer me as some kind of sacrifice."

A single silvery brow quirked. "Sacrifice? Murder? The honorable Senator?"

"He wasn't an honorable man…"

"But you just married him…"

"Under duress. He was going to kill my sister and my father and…" she couldn't verbalize Cody's name. "If I didn't. His men were prepared to shoot you and all of us if I said anything."

The President's expression turned to granite as he glared at Nathan's flock. "Those men?"

"Yes, Sir." On a whisper, Melissa said, "They ritually sacrificed young women. They bragged about it to us. It's so very awful. You can't trust my husband. You have to find him and stop him at all costs. I fear your life is still in danger." She buried her face against his shoulder, wetting his shirt with her tears. "And mine."

Lifting his arm, he pointed at the brethren. "Arrest those men!"

The agents ran, guns drawn, upon Brother Larry, Brother Daniel, and Brother Thaddeus, who didn't run fast enough to escape. One aimed his gun at Cody as well.

"No! He's not one of them." But no one seemed to hear her.

"Arrest them!" The President wiped off his slacks, scowling.

"I can explain, Mr. President," the tall skinny former Secret Service agent said. "I went undercover to infiltrate…"

The President's eyes narrowed. "Save the suck up for the investigating committee. That bomb in the Presidential limo is a strong witness against you." He turned to his aide. "Get him out of my sight."

"Yes, Sir!" The aide stood at attention until the President turned away, and then took the double agent into custody at gunpoint.

Melissa's gut twisted when Cody was handcuffed and taken into custody. He had saved her neck more than once. Nathan had tried to kill him so they obviously weren't in league anymore.

Shouldering her way through the men, she approached the president.

"Mr. President! Mr. President!" Melissa yanked off the agent that tried to hold her back. Her dress was in shreds, mud and grass stained. Her hair hung in clumps about her face. "You're making a mistake." She started to grab his arm in her distress and then pulled back when she realized the inappropriateness of her action. Her hands fell limply to her sides.

"What mistake is that?" He smiled at her kindly. Weariness flickered in his eyes. His shoulders drooped as he tore his tie off and yanked the neck of his shirt open.

She pointed at Cody, who was in the middle of the throng of men being taken into custody. "He's not part of them. He saved me."

Pity flashed in the president's eyes. "The other men say he's working with them…"

Frantic with worry, desperation rose in her voice. "He was helping me try to stop them. To save you."

"No offense, Ms. Vanderbilt-Smythe, but you've been traumatized. Kidnap victims are very often brainwashed by their captors."

"I've not been brainwashed. Cody didn't kidnap me…"

"That's contrary to the information we've collected." He nodded at his men.

Strong hands clamped around her arms, dragging her backwards, away from the leader and chief. "Come with us. We have a few questions for you."

"Where are you taking me? Take your hands off me." Struggling with all her might, she spat at the men.

"Settle down, Ms. Vanderbilt-Smythe. You're not being charged with anything— *unless* you resist cooperating by answering our questions."

With one final thrust, she knocked the agent off her arm. "I'll go peaceably provided you unhand me." She lifted her nose imperiously. "Just *where* are you taking me?"

"To the FBI Building in Los Angeles. Your sister will be our *guest* also."

"Can I say goodbye to my father first?" Melissa spotted him by the back porch and waved. "Will you protect him in case the Senator returns for revenge?"

"You won't be gone long, don't worry. Just a few hours. We'll provide guards for your father." The man stood tall and straight and was devoid of emotion. The setting sun cast him in the shadow of the gazebo so she couldn't fathom the expression in his eyes. However, his stance was rigid.

"What are they doing to us? Where are they taking us?"

Christina cried as she was escorted to the black sedan where Melissa waited impatiently. “I thought they were the good guys.”

“We *are* the good guys.” The blond agent in the front passenger seat turned around, semi-smiling.

“Yeah?” Fire flashed in Christina’s blue eyes. “Then why are you *hijacking* us? I thought there were laws against seizure and kidnapping in this country?”

“We’re taking every precaution to protect the President. We believe you have vital information to crack this case.”

The driver cleared his throat loudly and scowled at his partner as he shook his head.

Melissa watched his face in the rear-view mirror. He didn’t look as if this would be a routine interrogation. But to soothe her sister, she said, “They just need to talk to us. To learn what we know so they can lock up Nathan’s loonies once and for all.” She embraced her sister, shushing her sobs and stroking her hair. “We’ll be all right. I won’t let them hurt you.”

If they tried to hurt Christina, they’d be the sorriest sons of bitches on earth. First Nathan and now these bozos. Melissa was tired of people pushing her around. She didn’t care if they wore badges or not.

Christina hiccoughed, brushing tears from her over bright eyes. “I don’t know how much more I can take.” Her lips quivered. “I thought Nathan loved me. I thought he was a good man. But he was such a *monster*!”

“I never dreamed he’d turn on you. Or I’d have castrated him before I left.”

Christina pulled back, gazing at Melissa with wide luminous eyes. Shock registered on her face.

Her vocabulary had become more *colorful* since she’d lived at the carnival. She’d forgotten her sister was still a genteel society woman, unaccustomed to such language or sentiments. She’d try to curb her tongue around Christina, but Melissa wasn’t the same person anymore. She’d grown.

Traffic picked up as they approached downtown and the sun set before they reached their destination. The paparazzi followed, snapping photographs, so she tried to cover her face with her arms and hands. Christina did the same.

They passed through a guarded gate into a parking garage that wouldn’t allow the press to follow. The driver parked the car and unfolded his long length from the vehicle.

“Shall we, ladies?” The blond agent opened their door and held it for them.

"Follow me," the dark haired agent who had been driving tilted his head. His voice was gruff. He set off at a brisk pace, his footsteps echoing in the parking garage. At the first checkpoint, he showed his badge and signed in after exchanging a few words with the guard.

Melissa stared around FBI Headquarters, aware that people stared at her. Brightly lit offices were filled with desks, computers, and papers. Men and women in sedate suits bustled back and forth quietly.

"In here, please."

Both agents wore their badges prominently on their jacket pockets now, so Melissa could see their names. The blond good-looking one was Brent Sitorsky and their driver was Randall Herman.

Herman acted like the senior partner. Circling his wrist, he gestured to the oblong table in the center of the floor surrounded by hard wooden chairs.

"Would you like some coffee?" Sitorsky asked, smiling.

"No." Melissa shook her head. Nauseated, she didn't want food or drink.

An attractive young lady with dark brown hair scraped back into a bun and wearing gold rimmed glasses slid quietly into the room with a tape recorder. She busied herself setting it up.

Herman straddled a chair backwards, staring at them. "Agent Neubauer will record our session. It's standard procedure."

The young woman glanced up and smiled, nodding.

Sitorsky closed the door and perched on the side of the table, his expression quizzical. His pants leg hitched up, revealing a black sock and an expanse of blond hairy leg.

"Let's get this show on the road," Herman said. Pinpointing Melissa with his gaze, he asked, "Tell us the events leading up to Senator Alexander's escape and Agent Mulligan's death. And what you know about a bomb being planted in the President's car."

She didn't like the sound of this. "Don't we have the right to have an attorney present?"

Christina nodded sharply, her lips pursed.

Herman favored her with a sigh. "I thought you were innocent?"

They were! Well, except maybe for *borrowing* and crashing that small plane and doing the same with the car, running from the police. Trivial, nothing compared to trying to kill the President of the United States. Still, they sounded as if they might crucify her anyway.

"I'm not saying another word until we have legal representation." Melissa crossed her arms over her chest mutinously.

Christina nodded again, smiling. "Our family attorney is John Rascomb, Esquire. He handles all matter for the Vanderbilt-Smythe Estate. We demand you call him."

Herman sighed and flicked his head at Sitorsky. "Call him in here ASAP. Better yet, send a squad car to pick him up." He cast an apologetic smile at Agent Neubauer.

The female agent pursed her lips as they quirked into a momentary smile.

"I'll take tea or soda if you have it," Melissa said. Her throat was parched. Looking at her sister, she asked, "What about you?"

"Hot tea will be fine."

"I'll see what we have." Sitorsky unfolded his long length and ambled into the hall. The door stayed open half a crack and they were able to hear snippets of a passing conversation.

"Two rogue generals and their followers seized a missile complex in Missouri and are threatening to launch missiles at Lebanon, Washington D.C., and China. They were told in the event that the assassination attempt was thwarted, to launch."

Sitorsky and Herman lunged for the door and shut it.

Melissa and Christina exchanged worried glances. She read fear in her sister's eyes. Answering fear leapt in her heart.

My God, was this Nathan's doing? Had she heard right? Rogue generals, fueled by Nathan's failure to kill the President, were planning to launch nuclear weapons? She wanted to ask but knew better to wait for John.

Chapter Fifteen

Cody was thrust into a dark room and made to sit on a hard chair. A spotlight blinded him; he closed his eyes.

A voice boomed out of nowhere, everywhere, reverberating eerily in the blackness. He couldn't see the owner of the voice with the light glaring in his eyes.

"Your boy Alexander is creating one hell of a mess. If you cooperate, you might get off with life in prison instead of the death penalty."

Death penalty? A mess?

"What mess?"

"Don't play dumb with us, Richards. We know you're on Alexander's payroll. Do you deny it?"

"Yes. I mean *no*!" That sounded real convincing.

"It can't be both. Which is it?"

Cody expelled a huge sigh. His ribs ached where he'd been beaten by the good Reverend and the Lions.

"I was retained by Alexander to find and retrieve his fiancée, Melissa Vanderbilt-Smythe. I was told she'd been kidnapped and needed rescuing."

Impatience snapped in the interrogator's voice. "We've been told you were much deeper into the organization than that, *Mister* Richards."

"That's *all* I did. I found her and she set me straight on a few facts."

"What facts?" The disembodied voice was getting more and more disconcerting, rankling on his nerves. His muscles were cramping, sitting in one place so long. Rolling his shoulders, he worked out the kinks.

"She told me he was very abusive to her. That he was forcing her into marriage."

"So you still turned her over to him?" Derision laced the man's voice.

"No!" Cody jerked upright in his chair. "Once I knew what he'd done to her, I wasn't going to hand her over."

"But you did."

"No, I didn't. Alexander's men kidnapped us. FBI Agent Mulligan ambushed us. He was Alexander's right hand man. He set me up. He and that *Brother Larry*." Contempt dripped from his voice. He hated hypocrites. "Talk to Brother Larry. Maybe you can get it out of him."

"Agent Mulligan was on assignment, infiltrating some suspect cult."

Fury boiled in his veins and Cody jumped up. "Well, then he was turned. Ever hear of a double agent? He was as rotten as they come." He paced the room, going in and out of the light.

"Sit down, please. Now who do you expect us to believe? An agent with a spotless service record? Or a no account ex-cop with a rap sheet?" The voice grew deadlier. "We don't have time to play games. Tell us where Alexander would hide? What he plans to do next"

"I don't have a clue. He's crazy. He wants revenge for Waco." Cody scowled, trying to think like a crazy man. "What would your typical religious fanatic do if pinned in a corner?"

"Who's the mole in the government telling these generals what to do?"

He peered into the light. "What generals? What mole? It was probably Agent Mulligan. Maybe the good Reverend himself."

Voices whispered together. "Look, we'll cut you a deal. You help us stop the missile launch and apprehend these rogue generals and their units, and you'll get amnesty."

Cody roared in frustration. "What rogue generals? What missile launch?"

Frustration colored the interrogator's voice. "Bring the others in. Maybe one of them will slip and tell us what we need to know."

"My God! What missile launch?" Picking up his chair, Cody hurled it at the voice with all his might. "Goddammit! You're holding me illegally, now I demand some answers."

"You're in no position to demand anything, Mr. Richards. You could be looking at death row for crimes of this magnitude."

"I'd love to help, but that's all I know. Other than these guys are religious fanatics. They're totally nuts. They're hiding in the woods, holding sacrificial rituals."

"You thought this information unimportant?" The voice became deadly quiet.

"Of course not! Hell, we were captives. We couldn't get to a phone to call you. It's some friggin' nightmare." Cody felt like a trapped animal and dug his fingernails in his palms to stop from punching a hole in the wall.

"It's a nightmare all right." The disembodied voice of the

interrogator reverberated in the small, sterile room.

The door opened and light filtered in. Dust mites shimmered in the air as Brother Larry, Brother Daniel, and the other gruesome cult members filed in. All were handcuffed and chained. They clanked as they shuffled their feet.

"Maybe your colleagues can shed more light on this situation." The interrogator's voice adopted a singsong quality.

"They are not my colleagues," Cody mumbled in disgust. "They're some wacko Koresh-type cult. Every one of them is certifiable, especially Brother Larry. He tried to kidnap Miss Vanderbilt-Smythe back in New Jersey."

"I was trying to help the young lady," Brother Larry denied, in a church-like voice. "I saw this man trying to kidnap this young woman…"

Seething, Cody rounded on Brother Larry. "I saved her from you. All anyone has to do is ask the lady, she'll tell you. What kind of *mess* have you and the good Reverend made? What's going on? Rogue generals? Armed missiles?"

Brother Larry lifted his voice with a sermon-like quality. It resonated in the dark room. "Dear brothers, we live in an evil world. Only a handful of disciples are fit to survive and start a bold new order. But we are willing to make the ultimate sacrifice, for God's glory."

"Shut up!" Brother Daniel lunged at Brother Larry. "Stop rambling like an idiot."

Survive? Sacrifice? Cody's blood chilled and he was bone cold. "What brave new world?"

"Don't say another blessed word." Brother Daniel's voice reverberated, dangerously quiet.

"You're not the *lamb*." A wicked smile flavored Brother Larry's voice. "I don't take revelation from you."

"You'll shut your mouth or I'll shut it for you permanently." A tussle broke out and Cody stepped back out of the way.

"Break it up!" Annoyance rang clear in their host's voice. "Tie them up if you have to."

"Police brutality! We'll get outta here on technicalities." Brother Daniel chuckled. "You can't treat us like this. I know the law."

"In matters of national defense, we can do whatever's necessary." Supreme assurance tinged the interrogator's voice.

"What time is it?" Brother Larry asked.

Cody had no clue. His watch had been confiscated and he felt as if he'd been caged in here forever.

"Two a.m." The voice came from the darkness.

Brother Larry clapped his hands and laughed maniacally. "Praise the Lord! The time of deliverance is upon us. You can't stop us now."

"Stop what?" Every cell of Cody's being echoed the words. What diabolical plan were they hatching? How evil a megalomaniac was the Reverend?

"They're going to make their demands any moment." Brother Larry snickered and crossed his arms over his chest.

"What demands? Who?" The interrogator's voice sharpened, booming into the room.

"The Reverend and the generals are about to demand that the President abdicate power and that the Reverend be made the Commander in Chief—of the world. And that we be released and granted full pardons." Brother Larry nodded at Brother Daniel, a smirk playing about his lips.

"We don't deal with terrorists. The United States never has and it never will." Steely determination rang in the interrogator's voice.

In all Cody's years on the police force and in detective work, he'd never been involved in such a dangerous situation. It felt surreal. Cold sweat broke out all over him. They were talking about crazy things—annihilation of the human race. Armageddon…

"You *have* to deal with us or we'll nuke the whole east coast. The four beasts will avenge the Lamb." Brother Larry got up on his evangelical pedestal to preach.

"And China, and Lebanon," Brother Daniel added, sneering. "The whole government will be blown to smithereens and half your population with it." His cheeks puffed out and he made a whooshing sound. "Brimstone will fill the sky and the revelations will be fulfilled!" His hands fanned out in an arc, his fingers fluttering in the air, mimicking nuclear fall out.

Brother Larry's eyes twinkled, maniacal like Alexander's. "Then China and the Middle East will retaliate. And the skies will be filled with hail and fire mingled with blood. Mountains will be cast into the sea. Stars will fall from the heavens. The sun will be smitten. Woe to all sinners. Woe to you who do not believe. Woe to you who slay the Lamb. For *you* will fall into the bottomless pit of despair."

"Cut the Biblical mumbo jumbo. What's the code word to stop these lunatic generals from launching?"

"Oh ye of little faith." Brother Larry shook his head and a

lock of his oily hair fell across his forehead. "The only way to stop the beasts from devouring your planet is to give us what has been decreed from the beginning of time. Hand over the President and exalt Reverend Alexander to his ordained position by God—Prophet and ruler of the World."

"You'll never get your demands met if you're dead."

"Our souls are prepared to die. Are yours?" Brother Larry started mumbling a mantra, his eyes rolling back in his head. His pupils dilated.

They were at an impasse, or so it seemed. Cody knew never to deal with terrorists; however, he'd never met such zealots.

"How long before they launch?" The voice became more demanding.

Brother Larry chanted tunelessly for a few more moments, his eyes clouded over. "They will launch at three a.m. Pacific time if our demands are not met."

"Key-rist! That's not enough time to give them the President even if we wanted to. We don't have that kind of authority. The United Nations would have to decide something of this magnitude. I don't even know if they're in session." Panic laced the interrogator's voice.

"Nevertheless, Brother, you only have until three a.m. or the Beasts will devour the enemy." Brother Larry looked very serene for a man on the brink of death, almost as if he welcomed it. Enjoyed it.

"Where are the generals? Which generals? Which missile silo have they taken over?"

Brother Larry smiled widely and squared his shoulders. "They're in Zion, home of the Lamb."

Cody closed his eyes, remembering his Sunday school teachings. Zion lay in Missouri. But was it merely the state of Missouri as was drawn on the map now? Didn't it include a longer, broader section of the middle of the country? Perhaps Kansas? Nebraska? The Dakotas as well?

"What military installations do we have in Missouri and Kansas? They have silos, don't they?"

"Let's say we want to hand over the President to you and your generals, at *what base* do we do this?"

"McConnell Air Force Base in Kansas," Brother Daniel said. Bags puffed under his milk chocolate eyes.

"Get 'em out of here! Put them in complete isolation from everyone else and from each other."

As they were marched out single file to their new cells, Cody overheard, "Self-righteous bigots. We ought to put them on a deserted island and nuke them." The voice running the show sounded thoroughly disgusted, even scared, now.

As soon as Cody was separated from the other captives, he was escorted back to the room. "What's going on?" he asked when he was shoved into the room. This time the lights were on and several men sat around a long rectangular table.

"Have a seat, please." A dignified black gentleman with close-cropped graying hair, a clean-shaven face, thick glasses, and a perfectly tailored three-piece gray suit, rose to his feet and motioned to a chair. "I'm Chief M.J. Devereaux, and we have a proposition for you, Mr. Richards."

Cody hitched up his pants to sit down, feeling grubby next to the well-dressed agents. "What proposition? Shouldn't you be saving the world from apocalyptic Jim Jones-like Alexander and his *disciples* instead of dickering with me?"

"We want you to help us save the world, Mr. Richards, from megalomaniacs and self proclaimed messiahs like David Koresh. In fact, we're depending on you to avoid another Waco type disaster. They've been planning their day of reckoning for a very long time and this seems to be it. Only this one's for the whole *world*." Devereaux peered long and hard at him.

"What can I do? I'm just an ex-New York cop that got drummed off the force for misconduct." Sarcasm slipped from his tongue glibly. He slid a sly glance at everyone sitting around the table. "Besides… I thought you believed me to be in league with those cultist crazies. You would allow me within a hundred miles of nuclear devices?"

"Mrs. Alexander swears under oath that you're not involved with those men. I don't think you are either or I wouldn't even be telling you this." The man's voice deepened and he stripped off his thick-lensed glasses and squinted at Cody.

"Then why do I need to make a deal to be absolved of charges? Why blackmail me?" Cody crossed his right leg over left knee.

"Because we need you…"

"Because I'm *expendable*?" Cody sighed deeply.

"Because we hope you're patriotic. Because you have experience with these men. Because you've studied the breed. You know them. And because you look enough like the President that with make-up we can exchange you in his place."

Cody jerked straight up. "You want *me* to impersonate the President?" He looked down at himself, incredulous. "In case you haven't noticed, he's about thirty years older than me, for one. Secondly, you're out of time to do a make-over."

"Stand up," Agent Herman said, his voice devoid of emotion. He took out a tape measure and took Cody's length, and girth, murmuring, "Hmm," at various intervals. Looking up at Devereaux, he nodded. "He's six-foot-two-inches. The President's six-one. Close enough to fool them. They're both about the same build. They have the same facial structure. It can be done."

"Aren't we out of *time*?" Wasn't anyone listening to him? Or was he only talking in his dreams?

Devereaux quirked his lips. "It's only eleven p.m. We lied to them. We have a couple of hours to work with. We'll get you into make-up and wardrobe and Air Force One will carry you to *Zion*."

"So I can stop the *beasts*." Hopefully they weren't like the Heaven's Gate members, convinced they could move up a notch in human evolution by shedding their *containers* and catching a ride on a spaceship on the tail of another comet—or nuclear warhead. Why couldn't these society dropouts focus inward instead of trying to destroy humanity?

Cody was as patriotic as the next guy, but he didn't like the turn of his thoughts. These killer cults made him crazy. How had Melissa ever managed to get involved with one of the worst of the megalomaniacs in history?

"I don't suppose they want to dance with me once they get me? And unless you're like the Mission Impossible guys with facial masks and voice synthesizers, they'll never buy the switch. They're crazy, not stupid."

A tall, slim woman stood up and sauntered over to him. Her nametag read, 'Agent Lynne Decker.'

"Where do you think television got the idea for that show? We're the originals. My crew can make you over so that you won't even know you're not the President when you look in the mirror."

Devereaux leaned on the table heavily, staring at him. "We're counting on your police training, rusty though it may be, to help us overtake these lunatics. We cannot let them launch their missiles, or else millions, maybe billions, of innocent people will die. Our government will be in ruins. World War will ensue; nuclear winter." He banged his fist into the table, making all its contents jump.

Cody gulped as his Adam's apple worked overtime. "Is that

all you want from me? *Piece of cake.*" Did these guys remember he had a rap sheet? That they weren't sure he wasn't on the bad guy's side?

"You can tell us *no*; however, you probably won't be alive past tomorrow to regret your decision." Devereaux stared him down, his eyes mere slits in his dark face.

"Don't you need someone more seasoned? Someone with better and current training?" He'd made up his mind to help; however, Cody wasn't sure just how good a choice he was. He'd not even been much protection for one runaway heiress and now they wanted him to save the world.

"Not with our limited time. We'll have a team behind you. But we need you to get inside and cause a commotion so that our boys can stop the launch." Devereaux looked pointedly at his watch. "Are you copasetic with that, soldier?"

Cody stifled a groan and nodded. The military mindset made him sweat, even though these were the supposed good guys, and although the FBI wasn't officially military, they were close enough. He didn't work and play well with others. Wasn't that one of the reasons why he'd been cut from the force? Isn't that why he worked as a lone bounty hunter now?

"I hope you're a good actor." Devereaux slapped his shoulder, grinning, but his eyes remained dead serious. "Go get into make-up. Win the Academy Award. You're our last hope."

Cody grunted, biting back a snarl. The idea of these self-proclaimed divinities, intoxicated with lust and power, running loose in armed missile silos gave him big time indigestion. The satanic rites he'd run across in the past, like the Lions had described, made him shudder and he never wanted to see these bloodsuckers again. And he'd run across some weird ass cults in his mission to save innocent kids like his sister and Melissa, like that Kentucky Vampire cult he'd investigated a few years before.

His patriotic fervor won over, as it always did. Or was it his intense anger that these idiots seemed intent on opening the gates to Hell, too often in the name of Heaven? Cody wanted to cut their nuts off and stuff them down their throats every time he thought of his sister and those other lost kids. Maybe if he castrated them in the process of saving Mother Earth, he'd chase away his personal demons, too. If he was successful at this all-important mission, maybe he could finally put the ghost of his sister to rest. At the very least, he'd save Melissa.

He'd be damned if the Senator, or his spirit, got in his way.

"Can I see profiles on these *generals*? Do you know who any of their men are?"

Devereaux followed Cody and Agent Decker down the antiseptic hall, their footsteps reverberating in his ears. "Alexander's as lethal as any Jones or Koresh or Manson. He's got to be in the silos or pulling the strings."

Decker, who had been quiet throughout the ordeal, shook her head. "They're launching from Zion, of all places. Why is Missouri such a magnet?"

"We first ran into Brother Larry in New Jersey." The nightmarish memories sent shudders down his spine.

"In here." Agent Decker held out her hand. "My team's waiting to groom you, Mr. President." She winked and a dimple came out of hiding in her cheek.

The team consisted of two women and two men. Latex, glue, wigs, fake eyebrows and hair littered the table. Heavy, porous make-up clustered on a nearby vanity.

"Meet Rosa Patterson, who is our wonder beautician." Agent Decker pointed at the second lady. "Julia Jacobs will do your make-up." Turning to the men in the group, she smiled professionally. "This is Scott Thurlowe and Artie Unger. Scott does magic with latex. Artie is the best tailor this side of the Rockies." She backed toward the door. "We'll leave you in their capable hands, *Mr. President*."

Devereaux saluted smartly, clicked his heels and pivoted on the balls of his feet. His chuckle echoed down the hall and Cody turned to his transformation crew.

"Doctors Frankenstein, I presume?" he asked dryly, eyeing his team of makeover whizzes quizzically.

As they were giving him a new face, he hoped they'd found a better brain to give him…for he'd obviously lost his mind.

Chapter Sixteen

"I demand to see him!" Melissa shook with fury and turned to her attorney. "John, represent him. I'll pay your fees. They have to let you see your own client." She crossed her arms over her chest and stared into John's kindly brown eyes.

The lawyer laid his hand on her shoulder and squeezed. "I'll represent him, but you have to let me handle this."

Out of sorts, scared, confused, she implored John with big eyes. "Can't you get me into see him for at least a minute?" She recalled the snatch of conversation she'd gleaned from the hallway. If she didn't see him now, she might never see him again, and she needed to tell him she was sorry and that she loved him. Soul-searching combined with fear made her realize he wasn't the scoundrel she'd accused him of being. Fate might snatch away her happiness again but at least she could set things straight first, couldn't she? "I love him."

"This isn't a regular prison and he's in the middle of questioning. I don't think even I can see him so fast."

Agitated, Melissa jumped to her feet, biting her finger. She paced, glaring at Sitorsky. Herman had disappeared long ago. "Can't I see him for at least two minutes? *Just* two minutes?"

Sitorsky pursed his lips, and shook his head. "Maybe later. Not now."

"He's innocent." She counted to ten silently, holding her temper in check as best as she could. "He's a hero. He saved the President. He saved me. What is there to be suspicious of?" She pinpointed the man with a haughty look. "He's a hero. You should be pinning him with medals, not blackmailing him like this."

"Please calm down and be seated, Miss Vanderbilt-Smythe. Please…" Sitorsky rose, towering over her.

Through gritted teeth she said, "I am calm. And I'm not going to sit down and let you walk all over us. We have rights."

Cody's voice floated in the door and she froze, her ears perked. "These are the general's dossiers? Did you locate the Vice President yet?"

"We'll finish briefing you on Air Force One. Time's running out."

Bolting past Sitorsky, ducking his grab for her, Melissa ran into the hall, ignoring the agent's shouted "Stop! Come back here!"

When hands grabbed her arms, she shook them off. "Cody!" She flung herself at the man.

"Melissa!" Heavy footsteps bounded down the hall toward her.

But it wasn't Cody who came face to face with her, but the President. His hands held her shoulders.

Mortified, she stared at him. Her eyes scanned the hallway behind him for Cody but she only saw a group of agents, a distinguished black man with graying hair at the front of the group.

"I-I'm sorry, Sir. I thought you were someone else." When she tried to pull back, the hands clamped more firmly on her.

"Lisa." Firm lips descended on hers, coaxing a response from her.

Melissa stiffened, confused, and pulled back. Then she realized that Cody's intense eyes gazed at her from the President's face. "Richards?"

The leader marched hurriedly, looking around. "Get in the room!" He ushered them into the room where John and Christina waited and closed them in. "National security's at stake. We can't afford a screw up now."

"What's going on?" Melissa asked.

"Captain Devereaux…" Sitorsky began, sliding a sideways glance at Melissa.

The black man glared at Sitorsky over the rim of his wire-rimmed spectacles. He wore an impeccable dark blue suit with an air of authority. His face didn't match his body. Long, heavy jowls tugged at his mouth, and he had a broad, lined forehead and slightly receding hairline. Yet he looked fit, and moved with a lithe grace a man twenty years younger would envy. "Why was the door open? They shouldn't know…" A deep, rich voice resonated through the hall even though he lowered it several notches.

"Know what?" Melissa circled Cody, looking him up and down. "That you're impersonating the President?"

John strode over to her, scowling. "Let me handle this." When he tried to escort her back to her seat, she shook him off.

"What about the *missiles*? Did Nathan's soldiers seize them?" She bristled outwardly but was scared to death inwardly.

"Why is Cody impersonating the President?"

Cody's lips set in a grim line and he frowned.

Revelation flooded her. "My God!" She rounded on Devereaux, the blood draining from her head; she felt faint. "You're sending him into the silos because he's *expendable*. You don't expect him to survive." Trembling, she hugged Cody. "You're not taking him."

She'd already lost Jesse. Not Cody, too. Not now when she'd finally realized what a fool she'd been.

"I have to do this." Cody lifted her chin with his finger, forcing her to gaze into his eyes, willing her to understand. "The alternative is certain death for all of us."

Eyes narrowed, she lifted her chin imperially and squared her shoulders. "Then I'm going with you."

"She can't go." Devereaux rubbed his short hair. Light reflected off his glasses so that she couldn't read the expression in his eyes. "This isn't a trip to Disneyland, Miss. Essential personnel only." The words were clipped, terse even.

Melissa quelled the part of her that the man intimidated; adopting the air of authority she'd learned to run a large estate. "Nathan might listen to me. You need me."

Cody's eyes widened and he stiffened. "No, Melissa. He almost killed you before. He kidnapped you. He's desperate and has nothing to lose."

Thinking of the alternative, waiting for the world to explode, she said, "Neither do I."

She lifted her chin and stared at the man straight on. "Like it or not, I'm your best shot at reasoning with him." Or bargaining with him. Acid burned in her chest at the thought that she might be forced to go with the man again. She pursed her lips and waited for her invitation.

The Captain glowered at her, his heavy-lidded eyes narrowed to mere slits. "I don't like this one little bit. Regulations do not allow us to put civilians in danger." To Sikorski, he said, "Put it on record that I'm taking Mrs. Alexander on this mission under protest and against my better judgment."

"Against mine, too." Cody whispered so that only she could hear him. "Please stay here, out of danger. I'd feel much better knowing you're safe."

"Safe?" Visions of a big bang and rising mushroom clouds filled her mind. If she had to die, she'd rather it be at Cody's side. "No one's *safe* until Nathan and the Lions of Judah are stopped for good."

Melissa neglected to add the second portion of her thoughts aloud for the ex-cop's benefit. Just because he was worried about her didn't mean that he wanted to spend the rest of his life with her. They had a lot to talk about when this was all over.

Devereaux snapped his fingers and then nodded to his men. "Get them to safety."

~ * ~

How his disguise fooled the array of officers and enlisted men who took him from Air Force One, Cody didn't know. He supposed the Doctors Frankenstein were marvels at their job. He just prayed his luck held out. He wondered how long this latex would stay put? Twelve hours? Twenty-four hours? Thirty-six? If he could just get inside and cause a distraction for a couple of moments, the special task force would do the rest. He just had to make sure the Lions didn't launch the missiles prematurely, before the good guys could disarm the warheads.

"Here's the President, Sir." A young Lieutenant whose nametag read 'Lt. Lamont' shoved Cody forward at gunpoint as he dared Melissa and Devereaux to disobey.

General Hyram Potter squinted at him over the giant circles that bagged under his eyes. He sported a crew cut and wore black Army regular issue glasses. "It's about time you got here. The Senator's been crawlin' up my ass." He practically growled the words.

"What happens now, *General*?" Cody's extra emphasis on the man's title belittled it. He took in the dynamics of the dark, daunting room that wasn't much larger than the plane's compartment; noting that it was dim for the most part with a myriad of red, white, and green blinking lights. Digital displays flashed and he heard the occasional ping above the hushed voices.

Melissa stood between himself and Devereaux, uncharacteristically silent, her hands folded demurely in front of her.

Uniformed men quietly bustled around, shooting him haughty looks, even snickering.

"This the girl the Senator wants so badly?" The General looked Melissa up and down dispassionately.

"Yessuh." He swallowed the *sir* as if he hailed from Alabama or Louisiana. Lieutenant Lamont was a good-looking young man. Almost a man at any rate. He looked to be fresh out of college. Tall and lean, with classical dark looks, he'd fit better in a college frat house than this missile tomb.

Tension made the air oppressive, although Cody doubted it ever felt comfortable, much less pleasant, to be inside this rocket silo. He wouldn't want the job of turning one of those keys and annihilating all mankind. Death lurked here, laughing, waiting, trying to trick the unwary to turn the keys as if in a Stephen King nightmare… He finally spied one of the keys. It seemed to glow, radiating negative energy.

"Hello, Melissa." Nathan swaggered up to them as Cody stood stoic, holding his breath, biding his time.

"Well, well, Senator," Cody drawled in his best imitation of the President's voice. "You've got what you want—me and this young woman. Call off your goons. Disarm the warheads."

The Reverend drew Melissa away from Cody by both hands. "There's only one way I'll disarm them." He didn't waste his glance on Cody—they were all for the woman. "Concede all power to me *now*. Declare me ruler."

"Ruler?" Cody's skin crawled. He faced a truly crazy man. "Emperor of the United States? Or King of the world?"

Nathan turned feral eyes on him. "Why, emperor of the world, of course."

"Our government doesn't work that way. I don't have that kind of power. Even if I was willing to hand over power to you, which I'm not, I don't have the authority to speak for all other countries…"

"Oh, I have the *authority*. I think I have about fifty tons of *authority*."

Nathan drew and cocked a handgun, and aimed it at Cody's head. "You do exactly as I say, the way I say, or we'll send this world back to our Maker. Our society will disappear in a flash—just like Babylon. Because of you and your government, this world is too evil to survive. Drastic measures must be implemented, and I've been ordained to lead His disciples."

Melissa's eyes widened as all color drained from her face. "Who chose *you*?"

"Divine revelation was revealed to me." Nathan lifted his face and arms to the sky as if he were nailed to a cross.

Several of the men glanced their way. Lt. Lamont stood at parade rest, his gaze straight ahead. His reholstered pistol gleamed under a beam of artificial light.

"You got me. Isn't that what you wanted? You still going to attack the American people and fill the sky with fire and brimstone?" Cody grimaced, shifting his weight from one foot to the other. "Call off your disciples. Do with me what you will."

Maybe Cody could avert global bloodshed if he sacrificed himself.

But Nathan chuckled and shook his head, cocking the firearm. "Where's the real president?"

Cody stiffened, barely able to breathe, his focus on the gun.

"You think I wouldn't recognize you under all that plaster? The make-up's good but you don't sound or act a thing like the real President." He clucked his tongue. "Your conceit continues to amaze me, Richards—first, you thought you could steal my intended bride and hide her from me. Now you thought you could fool these yokels with such a poor facsimile." He notched his arm higher so that the gun aimed at Cody's heart. "You know, it occurs to me that you'll let me shoot you, the noble hero, the martyr…" He reeled around and grabbed Melissa, putting the gun to her temple and cocked it. "But will you sacrifice your beloved lady love for the world?"

Melissa turned deathly pale, all blood draining from her face; but she didn't make so much sound as a whimper. Her eyes implored him to do what he must, even if it meant sacrificing her—which Cody wasn't about to let happen without a struggle.

"So what happens now? You're going to shoot your own wife? The love of *your* life?"

A purely crazy smile lit Nathan's face. "We'll be together through eternity. These are but our earthly shells. Bullets nor bombs can harm our eternal souls."

"Then why should I be scared of your guns or your missiles, Reverend?"

"Ahhhh, my brother, why indeed? I can see in your eyes that your soul is not prepared as is mine. You don't have one one-hundredth of my faith. You're afraid to die."

Unfortunately, Alexander was right. The thought of his world and all mankind exploding scared Cody to his core. Why should innocent children die because of this one man's insanity?

"So what do you want me to do? As you said yourself, I'm not the President. I can't make you ruler or emperor of anything." He tried some of Melissa's poker tactics. "Do you truly want to end the world?"

Nathan narrowed his eyes and seemed to ponder Cody's question. Finally, he swiveled the gun toward him and snarled. "No, just you. You've been a thorn in my side ever since I hired you."

"No!" Melissa bit Nathan's hand, and stomped as hard as

she could on his foot, just as the bullet exploded from his gun.

The gun jerked upward towards Cody's head instead of at his heart.

Cody threw himself to the side, but felt a burning through his right shoulder, as he rolled to the ground. He couldn't tell if the bullet had impacted him as his shoulder had been throbbing wildly already, his earlier wound raw and probably infected by all the abuse it had been through.

Nathan yelled, as he backhanded Melissa to the ground amid the sounds of bones crunching. "Launch at the US Eastern Seaboard."

She hurtled backward, howling in rage and pain. Twin spots glowed in each cheek, almost nuclear red. "You're not a man of God, a Lion of Judah. Men of God don't hurt innocent people. They don't enjoy power and degrading others. You're a demon!"

"Women should be seen and not heard." Nathan strode over to her, towered over her, and aimed a deadly foot at her face. "Learn your place, *wife*."

"*No!*" Cody struggled to his knees and lunged for Nathan's legs just as his steel booted toe almost connected with Melissa's jaw.

She rolled out of the way just in time.

Teetering, Nathan kicked at him but Cody managed to roll and catch the other man's leg in the process, flipping him to the floor. The gun tumbled out of Nathan's hands; flame burst forth in mid air from the spiraling gun and a bullet ricocheted in the compound. A fist connected to Cody's eye and pain flared out of control. Blood trickled down his cheek as shouts of rage roared in his ears.

Lt. Lamont said in a deadly voice above him, "Lie still, or I'll blow your head across the room, Suh."

"Forget him," Nathan puffed. "I've got this handled. Help Potter get that key turned."

"Yessuh!" Lamont turned…and saw Devereaux, "Move away from the General or I'll shoot."

The elite task force burst into the silo, fanning out, before the lieutenant's voice stopped echoing.

"Launch, Goddamn you!" Nathan shouted, pulling himself forward on his elbows toward General Potter who struggled to turn one of the keys, Devereaux fighting to get it out of his hands.

"Help Devereaux. If that key turns, the birds will fly." Cody used the last of his waning strength to pull himself to his feet, and half limping, half running, made his way toward the agency director. Cody grimaced as blood stained his hand where he held his burning shoulder.

Nathan grabbed his arms more securely around Cody's legs, his fingers biting into Cody's flesh. "You think you can save the world?" He laughed maniacally. "Why bother? Satan's loose and winning the war. The world doesn't deserve to live."

"You're crazy. It's not your decision." Cody stared at him dumbfounded. "If God were going to choose a prophet, it sure wouldn't be you."

"Oh, but I am God's mouthpiece. He speaks to me, only to me." Nathan finally grabbed the gun on the floor and cocked it to Cody's head again. "As you'll soon see…"

Gunshots rang out; one so close Cody thought that his head was being ripped apart. If the blood splattering his face were anything to go by, it just had been.

Then a shadow fell over them.

"Crazy, sorry bastard." Devereaux shook his head, his gaze inscrutable, his gun smoking. "Someone should've taken you out years ago."

Cody pushed the Reverend's petrified form off, his skin crawling. When the man's head rolled to the floor with a thud, his lifeless eyes staring at the ceiling, Cody shuddered.

"You hurt?" Devereaux held out his hand to help Cody up. He had an amazingly strong grip for an old guy. He must be sixty-something at least. Wisdom shone from his sloe black eyes.

Swiping at the blood dripping from his nose with the back of his hand, Cody met Devereaux's gaze. The latex lay askew on his face, a piece ripped and hanging off. Tearing it off in pieces, he said, "I'll live." Glancing at the key, he added grimly, "You turned off the key?"

They stepped over a number of handcuffed soldiers lying face down on the floor to get to the key. Melissa had run to the protection of a number of Devereaux's soldiers. "Not a second too soon. One moment more and we wouldn't be having this conversation."

"You're hurt!" Melissa cupped Cody's face in her hands, gently exploring his bruises and cuts.

"So are you," Cody said, swearing under his breath. Good thing the bastard was dead or he'd murder him with his bare hands for hurting a woman, especially his woman. "Don't you care you're a widow again?"

Shudders ripped through her and she squeezed her eyes

tightly. "I suppose I should care that a man is dead, but all I feel is relief. We're finally free of him." She wrapped her arms around Cody's middle and buried her face in his chest. Almost as quickly, her head snapped back, and she ripped his shirt away from his shoulder. "Oh God, your wound's reopened. Medics! He's injured."

Cody's breathing grew increasingly shallow and he could barely stand, his knees wobbly. "I've survived thus far..." He slumped, despite his words, into Melissa and Devereaux's arms.

"Over here!" Devereaux's authority rang out sharply. "Man down."

"Don't die on me now, not after everything we've been through. I need to talk to you…" Melissa swiped at a tear that had the audacity to trickle down her cheek.

His heart flipped in his chest and he reached for her as strong hands lifted him and put him on a stretcher. "Don't leave me, now. I love you."

This time she let the tears flow. "I love you, too. I'm so sorry I didn't believe you, that I could have ever thought you would work with Nathan knowing what he was."

"Think you could marry a poor man, Princess? One who loves you with all his heart and soul?" Cody squeezed her hand as she walked by his side as he was being wheeled out. Behind her, he saw a sheet being pulled over Nathan's form.

"You mean marry the savior of the world? Am I worthy of you?" She chewed her lower lip and stared up and over him at Devereaux. "Are we still up on charges? Either of us?"

Cody looked up through a fuzzy haze, seeing two Devereauxs. Feverish, his head pounding, his shoulder burning as if on fire, he tried to stay awake.

Devereaux winked at Melissa and nodded to Cody. "I think we can work something out under these extenuating circumstances for you and our Mr. President. You've had a ringside seat to the biggest adventure of your lives."

The man obviously didn't know Melissa. Cody suspected this was just one of many big adventures he'd have, if she agreed to spend the rest of her life with him; although he hoped this would be the last adventure of this magnitude and danger.

Cody tried to smile but the teasing note in his voice would have to be enough. His cheek felt as if it was crushed and the muscles didn't respond correctly either, refusing to pull his lips up on command. "I'll take notes for the book I'm writing: *'I was the President'*." The remaining latex itched like crazy as he tried to peel it off.

He saw Brother Larry and the other Lions being escorted away in handcuffs. "I hope they lost their roar now that their leader is dead." He lifted a silent prayer that all the megalomaniacs would be nullified.

"I hope so." Melissa squeezed his hand, rubbing his knuckles with her thumb.

"Don't worry. We'll make sure of it. You could write that book, you know. I bet it would be a bestseller." Devereaux winked. "Spell my name right." An enigmatic smile played about his lips. "And name your first son after me." Saluting smartly, Devereaux spun on the ball of his heel and marched into the melee, shouting orders.

"What's your first name?" Melissa called out, her hands cupped around her mouth. Mirth danced in her jade eyes.

Cody prayed it would be something normal and manly like Robert or William or Steve.

Devereaux turned back, grinning. "Melvin."

"Melvin?" Cody scowled, instantly sorry when fireworks exploded underneath his face. "You'd saddle my son with a sissy name like Melvin?" Then the impact of her words hit him square in the heart. He struggled to sit up, commanding the pain to get lost. "You'll marry me?"

"Just try to stop me, mister." She coaxed him to lie back down with angel soft kisses. Against his lips, she said, "Two million women in America will disagree with you."

He racked his brain trying to figure out what she meant but had no clue. Never, as long as he lived, would he understand the workings of the female mind.

"About what? They should be kissing my feet for saving baseball, apple pie, and keeping our skies pretty and blue."

"Mel Gibson is no sissy." Her laughter tinkled in his ears and her smile lit up his soul. "You think you had problems with the Lions of Judah, just wait till they find out you think Mel is a sissy name."

He rolled his eyes. "How about I cut you a deal? We'll name our firstborn son 'Cody Melvin' and only call him *Mel* when his Uncle Melvin comes around."

She pressed her lips to his, and spread her palm over his heart. "You got it and you got me."

Cody's heart almost exploded with joy and pride. He was the luckiest man on earth, luckier than Mel Gibson.

As soon as Cody's gurney wheeled outdoors, the sun

nearly blinded him. Or was it about a thousand cameras flashing at them? Microphones were shoved in their faces and about a thousand questions shot at them in unison.

"Tell us how you saved the world."

"What was it like to be President?"

"Did you kill Jesse Elliot?"

"Are you going to jail for life?"

"Is your husband headed for the White House?"

Voices blended and grated, making it impossible to tell who said what.

Melissa lifted her chin in that regal manner that Cody had once despised but was quickly coming to appreciate.

"No comment, except I'd like to announce our wedding," she purred. "And Mel will be our best man."

THE END

Elaine Hopper

I've always yearned to be like Lois Lane and to enchant my very own Superman. Okay, so I can't have my very own caped crusader, at least not the real deal. Except in a book.

I'm a sucker for moonlight shining on a deserted stretch of beach while walking barefoot on the edge of the water, my hand tucked into the hand of the only man in the world. A pool under the moonlight will suffice when I can't get to the beach. A pool with a Jacuzzi will suffice even better.

I'm the mother of five of the most wonderful children in this or any universe -- three handsome boys and two beautiful girls. They keep me busy with swimming, karate, Friday night sushi and parties, Boy Scout meetings and campouts, and etcetera. My boss thinks he lays claim to my time, too, which he does, 9-5 five days a week. Sometimes even six days a week. Sometimes 9 - 7. I'm ex-Air Force and an ex-accountant. If I weren't a writer I'd live on a college campus. I could be very happy living on a university campus forever -- probably the University of Southern Mississippi, my alma mater which boasts a very lovely campus. Or Miami University in Ohio, where I'd always planned to get a degree in journalism. Isn't it funny how plans change? How life takes U turns and veers to the left when you thought it would veer to the right?

Obviously I'm a dreamer. I'm also a story teller and a hopeful romantic.

I can't NOT write and I can't stop dreaming. I'd rather stop breathing. I was born to sojourn into fantasy, to get lost in the hue and fragrance of prose, to create my own worlds and control countless destinies.

elainehopper@novelbooksinc.com
www.novelbooksinc.com/authors/elaine_hopper.htm
www.gate1.net/ElaineHopper/romance_cafe_home.htm

Continued on next page...

Desert Dreams by Gracie C. McKeever Paranormal/Suspense
Old World Evil vs. New Age Passion...Can their love survive?

The Anonymous Amaneunsis by Judith B. Glad Regency
Regency England is a man's world, until one woman writes her own rules...

No More Secrets, No More Lies by Marie Roy Contemporary
Secrets, lies, and consequences. What consequences does Sydney Morgan pay when all secrets are exposed?

The Blood That Binds by Rie Sheridan Fantasy
In Ancient Days, when elves were king...
the legends tell of wondrous things...

The Dragon's Horn by Glynnis Kincaid Fantasy
Three Dragons. Three Immortals. One Choice. But what will they choose? Will they rescue their loved ones, or fight to redeem the world?

Escape The Past by K. G. McAbee Fantasy
Can they escape their pasts and find a future in each other's arms?

Dream Knight by Alexis Kaye Lynn Medieval
Do you believe in the power of dreams?

Allude to Murder by Emma Kennedy Suspense
Balkan smuggling conspiracy entangles two Americans

Mating Season by Liz Hunter Contemporary
One lucky sailboat captain + His fetching first mate + Hurricane Season? Mating Season!

Unlawful by Dorice Nelson Medieval
Butchery tainted their first encounter... Enslavement separated them... Deception and deceit reunited them... Thus began their struggle of courage and conquest...

Available in HTML, Microsoft Reader, Adobe PDF and Trade Paperback formats

FATE

by:

Robert Arthur Smith

Science writer Judy Armstrong's nightmares about a murdered woman rapidly escalate into fugue states, during which she learns that the victim's son, Danny, will be the next to die.

Judy is desperate to help Danny, but this means risking her sanity, and ultimately, her life, by yielding to the dead woman's influence. When she realizes the murderer is closing in on Danny, however, Judy chooses to intervene, whatever the cost to herself, and flies to the victim's home to confront a killer.

ISBN #1-931696-05-5 (eBook)
ISBN #1-931696-94-2 (Print)

http://www.novelbooksinc.com
http://www.clockworkcat.com

OTHER BOOKS BY ROBERT ARTHUR SMITH

THE PREY

Werewolves and vampires pursue Morivania through Vienna and Paris during the French Revolution.

Trade paperback available: ISBN #0-595090-3-97
http://www.amazon.com & http://www.barnesandnoble.com

SILENT WITNESS

Deep in the Brazilian rain forest, a young girl makes a discovery about her father's Nazi past that will thrust her to the edge of sanity.

Trade paperback available: ISBN #0-595142-4-00
http://www.amazon.com & http://www.barnesandnoble.com